THE
SECRET
WEAPON

ALSO BY BRADLEY WRIGHT

Alexander King

THE SECRET WEAPON

COLD WAR

Alexander King Prequels

WHISKEY & ROSES

VANQUISH

KING'S RANSOM

KING'S REIGN

SCOURGE

Lawson Raines

WHEN THE MAN COMES AROUND

SHOOTING STAR

Santa Claus

SAINT NICK

THE
SECRET
WEAPON

Bradley Wright/King's Ransom Publishing
www.bradleywrightauthor.com

For Kade Alexander
I'm the shelter in the storm, the anchor in the tide, and the
whispering wind if ever you feel lost. My back is strong, son,
come aboard until you're ready to walk alone.

To think of shadows is a serious thing.

— Victor Hugo

It is madness for sheep to talk peace with a wolf.

— Thomas Fuller

THE
SECRET
WEAPON

PROLOGUE

March 9th, 2020

CIA SPECIAL AGENT FRED JOHNSON was feeling good after *finally* having the meeting that would shake things up in the war on terror. He didn't know it yet, but he unfortunately wouldn't live long enough to tell anyone about it.

The streets weaving through one of the liveliest neighborhoods in Greece were almost entirely deserted. As were most places around the world at four in the morning. It was the only time he could get the bartender to meet with him —after hours—when hopefully all the prying eyes would be asleep. After two years of undercover work in Athens, chasing his tail and reporting nothing but failure to his superiors, he finally knew not only *who* was running things in the fastest-growing terrorist organization in the world but also *where* that man was hiding.

Fred walked past the row of some of the most happening nightclubs and bars in the city. All were closed at that hour, but when open it was a murderers' row for places to get wasted on booze, women, or whatever else got sold in their bathrooms. Fred had spent a lot of his first year in Greece in those places. He spent the entire second year trying to avoid them. His apartment was just a street over now. Though he hadn't had a drink in months, tonight called for a celebration. Not only would he save countless lives with the information he'd just bought from a man connected to the terrorist cell, but the last two pages of important notes he'd just written in his notebook would propel his career immeasurably forward. Plus, if everything played out right, he could also finally get home to his daughter in South Carolina. A day he'd been praying far too long for. Now it was within reach.

As he crossed the street, he heard a woman's laughter echo behind him. Someone kicked a glass bottle in the distance, and it clinked and clanked across the pavement. A block away a dog was barking. Otherwise, it was as quiet in his neighborhood as he had ever heard it. And maybe twice as dark. He couldn't remember the last time he was out at night and the neon lights from the bars weren't guiding him home. Now there was just the one streetlight a couple hundred feet away and a few lamps in windows belonging to fellow members of the insomniacs society he'd unwittingly joined about six months ago.

The stress of the agency breathing down his neck for answers as the attacks mounted around the globe had stolen his ability to sleep almost entirely. However, he couldn't help but think that tonight, after a glass of wine or two, he might just sleep like a baby.

Fred crossed the last street to his apartment complex.

The thought of maybe being able to leave that place for home, and to be with his daughter, gave him a little extra bounce in his step. He would certainly miss the gyros and the Greek goddesses that seemed to be everywhere, but he wouldn't miss Athens as a whole.

He started up the outside stairwell that led to his place on the fourth floor. Just as he was making the turn for the second floor, some movement caught his eye below him. He slowed his pace, and instead of living in the future with his thoughts, he keened his senses back to the present. He stopped, listened intently, but didn't hear anything below him. That area of Athens could get a little rough after hours, but he hadn't run into much more than a drunken partyer or a beggar in all the time he'd lived there.

Fred continued up the stairs, conscious of his surroundings but not really worried. He turned the corner to the stairs bringing him to the fourth floor. All seemed quiet, so he pulled out his keys and walked to his door. Just before he inserted the key, something told him to walk around the wall and check the outer walkway. He poked his head around the corner. Nothing. He shrugged and walked back to his door.

Once inside the apartment, before he even took off his shoes, he did what he always did when he came back from speaking with an informant or, for that matter, any meeting regarding his business with the CIA: he walked over to the painting hanging above his mantle in the living room, pulled it off away from the wall, lifted the piece of tape that held the paper backing down at the corner, and placed his notebook full of secrets in the hole there. He replaced the tape and moved the painting back, flush against the wall.

His next move was toward the kitchen. He had a bottle of red that he'd been saving for a special occasion. He couldn't think of a better one than tonight. Fred found the bottle in the cabinet, grabbed the wine opener and a glass. When the cork popped, the sweet aroma of black cherries, chocolate, and hint of oak emanated from the bottle. He laughed at himself for knowing and recognizing such things. Before swearing off booze for a while, he'd become quite proficient with tasting wines and discerning their aromatic notes. The life of a lone spy is a lot more mundane than most would expect.

Fred tipped the bottle and watched the dark red liquid slosh into his glass. He set the bottle down, picked up the glass, and gave it an aerating swirl. With his free hand, he took out his phone. He wasn't supposed to check in with his superior for another couple of days, but he just couldn't wait to share the groundbreaking news.

Just as Fred was about to tap on Deputy Director Rodgers's contact, there was a knock at his door. It caught him so off guard that he dropped his phone, but he managed to keep his glass in hand. He set down the wine and pulled his Beretta from his hip holster. There was no reason anyone should be knocking on his door, at any time, much less at four in the morning. His heart rate ticked up as he looked through the peephole.

It was a woman.

Her hair was a mess, her mascara was running down her face, and she looked terrified. It must have been her whom he saw when he was coming up the stairs. He hoped she was okay. He holstered his gun and took a deep breath to calm his jangled nerves.

Fred swung the door open. "Are you all right?"

At first he thought the man who came around the corner with a gun in his hand was going to shoot the woman. But as Fred struggled for his own gun at his hip, he noticed a smile across the woman's face. Then the man's gun went directly to his own head.

"Do I get my money now? I fooled him, just like you asked," the woman said to the gunman.

Three more men came around the corner. The gunman shoved Fred back inside his apartment and took his gun. He knew what they were there for. He knew he was going to die. Fred just didn't want to be tortured.

"I already called my superior," Fred told the gunman, who was large, olive skinned, black cornrows in his hair, "and told him everything I know. Everything your man at the bar spilled to me. I know who your leader is . . . and where he lives. You're too late."

"In that case," the man said, looking around the room, "you're going to give me all of your credentials and your protocols for checking in. Or I'll not only kill you but your entire family."

Fred knew then that he wasn't going to get his wish. These men were going to torture him. He just hoped they wouldn't find out he had a daughter.

Hours later, after he'd bled all that he could bleed and the gun was to his head one final time, the last thing he thought of was the notebook. He hoped that whoever the CIA sent to investigate his death would be the one to find the notebook instead of these terrorist thugs.

But that was information Fred would never have the privilege of knowing.

1

6 DAYS LATER

South of London, UK

ALEXANDER KING TOOK a moment to steady his breathing. He'd waited a long time to kill the man who was less than a mile away from him now, but he couldn't let the anticipation affect his performance. Tonight, like every other night in his line of work, there was no room for error.

He slowed the rental car as he made a right turn off the A21 motorway onto Bewlbridge Lane. The hour long drive from London had been quiet. By eight o'clock in the evening most had settled in after a long day of work. However, King's workday had only just begun. He glanced up through the windshield at the colorful sky—an orange glow across the entire expanse hovering below a fiery layer of red. Those colors were the daylight fading, and long shadows began to throw their cast. Which was perfect, because for the last year those shadows were where he'd done nearly all of his work.

Though his flat was in the Soho neighborhood of central London, King had no need for a map to get where he was going. This was the thirty-third day in a row he'd made this particular drive. Long enough to watch hints of spring begin to blossom in the countryside southeast of the city. Every time he traveled this far into the country, a longing for where he grew up tugged at him. As he took in the rolling hills that reminded him of Lexington, he would have to blink away the running Thoroughbreds he knew weren't actually there. Kentucky—once a place he could always come back to after the wars he'd fought for his country—now seemed a place that only existed in his dreams.

King turned left and steered the car toward a small boat dock that served as an entryway into the Bewl Water reservoir. In all of his previous thirty-two trips, this was only the second time he'd made it to the docks. When you are someone who never wants to be noticed, you never keep the same pattern. Even when you *know* no one is watching. It was the same reason the car he'd driven tonight was also the thirty-third different vehicle or mode of transportation he'd taken to get there.

One can never be too careful.

King turned left off the main road and slowed to a stop. The small parking lot's streetlamps popped on overhead as he exited the vehicle. Cool air rushed him, carrying with it first the scent of mildewed wood, finishing with the sweet smell of English bluebells that carpeted the nearby fields. He could hear the boats rocking a few feet away, but nothing else.

More importantly, he could hear *no one* else.

8

He glanced down at his watch. Just about twenty minutes now.

He stepped from the pavement onto the wooden dock, counted four boats down on his left, and stopped when he came to the small green fishing boat. It had a large blue tackle box in the front, just like Sam had told him it would. Not that he'd doubted her. She was almost never wrong.

King stepped down into the boat, and it wobbled beneath him. His six-foot-three-inch, two-hundred-fifteen-pound frame sank the bottom a few inches. Though it had been almost five years since his last mission with the Navy SEALs, he'd never stopped the daily workouts that had become second nature. He was all muscle, but it was lean muscle. He was strong as a bull, just not so much that it took away from his agility. The things he did for a living required a lot of stealth, and a squad leader once told him, "A bull of a man never snuck up on anyone." The last few years of vigilante work and subsequent missions with the CIA had taught him as much to be true.

He untied the damp rope from the metal cleat attached to the dock and pushed back. As soon as he cleared the boats on both sides of him, he reached back and yanked the starter on the outboard motor, then grabbed the steering handle. The small engine barely roared to life, but the power of the boat was not his concern. He turned right once he cleared the dock and started down the lake. He didn't have far to go, but because he was anxious to get his hands on his target, the short ride seemed to take forever.

The light above him had been swallowed by the night, the glow of the rising moon behind him now his only guide. He took out the small set of keys left for him at a drop back in London, then scooted forward on the bench seat and opened the large tackle box. He raised the top shelf, reached in, and wrapped his fingers around the Glock 19 handgun waiting for him. It had been fitted with a suppressor can. A gift from the clandestine gods. Sam had also left him a Chris Reeve Sebenza 21 frame lock knife. Just in case a gun didn't make sense. That went in the pocket of his black tactical pants—the kind that looked civilian without losing efficiency. The last of the treats in the bottom of the box was a burner phone. He picked it up and dialed the number he'd memorized earlier.

"I see there were no problems with the drop," Sam answered, her British accent thick. He hadn't realized he was so on edge until he heard the sound of her voice, then felt the tension fall from his shoulders.

"Everything else in line?"

Normally he would have had a sarcastic line ready to throw at her, maybe something to rib her about a past failure. But not tonight.

"All I know is that no one has come or gone from the estate in the last twenty-four hours. The rest is up to you," she said.

"I'll check in when it's over."

King went to close the flip phone when he heard her voice.

"Listen, X," Sam said. X was the moniker Sam had chosen for him when she could no longer say his name in open communication. "I realize this is old hat for you. But this is the first of your targets in a long time that is personal. Just make sure you—"

"Sam," he interrupted. He could see his jumping-off point just up ahead. "I kill people who threaten my country's way of life . . . they're all personal."

He shut the phone and shoved it back into his pocket. He felt down beside his right foot, along the inside wall of the boat. His hand found the wooden handle of a single paddle. He pulled the oar into his lap and reached back to shut down the motor. The boat coasted forward, and he laid the paddle in the water at an angle that would steer him toward the shore.

Though he didn't want to think about it, he knew Sam was right. This one was more personal. This wasn't an assignment handed down from CIA Director Mary Hartsfield, the only other person on the planet who knew he was alive. This was something he and Sam had never stopped working on by themselves since the day King was forced to disappear in order to keep everyone he loved safe. He couldn't think about how close they all were to dying last year, and he couldn't focus on the fact that the man in the house just down the lake was one of the last people living who was responsible for putting everyone he loved in danger. To Sam's point, it needed to be about the kill. Not about *whom* he was killing.

The nose of the boat slid to a stop on a flat part of the bank. There was a thick wall of trees between him and the house he'd been watching for more than a month. Being so close spiked his heart rate. He let the sick feeling of unused adrenaline wash through his system as he stepped out of the boat and took a deep breath.

Though King never enjoyed taking another human's life, he'd be lying to himself if he said he wasn't looking forward to finally ending the man responsible for the death of so many innocent people. The man responsible for putting King's own loved ones in danger.

Andonios Maragos was a terrorist on the wanted list of every government agency in the world. Last year his money had funded the most terrifying attack on the White House in US history. King knew there were other people closer to the terrorist group, which Maragos was involved with, who were actually pulling the strings, but he didn't know who they were yet, and he had to start somewhere. The money was as good a place as any. And because bureaucracy had failed to pin this guilty man to any of his crimes, it was up to King to make him pay.

King wasn't sure if killing a monster like Maragos was playing God or playing the devil, but he also didn't care. Either way, the man was going to get what was coming to him.

And there was no one better suited for the work of giving Maragos what he deserved than Alexander King.

As he stepped into the shadows of the trees, King had never been more ready to do his job.

2

THE LIGHT FROM THE BACK DECK OF THE HOUSE NEAR THE Bewl Water reservoir helped guide King quietly through the trees. The goldcrests sang their happy tune above him. He knew what type of bird was prominent in this part of the world because of the dozens of hours he'd spent familiarizing himself with all things East Sussex. While he knew such information regarding the area's indigenous wildlife would be of no use during the assassination, he also didn't want any surprises. When it was life and death, no detail was too small, no stone would go unturned.

The mansion at the water's edge was sprawling, and so was the land on which it was situated. The reason Maragos chose it—its isolation—was now the very thing that made him all the more vulnerable to a man like King. During the past month, King had spent every visit scouring the property. He knew *everything* about it. Most importantly, he'd learned that there were no security cameras. Maragos didn't want any record of where he'd been hiding from the world, and he also didn't want anyone to have the ability to hack into them to find out his whereabouts. Maragos was familiar enough with technology to know that anyone with any tech savvy at all could reach right into a set of security cameras from a computer anywhere on the planet.

That was his reasoning to have around-the-clock guards instead.

A couple of weeks ago, there were four men walking the grounds. The past week, only two. Not counting the guard at the gate several acres to the north, who was not a concern because by the time the guards near the house realized they needed backup or Maragos himself was in trouble with the other guards down, King would be long gone.

The only other important thing King knew after watching from across the lake was that every night at eight thirty Maragos got on his treadmill on the top floor of his home. The window in front of the walking machine looked out over the lake below, but both times King had entered the house when Maragos was gone, he made sure the end of the deck below could not be seen from the treadmill. King had to be sure the deck was out of sight because of the guard who regularly paced back and forth on that very deck. As King watched now, the armed guard turned his back to the trees and walked toward the opposite end of the deck.

King made his move.

He crossed the grassy area between the trees and the deck like a mouse scurrying across a kitchen floor. At the foot of the stairs, he crouched and waited. He reached inside his pocket, pulled out the knife, and thumbed open the blade. Though his Glock was fitted with a suppressor, that didn't mean it wouldn't make a sound. It would make a noise like that of a hand slapping against a wall, which was better than a full blast but still loud enough to get the guard's attention at the front of the house.

All King could hear now was the whisper of the breeze, the chirps of the goldcrests as they settled into their nests, and the footsteps of the guard coming back his way. King could tell by the groan of the wood planks under each step that this was the larger of the two guards at the mansion. He squeezed the handle of the knife and placed his foot on the first step leading up to the deck. He listened for the footsteps to stop then start again; that way he knew the guard had once again turned his back.

The footsteps began moving away, and King matched the cadence of the guard's footsteps exactly as he ascended the stairs. When he reached the top, he sprinted for the guard. As the guard turned to see the commotion, King was already on top of him. King stabbed just below the man's beard to stop his shout, then twice to the carotid artery so he would bleed out.

As the guard grasped at his neck, trying desperately to keep his blood on the inside, King lowered him to the ground and took the semiautomatic rifle that was strapped over his shoulder. He ejected the magazine, plus the round that was chambered, and put both in his pocket, leaving the gun resting on the man's chest. He walked away as the guard slipped quietly into death.

Before he left the deck, he paused to look up at the windows above him. The lights were on, and when he really tuned his ears, he could hear the news on the television inside. His target was in position. Now it was time to eliminate him.

As he descended the stairs, he pocketed the knife and took the Glock in his hand. He squeezed the grip on his familiar friend as he rounded the side of the house. There was no need to chamber a round; it already lay waiting. One of the reasons he chose a Glock many years ago as his most important tool was because there was no need to fiddle with a safety since there wasn't one. The gun was always ready to go.

King sidled up to the edge of the brick wall of the home. He inched his head around the corner. The yellow light from the two porch lamps hanging from the house on both sides of the front door shone down on the man standing at the bottom of the driveway. This was the part of the job that King hated. He knew the man upstairs on the treadmill deserved to die, but this man guarding Maragos, did he qualify for the same fate? In any war, there was always collateral damage for the greater good. But King never liked this part. This man has a family, friends, maybe even kids, but a host of bad decisions led this man here—guarding a man responsible for the death of many innocent people—and though King didn't like being the hand that brought the consequences, it's the life he chose. Nobody likes everything about their job, but the work must still be done.

King raised his gun and squeezed the trigger in quick succession. The suppressor clapped twice, and the man dropped to the ground. He moved forward and once again removed the magazine and the bullet in the chamber from the dead man's gun. Then he found the keys to the front door in the guard's left pocket and moved toward the house.

Inside, the mansion smelled of cooked hamburger. Maragos's last meal. Every light on the bottom floor was on. The stone tile floor beneath King's feet made it easy to stay quiet—no groaning wood. The staircase turned left as he ascended then turned left again at the top to walk the hall that ran the length of the upstairs. The wood beams running along the ceiling gave the mansion a mountain cabin feel, but King cared nothing about that; he was focused on the open door at the far end of the hall.

The BBC was blaring from the television, almost loud enough to cover the *thrum-thrum thrum-thrum* of Maragos's sneakers skidding along the conveyor belt of the treadmill. As King stepped forward, his heart rate stepped up a beat. Over a year ago, the nanochips that Maragos had his terrorists implant in King's team members and also King's sister and niece could have killed them at any moment. *Would have* killed them if King hadn't been able to take out the only two people who knew how to set them off before it was too late. Andonios Maragos, his now deceased brother and sister—Gregor and Anastasia—were all part of a terrorist group that the United States had deemed defunct once Anastasia was killed.

But King had known better.

He knew the kind of radicalism coursing through the veins of this Greek family didn't come from the teachings of their wealthy father. They had come from somewhere else. And while the US government was okay with being able to tell the American people that it all ended with the death of the "ring leader"—Anastasia Maragos—King was being pulled by some unseen force to look deeper. Even past the man in the next room, Andonios, who most of the world saw as a harmless and wealthy playboy.

Money-funding terrorists are anything but harmless. That's why King's only ally, Sam, was currently in Greece investigating the lives of the Maragoses, how they grew up, who knew them as children. At that very moment she was following up on a lead about a caretaker the Maragoses had during their childhood. King wasn't the type of man who lived his life letting signs dictate his behavior and beliefs. However, he was a man who trusted his instincts, and they were telling him that what Sam was about to uncover in Athens would lead to the real people in charge of the terrorist organization that Maragos's money had been funding. Now it was time to cut off the money supply. King would worry about the head of the snake when the serpent was finally identified.

As King rounded the upstairs banister, Andonios Maragos came into view. For most people in this situation, their adrenaline would be gushing. Their heart rate would be spiking, and their breath would become short. All making it more difficult to get the job done.

Most people aren't trained killers.

Alexander King placed the Glock in his pocket, right next to his knife, as he stalked toward the open door. His breath was even and his mind, clear. There was no need to question Maragos, because King knew he wouldn't give up any information. King had no plans to prolong the visit at all. He'd already searched the entire house for clues, and there were none. There was only one thing left to do.

As King walked through the open door, Maragos turned in shock, looking like he'd seen a ghost. Which, for all intents and purposes, that was exactly what King was. When it registered that King had come to kill him, he jumped off the treadmill and ran for the desk sitting under the window at the far wall. He reached under the desk for the Walther PPK pistol that King had removed two days ago. His look of shock at the gun's absence morphed into determination as he rushed at King. A last-ditch effort to survive.

King stepped to the side at the last second and helped Maragos's momentum by pushing him headfirst into the wall. Maragos fell to his knees. King moved forward and landed a Thai kick to the ribs. Andonios grunted in pain as the breath was forced from his lungs. King lifted him by his shoulders, put his back against the wall, then clamped his right hand around Maragos's throat like a vise.

King looked deep into the man's eyes who just a year ago had put his family in grave danger. There was no need for words or explanations, because Maragos knew whose hand was wrapped around his neck. As opposed to hating having to kill the security guards outside, this moment King relished. The feeling of erasing evil from the world was always uplifting, even when it meant death. And because the Maragoses had decided to make it personal by targeting this CIA operative's family, well, that just made the squeeze all the sweeter.

It was a good night. The last of the Maragos family was slipping off into the afterlife, which meant so too was a lot of the money funding a violent terrorist organization. But King knew evil would always find a way. That's why, once Maragos was dead, King's mind quickly shifted to what he had to do tomorrow—the next step in the effort to keep his loved ones, and his country, safe.

The next step in finding the monster who was really behind it all.

3

The Next Day

London, UK

"We have a visual on Tango."

Special Agent Shawn Roberts rushed over to the window that overlooked Oxford Street in the Mayfair neighborhood of London. He searched the hordes of tourists and shoppers moving in and out of some of the most posh restaurants and boutiques in the city. But he saw no sign of Bentley Martin.

"Negative on a visual," Roberts told his man on the street.

"Sky-blue tracksuit, white running shoes, hair in a pony-tail. Looks like she's stretching for a run."

Roberts found her by her dark hair sprouting out from under a white hat, contrasting against the light blue tracksuit

Agent Anderson just referenced. When she stood from her stretch, Bentley looked to be a normal teenager, but Shawn had learned the hard way, in his line of work, that looks can be deceiving. Intelligence had produced communications coming out of Athens, Greece, that she was an asset to a terrorist cell the CIA had been attempting to collect more information on for the past six months. The details of her involvement with them were unknown, but over the last several days a couple of the few known members of that terror organization had been spotted in London. The tail end of a tapped cell phone conversation between one of the terrorist cell's members and someone back in Athens produced the time and location of activity that somehow involved Bentley. Roberts's orders were to follow Bentley in hopes that she would lead them to some of these high-value targets.

The CIA hadn't yet determined the level of Bentley's involvement. She could simply be an unknowing messenger, or she could have been recruited a while back. Her internet history hadn't proved to be the cleanest. Months ago she had researched this very terrorist cell from her laptop. This was the only reason they'd found her. Bentley wasn't a common name, and there weren't too many who lived in the surrounding area. When they matched her internet history with her name, she was the only logical suspect. And it didn't really matter if they found her or not. Knowing where she lived just gave them a focal point. What mattered was they had the date and place, so any suspicious behavior was going to be monitored on this street regardless.

"I can bring her in now if you want," Agent Anderson said.

"No," Roberts said. "Stay with her. Let's see where this

little run takes her. I don't like the looks of that fanny pack she's wearing."

"Why?" Anderson laughed. "Because she could have something dangerous in there she's passing along or because it's a terrible fashion statement?"

Bentley eased into her jog down Oxford Street.

"Both." Roberts smiled. "Just stay with her and keep your eyes open."

"Copy that," Anderson replied. Then Roberts heard him shout through his earpiece, "Hey, watch it, man!"

Roberts scanned the street below until he saw Agent Anderson facedown on the pavement. Coincidences certainly happen, but in espionage they were rare.

"What the hell happened, Anderson? Tired of running already?" Roberts said.

"No, some douche bag in a gray hoodie ran right over me."

Roberts especially didn't like the sound of that. He moved his eyes up and down the sidewalk until he spotted a man moving at more of a sprint than a jog.

Shawn clarified, "Gray hoodie with a black backpack?"

"Yeah, he was really moving."

He *was* really moving and had almost caught up to Bentley. The man couldn't have looked more suspicious. The hoodie was baggie, as if to conceal the man's body type. His hat was pulled low, the brim touching sunglasses that sat just above a bushy beard.

"I don't like this," Roberts said. "Stay with him!"

The man in the hoodie began waving his arms like mad.

Agent Anderson spoke through his earpiece. "He's shouting something. I think he's trying to get people to move!"

Obviously something was off.

"Agent Jones," Roberts said to the third agent on the team who was positioned at the next corner, "Tango and suspicious gray hoodie are coming right for you. Be ready to move in! I'm coming down—"

Before Agent Roberts could finish, the man in the gray hoodie grabbed Bentley and tackled her to the ground away from the street. If he hadn't, the exploding car to her right would have killed her. A ball of fire flared from the car, and black smoke plumed skyward. The explosion reached all the way to the building where Roberts could feel the rumble beneath his feet. He turned and sprinted through the doorway, turned left down the stairs, and rushed out onto the sidewalk across from the chaos. He watched as the hooded man pulled Bentley to her feet.

"They're moving, Jones, don't lose them!"

The fire still burned in the ruined car. Onlookers screamed in panic. Roberts looked past the explosion toward the corner toward the northeast corner of the intersection. He dodged a few stopped cars as he crossed the street to try to block the hooded man and Bentley. Agent Jones began moving toward them as well. Then he watched as, just before Jones made it to the corner, the hooded man pulled Bentley by the arm and jerked her down the stairs into Bond Street Station.

"They've gone into the underground!" Roberts shouted. "I'm almost to them! Agent Freeman, if there's a train down there, get on it now!"

Agent Freeman was the fourth and final member of Roberts's detail. Roberts had positioned Freeman in the Tube for this very reason.

"Copy that," Freeman said. "There's actually two trains. One at the Central line and one at the Jubilee line."

Roberts maneuvered around two more stopped cars; he was almost across the street.

"Tango and Gray Hoodie are headed your way. I need to know where they're going. Stay with them in case we don't make it to the train in time."

"Copy. I'm at the split. I'll follow them and let you know their 20."

Roberts ran around the blazing car, dodged the stunned bystanders, and followed Jones and Anderson through the entrance to the underground train station. They sprinted down one set of stairs, then down another, and continued dodging people as they rushed through the station and jumped the turnstiles.

"Freeman?" Roberts shouted.

"Jubilee line. They just ran past me."

"Stay as close as you can and try not to get made. But do what you have to do. Don't let them get on that train without you. No matter what! We can't lose them!"

The urgency in Roberts's voice suggested his concern not for the safety of Bentley Martin but for the information she likely possessed. The terrorist cell based near Athens had become the deadliest in the world. Factions were spreading across Europe like a cancer, taking credit for a record number of small and large attacks in multiple countries. They'd been listed priority one by CIA Director Mary Hartsfield. This was the closest anyone in the agency had been to any sort of lead in months. They needed *something*. Countless innocent lives depended on it.

Freeman came back in Roberts's ear. "They're at the escalators. I haven't been made."

"We aren't far behind you," Roberts said.

Roberts and his men continued weaving through the turns to get to the escalator that led down to the Jubilee train's platform. After one last turn and a sprint down a long hall, he could see the escalators.

"Escalators in sight. About to reach the train—"

Before Shawn could instruct Freeman to take down the man in the gray hoodie, three men came running out of the crosswalk hallway in front of him and sprinted down the escalator out of sight.

All three of them were holding guns.

"Freeman! Three men coming up on your six! All of them armed!"

Gunshots rang out through the tunnel system. Screams followed as civilians began panicking.

Anderson dodged several frightened people turning away from the chaos and looked back over his shoulder at Roberts as they approached the escalator. The look of fear in his eyes was chilling. Roberts was certain Anderson had found the same shocked look on his own face.

"Freeman!" Roberts shouted.

No answer.

The three agents sprinted down the escalator, and about halfway down the bullets were turned on them. More screams, more loud bangs, and more clanking metal all around them. Roberts yanked both of his agents by the backs of their shirts as hard as he could. When his ass hit the moving steps that were pulling them downward, he pulled his pistol and moved backward up the escalator steps with all he had. The relentless motion of the escalator pulled them down as they scrambled upward. Roberts watched as Anderson took a bullet in the leg and Jones took one in the arm. He began to return fire as the three of them backpedaled away from the gunman who waited for them at the bottom.

He wasn't sure who these men worked for, but he could only assume they were the terrorists they had hoped to find.

Careful what you wish for, he couldn't help but think as he squeezed the trigger on his Glock.

Two gunmen were firing on them from around the corner at the base of the escalator, not far from the train.

No sign of the third gunman.

No sign of Freeman.

No chance to stop the hooded man and his hostage, Bentley Martin.

This operation had just gone horribly wrong. And the only thing Special Agent Shawn Roberts could hope for right then . . . was a whole lot of help.

4

ALEXANDER KING HAD YET ANOTHER LIFE-AND-DEATH decision to make. He had half a mind just to let the American agents who were currently taking fire on the escalators get what they deserved for possibly blowing a clean getaway for him. After all, he had what he came for: Bentley Martin in hand and a clear path back to his flat. He had spent too much time and effort getting to this moment to let his old "save them all" mentality ruin this. If Bentley could help him, innocent lives would be saved. Not only had he just risked blowing his cover, but if he returned down the tunnel to help, he would most certainly lose Bentley.

He didn't know how many American agents there were in total. He only knew of two for certain: the man he'd run over on the sidewalk holding his hand to his ear and the "homeless" man with perfectly clean sneakers and a fresh haircut at the Central and Jubilee line split. Either the CIA was short staffed or they were just getting sloppy.

The gunfire continued as the train pulled in. It was decision time. And even though he didn't like it, there was only one decision to be made.

"If you want to survive this, don't move."

"Who are you?" Bentley looked up at him. Her lips were trembling and her eyes were wet with emotion.

King removed his backpack, digging inside and pulling out the change of clothes he'd brought for her. They were huddled against the wall inside the train platform. Everyone around them was staying low to the ground, anxious to get on the train before the battle down the tunnel made its way to them.

"I'm the guy who just saved your life. You might want to listen to me. That car bomb would have killed you, you know."

King handed her the clothes. She didn't take them immediately.

"Clothes? What am I supposed to do with these?"

"Put them on." He shoved them into her chest. "Do everything I tell you or you really will be dead."

The seriousness of his tone brought the fear back to Bentley's eyes. Across the platform the train had stopped and the doors opened. People rushed in, knocking passengers to the ground as they tried to exit. The gunfire was still echoing all the way to the train platform, deterring anyone trying to exit from doing so. Everyone packed themselves into the train. Bentley turned quickly toward the train, but King caught the back of her arm.

"What are you doing?" she cried. The shock of being stopped from saving herself was clear in her raised voice and crazed look in her eyes.

"We can't leave. Put the clothes on and wait here—"

"Wait here?"

King looked over Bentley's shoulder and pulled his Glock from his concealed hip holster. In the sea of people moving inside the train, there was one figure moving against the tide. King yanked Bentley down to the concrete by her arm with his left hand as he fired three shots at the man who had emerged and was now in the process of raising his gun to fire on King. Several people screamed as the gunman dropped to the ground beside them. If Bentley had been frightened before, now she was terrified.

King helped her up from under her arm as her gaze volleyed back and forth between King and the man who'd almost shot them.

"How did you know he was—please, let's go! Get me out of here!"

She attempted to pull away toward the train again, but King held her in place.

"The door's about to close, what are you doing?" She looked past King down the tunnel where the gunfire continued. "They'll come this way. They'll kill us!"

The doors closed on the train, and it began to pull away.

Bentley was incensed. "You just got us killed! Why are you doing this?"

King was calm. "Put the clothes on and stop talking." He nodded toward the gunfire down the tunnel. "You want them to hear you?"

Bentley shook her head no.

"Just put these on right over your clothes. Keep the hat on and pulled low." He gestured over her shoulder. "Get behind that pillar and don't move until I get back here."

"Get back here?" Bentley said in a shouting whisper. "Where are you going? You can't leave me here!"

"Just stay put. The next train will be here in ten minutes."

Bentley continued to protest, but King had already begun moving down the tunnel. There was a break in the shooting, so he kept his gun at the ready in case someone were to run his way. As it always did, the adrenaline felt good moving through his system. As he approached the turn in the tunnel toward the foot of the escalators, gunshots once again rang out, but they were now farther away. The terrorists looking to kill Bentley had pushed the CIA back toward the entrance. The situation was bad, but if the shooting made it out to the street, things would get a lot worse.

King moved with speed through the tunnel, and with his back to the next wall, he peeked around the corner. The homeless man King had pegged as CIA lay dead at the foot of the escalator, a pistol in his hand. Beyond the dead agent, the lengthy escalator was empty. He headed up the escalator, remaining in a crouch position, and let it carry him toward the gunmen. Once he made it to the top, there was no turning back; he would be exposed. Shoot first would be his only strategy.

He crested the top of the escalator, his aim unwavering, but there was nothing to shoot at. He moved forward as he heard a couple more bangs pop off near the entrance of the Tube. When he made it around the last corner, he watched a man drop to the ground on his left as well as a man rise up to fire on his right. Across the turnstiles, the sun was bright behind the silhouette of a man. King aimed down his sights and shot the man on his right in the leg. As the man dropped, King surged forward.

"Put your gun down!" a man with an American accent shouted. It was the owner of the silhouette, who King knew was one of the CIA agents.

King ignored the command, moved over the man he'd just shot, and removed the pistol from his hand. He put his knee heavy on the man's chest and pressed his own gun against the man's olive-skinned forehead.

"Who do you work for?"

"Hey! I said put the gun down!" the silhouetted man shouted again.

The man beneath him closed his eyes, expecting death. It was obvious this man was willing to die, so the only way King would get anything out of him would be to surprise him.

There was no time for a back and forth, so King took a chance.

"Husaam Hammoud," King said.

Husaam Hammoud was a notorious terrorist leader, also connected to Greece, which meant he was also connected to the man King had choked to death the night before. The Maragoses were all from Greece. King's instincts had told him from the beginning that Andonios and his family were likely connected to Hammoud, but he hadn't yet put all the pieces together. He was hoping Sam was about to change that with her investigations in Athens.

King knew the man pinned beneath him would never say who sent him, but he hoped his reaction to Hammoud's name might give it away. As soon as the name left King's mouth, the man's eyes shot open. But it wasn't the reaction King expected. The man was . . . confused.

"Silence isn't an answer," King said, pressing his gun deeper into the man's forehead. "Who do you work for?"

The man's accent was Middle Eastern. "I don't know his name. But he sent a lot of money for this, and he was American. I swear it's all I know."

Now it was King who looked confused. He hadn't seen that coming. But there was no time for more questions. King looked up over the turnstile, and the silhouette had begun moving his way. He looked back down at the man under his gun, tapped him twice on the forehead with the tip of his Glock, and gave him a smile.

"Have fun in prison."

King pulled back his gun and sprinted around the corner.

"Stop! Stop right there!" the agent shouted at him through the tunnel.

Just before he got to the escalators, he heard a man say to someone else, "Make sure he doesn't go anywhere. I'm going after the hoodie!"

King knew that with the timing of the train arrival still being a couple of minutes away, he was going to have to face this American agent one way or another. He rushed down to the bottom of the escalator, turned right toward the train platform, stopped as soon as he was out of sight, and put his back against the wall. If he had to deal with the agent, he was going to meet him on his own terms.

5

KING WAITED PATIENTLY AROUND THE CORNER FROM THE escalators. His face was beginning to sweat under the fake beard, and the sunglasses were annoying him at the bridge of his nose. Unfortunately, he still couldn't remove either one. He could hear the train moving toward the platform behind him. He didn't have a lot of time to deal with the American agent coming his way. If Bentley made it on the train and he didn't, he knew he would lose her. And he hadn't spent the last six months putting things in motion for this day just to lose it because of someone on the same side of this battle.

King heard the footsteps running down the escalator come to a stop. He figured the agent was backpedaling slowly to keep his distance. He assumed the agent had his pistol extended, waiting for King to make a move. Soon, the sound of the train would make it to the agent. It was mostly quiet in the tunnel now. Only murmurs from people still huddled in fear and a bit of street noise from above.

The train screeched to a stop at the platform—easily heard by anyone underground. The agent would need to make a decision, which King was prepared to capitalize on. He knew the agent could not let him get on that train with Bentley Martin.

As soon as King heard the first heavy footstep at the bottom of the escalator, he ducked down, surged forward around the corner, and caught the agent off guard by tackling him at the waist. It was fairly easy for King because he had him by at least thirty pounds, the agent was built more like a distance runner. King drove him down, pinning his back against the ground just below the moving stairs. He grabbed the agent by his right wrist and slammed his gun hand on the ground. The pistol dislodged from his fingers, and King moved into mount position—shoving his right forearm under the agent's chin and pressing his full weight against him. King didn't recognize the man with the buzz cut and short beard-covered iron jaw. Why would he, though, since he'd had almost no contact with the agency over the last two years.

"I'm not your enemy," King said. "Clean up the mess on the street, and forget you saw me."

King eased the pressure he was applying on the man's neck, just enough for him to speak.

"Who are you?" the agent said.

"A friend. That's all you need to know. Don't follow me down to that train. Next time I won't play so nice."

"What are you going to do with Bentley? How did you know someone was going to try to kill her?"

The agent was looking for something, some morsel of information to take back to his superior. King could understand that. But the train was about to pull away, and he had to go.

"Andonios Maragos wanted to kill the president. Now that Maragos is dead, I'm sure the real terrorist he was funding has the same agenda. Find out who Maragos was in bed with and you'll find the head of the snake. Maybe I'll see you there." After sharing this little nugget, King picked up the agent's gun and rose to his feet.

"Are you CIA?" the agent asked.

"You know, I've never really been one for labels." King ejected the magazine and the chambered round. Then he dropped the gun and pocketed the ammunition. He started to walk away, then stopped. "And listen, have someone give you a lesson on blending in. Your team couldn't have been more obvious."

"Who are you?" the agent asked again.

King shook his head. "Remember, focus on Maragos, and forget about me."

The train was seconds from leaving the platform, so King left him with that. He sprinted down the tunnel and readied his Glock in case more gunmen might be waiting on this train like the man he had to shoot on the last one. As he made the final turn, he could see the red Jubilee line train there waiting. Then he heard the two beeps signaling the door was closing. He surged forward. There was no time to check if Bentley had already boarded; he just had to trust that she had. At the last second he launched himself forward, diving through the closing doors onto his stomach. Pete Rose would have been proud.

When he looked up, it was clear that Bentley wasn't impressed. She'd thought she was going to get away without him catching up. King got up and walked over to her.

"Sorry to disappoint."

King wobbled when the train sped forward. He could barely see the agent he'd left at the escalators running down the tunnel before the window of the train disappeared behind the wall. He and Bentley were the only ones on the train. All other passengers had managed to pile in the earlier train, and police must have kept more from boarding this one. He was lucky authorities were letting the trains run at all. This would make his exit a whole lot easier.

"You know there are thousands of cameras all around these trains," Bentley said. "They will just follow from camera to camera wherever you take me. You won't be able to get away with this."

"Beauty and brains," King said. "Bet you had to keep a stick handy to fight off the boys at school."

King pulled a phone from his pocket and powered it on.

"Is this funny to you? People are trying to kill me."

"And you would already be dead if it wasn't for me, so maybe try to be a little grateful."

King typed one word—*Go*—and hit the send button to the only contact saved in the burner phone.

"Okay, you did save me," Bentley said. "But now you're holding me against my will. So I'm sorry if my mood isn't to your liking. It will be a lot better when the police are waiting at the next stop to take you in and let me go."

"News flash, Bentley, the people behind the car bomb that was meant for you are your enemy. Not me. And the police? We won't be seeing them."

Bentley started to reply but stopped when the power to the train shut down and the lights went out. The train slowed to a stop, and King put his sunglasses on his hat, stood, and moved to the back of the train.

"You coming?" King said. "Wouldn't want your bomber friends to find you wandering the streets alone."

That was all he needed to say. She walked over to him, and they both walked out the rear exit of the train. King knew exactly where he was. He'd been in that exact spot three times in preparation for this very moment. It's easy to spend a lot of time planning when everyone on the planet thinks you're dead. The "deceased" don't have a hell of a lot of social distractions.

He followed the course he'd plotted down the walking tunnel along the right side. He used the phone's flashlight to guide the way. The power returned to the train, and it sped away from them toward the next stop. The tunnel went quiet. King once again removed his backpack. He removed his hat and hoodie and stuffed them in the bag. He had a white MIND THE GAP tourist-special T-shirt underneath. He handed Bentley one as well. She changed without him having to ask—progress—and the two of them walked the maze of dark tunnel until they found the door he'd been looking for.

Beyond the door they walked up a flight of stairs, and at the top, King eased open another door and gave things a look. It led to a public tunnel above ground for a different train line, and the camera that usually faced the door had been removed for "maintenance," just like he had paid for it to be. He and Bentley walked out onto the sidewalk and settled into the crowd, as if they belonged there like everyone else. Immediately King spotted the car waiting for them. The two of them casually climbed in, and the car pulled away. No one was the wiser.

6

RAFINA, GREECE

Thirty kilometers east of Athens

A FEW MILES northwest of the port of Rafina, Greece, on the Aegean Sea, the quaint coastal town turns into a rural wooded area before the landscape climbs the peaks of the Penteli Mountains to the west. Somewhere nestled in between there exists a gathering of twelve small homes, situated on a couple hundred acres of private land. Twelve years ago Saajid Hammoud and his brother, Husaam, moved from their family's small flat in Athens to this expanse of property in order to expand operations. After their father, Majid, died at the hands of American soldiers, keeping him from building Allah's army to fight what he deemed the growing cancer that is Western culture, Saajid vowed to carry on his father's legacy.

Last year Saajid thought all of his and his brother's hard

work was going to pay off. They had aligned themselves with childhood friends who were heirs to a Greek tycoon's fortune. Saajid's mother had actually been their nanny. Thanks to the negligence of their ultrarich parents, Anastasia, Andonios, and Gregor Maragos partially grew up in the slums where Saajid's home was. The home where Saajid's father had opened the children's eyes to the sins of the West and how it would ruin the world if it were able to continue to thrive.

Over a decade of plotting and planning had been set in motion last year. They had built the perfect weapon, and been able to keep it off the radar of the world's intelligence agencies. Until Gregor Maragos—the brains behind the nanotech weapon they attempted to unleash on the United States and their leaders—got sloppy. Anastasia and Andonios were supposed to keep their brother Gregor focused solely on the building of the weapon. However, when one of his techs leaked information about the weapon to an American agent, Gregor decided to take matters into his own hands. He'd hired an assassin to kill the American agent, and the plan quickly unraveled after that.

If Gregor had consulted Anastasia and Andonios first, they would have contacted Saajid, and Saajid himself would have been able to dispose quietly of anyone who knew about the weapon they were building. Instead, the CIA found out about their agent's death and subsequently sent in one of their best to clean everything up.

Alexander King.

Despite King and his team throwing a wrench into everything they had planned, Anastasia and Andonios had almost managed to pull it off. They had unleashed the deadly nanotechnology on the White House, but King had been able to stop it before the president was harmed. He did so by killing Anastasia before she could reach the president. Losing her had been a great loss to the cause, because she was unwaveringly dedicated. And it had been a great personal loss as well, because she had always been like a sister to Saajid. The fact that Alexander King was dead—paying for his interference with his life—offered very little in the way of a sense of retribution. Anastasia was still gone, and the plan to strike a blow to the power in the West had still been a failure.

The only positive for Saajid was the way he and his brother had managed to keep completely clean and undetected during and after all of that mess. This was by design, but when people you plot with for years, like Anastasia and Gregor, die trying to commit an "act of terror," it's hard to stay clear of the debris. Their deaths were most likely the reason for Saajid remaining free from suspicion, because it gave the United States a bookend to tell their people that it was all taken care of. The US government could tell the American people they were safe, because they had killed the bad guys.

The only Maragos who had managed to stay alive after the failed mission had been Andonios. This was great for Saajid and Husaam because they had always been closest to him, but now it was the reason that Saajid was sitting in his backyard watching the sun disappear behind the mountains with a stomach full of anxiety. Saajid had called and texted Andonios several times over the past twenty-four hours. Andonios always answered within the hour. It had now been an entire day.

Saajid heard the laughter of his children as they rounded the side of his house. As they ran over to him, he forced a smile. His daughter was twelve, and his son was nine. Both of them were as curious as he had been at that age about the teachings of Allah. However, they were far more knowledgeable than he was. The commune Saajid had built around their house had ensured as much. He loved the two of them. It was one of the reasons the failed mission a year ago had disappointed him so deeply. He wanted it for them. He wanted them to be as proud of him as he had always been of his own father for working for his people and their culture. For shielding him from the sins of the ignorant.

He checked the burner phone one last time. Still nothing from Andonios. He swallowed his growing worry and embraced his children. He needed to hear himself preach the teachings of Islam as much as his family needed to hear it then. It always brought him comfort.

As he gave them a smile, he said a prayer that Andonios would be okay. The next mission Saajid had been working on so diligently for over a year was all but ready to go. But he didn't want to do it without Andonios.

7

KING AND BENTLEY made it back to his flat, took the lift to the fifth floor, and casually walked down the hall to his door. They had driven over to Westminster first, changed cars as a precaution, then finally circled all the way back to Soho. Just blocks from where the car bomb had exploded earlier. King had chosen the location in Soho, between Oxford Street and Marlborough Street, because of its vibrant activity during the day and its active nightlife. Not because he had ever planned to partake, but because a lot of movement around his residence, day or night, made it much easier for him to come and go unnoticed. Blending in was essential when the last thing he wanted to do was stand out. Soho made this easy for him. And the Oxford Circus station right outside his building also enabled him to travel anywhere in the city with ease. It was a stark contrast from his home in Kentucky.

Or what used to be his home.

King opened the door for Bentley and let her in. Other than asking why they had to change cars, she hadn't said a word since exiting the tunnel. King's flat was a two bedroom. The kitchen was open to the living room, which was where they were standing now. It was painted a neutral tan color that complemented the hardwood floors. There wasn't much in the way of decoration, mainly just a couch in the middle of the room that faced the TV. The only real glimpse into his personality were the books that packed the inset shelves behind the TV. When you're constantly alone and there is a bookstore around the corner, books worked well for passing the time. Sometimes you don't choose your hobbies, they choose you. He was surprised how much he enjoyed the slower pace of reading. He'd been consuming all of Vince Flynn's Mitch Rapp books. They were excellent and surprisingly realistic.

King turned and locked the three dead bolts on the door. Then he pulled out a key to lock the last one.

Bentley noticed what he was doing. "You lock people inside your home often? That's pretty creepy. And I've got to be honest, it doesn't make me feel warm and fuzzy."

"It should. Keeping you safe is the reason I've added the lock. If you wander the streets now, they'll find you."

"Who the hell are you?"

Bentley's accent reminded him of Sam. So did her feisty nature. Samantha Harrison had been King's closest ally after he left US Special Operations. When their paths crossed in a violent way a few years ago, her grit and determination in a horrible situation had linked them together for life. Shortly after, Sam left MI6, and because King had saved her life, she vowed to fight beside him in whatever way he chose. She ended up returning the favor more than once by keeping him from certain death. He really needed to check in with her. She'd called and texted several times that day. King knew she'd be worried.

"Earth to bearded guy. I said, who are you? And why are people trying to kill me?"

King walked past her and over to the kitchen. He reached into the cabinet, grabbed two glasses and a bottle of King's Ransom bourbon. The bottle was the only reminder in the house of what seemed now to be a very distant past.

"I'm trying to get those answers myself," he told her. "You should be able to help me clear up a lot of things."

"Me? I was just going for a run, then back home to study for an exam I have tomorrow. Why would anyone want to kill me?"

King studied Bentley for a moment. Though her hat was still pulled low, he could see that she was a beautiful girl. Olive skin, dark brown hair, tall and slender, and hazel eyes just like her father. Not the typical look of a Brit. But that's because her father was Greek. He examined her expression trying to determine if she actually had no idea what was going on or if she was bluffing. So far she was pretty convincing.

He poured a couple of fingers of bourbon for himself, then raised an eyebrow at Bentley.

"You do know I'm only seventeen."

He did, but she certainly didn't look it. She looked more like twenty-five.

"And? You think I'm so out of touch that I don't know you're partying? I'm thirty, not seventy. Do you want a drink or not?"

"I'd rather have some answers, but I could use a drink too."

He poured one for her. Both of them were quiet as they

44

sipped. King found it hard to believe that she could be completely in the dark. But he'd been watching her every move for over a month and hadn't seen anything to make him suspicious. It was more likely she was a pawn in a much larger game. The unsavory associations her biological father kept played a hand in making her look guilty. King was also trying to assess what communications she may have had with Andonios Maragos. From everything he'd seen, there were none. And after last night, there sure as hell wouldn't be any in the future either.

However, King was really just getting used to being a *spy*. His assessment thus far of his own covert abilities was a five on a scale of one to ten. His expertise lay much more in the art of assassination. The difficult thing for him was that he was used to relying on Sam for all the technical legwork. Over the years they'd been the perfect combination of her setting things up and him knocking them down, sealing the deal. This was still how their current relationship worked, but this bit of special operation with Bentley had grown from a passing conversation overheard by Sam, to a bit of a side project for him. CIA Director Mary Hartsfield knew that King was still working to get answers for what happened about a year ago—the reason he had to fake his own death—but she thought he was only doing work through the CIA. Sam, of course, knew King had found Andonios, but they both agreed not to tell Mary because they didn't want it to get botched somehow by other agents. Mary wouldn't be too happy about King running his own side mission—neither would Sam regarding Bentley, for that matter—but as King had always played it since leaving Special Operations, what they didn't know wouldn't hurt them.

He couldn't help but think Sam would find out about

this one, though. It was going to be all over the news. And when the American agent he locked horns with back in the underground reported back to the agency that an unknown American man had saved his life, and walked away with The Asset they were searching for, word would make it back to his two leading ladies. That much he was sure of.

"I said, what are we going to do now?" Bentley finally got his attention.

King finished his drink as he thought about the plan. He knew she was just going to have to sit tight while he determined whether or not she was truly uninvolved with the terrorists her father Andonios had been in bed with. If in fact she wasn't, he then had to figure out why in the hell the terrorists would want her dead. If that was even still the case. The terrorist in the tunnel saying it was an American who'd paid them for the car bombing was as tricky a curveball as King had ever seen. Even if Sam didn't find out it was him who'd saved Bentley today, he was going to have to tell her. He was going to need her help in a major way.

"Look, Bentley, this is an extremely complicated situation. You were just the central theme in a terrorist attack. If you don't know why, I have to find out for you."

"I don't understand. What's in it for you? Are you CIA or something? If so, why would you take me back to your place? Why not take me to your offices or whatever?"

King poured another one for himself. "That's not how it works. Not for me anyway."

Bentley rolled her eyes and turned away from him, taking in the small living room.

He pulled his phone from his pocket. More missed messages from Sam. And it was getting late. He needed to get to the rest of what needed to be done that night.

"Listen, I have to go. But you'll be safe here."

Bentley whipped back around. "You can't just leave me here. What if they followed us?"

For the first time, her innocent look of fear revealed her teenage demeanor.

"They didn't. You're just going to have to trust me. I haven't let you down yet, have I?"

He watched her search for a reason to say yes.

"No. But what am I supposed to do here?"

King pointed to the shelves covered in books. "You could start there. But I also have Netflix . . . oh, and pizza in the freezer."

"If I'm not a prisoner, can I have my phone back?"

King walked around the center island. "Sorry, kiddo. It's for your own safety. No one can know you're here."

"This sucks." She pouted.

"It could be a lot worse."

8
_____

THE SCHOTTENSTEIN CENTER IN COLUMBUS, Ohio, was buzzing. The crowd of nearly twenty thousand were rattling the rafters as if a game-winning shot had just gone down from the Buckeyes' basketball team. However, there wasn't a game going on tonight. The mass of people had gathered to support the surging presidential hopeful Senator Bob Gibbons—Bobby to anyone who'd known him more than a minute. As he stepped away from the podium after another awe-inspiring speech, however, the gleam of the crowd was already far from his mind. Other matters that he'd been trying to distance himself from were at the forefront— matters that were quickly becoming the biggest threat to derailing his bid to be the next president of the United States of America.

He bypassed the outstretched hand of his campaign manager and hustled toward the tunnel on his way to the men's locker room where Ohio State University had arranged a small celebration for him and a few local influencers after the rally. The crowd continued its rabid excitement behind him, their echoes following him down the hall. As he hurried along the tunnel, he noticed a banner of himself hanging on the wall. The well-kept, silver-haired, sixty-five-year-old man on the banner exuded confidence. You could see it in his eyes. Bobby Gibbons wished he had that confidence at the moment, but he was actually doing his best not to sweat right through his suit—not because he was hot but because he was nervous about what was going on while he was giving his speech.

He walked through the doorway of the locker room. The room was circular, with wooden lockers fanned out along the wall, a red seat in front of each one. The round Ohio State logo that usually hovered over the center had been covered with a banner featuring Bobby's "Gibbons 2020" logo—complete with his grassroots slogan, "*A Better America.*"

The roomful of supporters, campaign workers, and media all let out a roar when Bobby entered. He feigned a smile, waved his hand, then walked right over to his wife, Elizabeth. As he gave her a hug, he whispered in her ear.

"Where's Doug? Have you seen him?"

She kissed him on the cheek. "He's waiting near the showers."

Bobby's stomach dropped. This was the first step in clearing himself of everything that happened with Everworld Solutions and the fallout of some of his fellow investors. He and a couple of other congressmen were heavily involved in the corporation founded by the current US president, Mark Williams. When President Williams was elected, he abruptly left the company, and a host of seedy information began to surface. The biggest consequence was that many people, most of all the two fellow congressmen who had convinced Bobby to invest, lost a lot of money because of some shady dealings. A lot of people were angry at the president for leaving the company vulnerable, but none more than Senators Jerry McDonnell and Graham Thomas. Bobby was upset with the president as well, but not like the two of them. It was all downhill after that.

Bobby never really wanted to be involved in the company in the first place. But Jerry and Graham had convinced him it was a sure thing. Millions would come easily. However, the biggest reason Bobby pulled most of his money out early was because, as things began to crumble, it seemed Jerry and Graham were in it for other, more sinister reasons. Things Bobby wanted nothing to do with. He had been upset that the president had left the company hanging, but he didn't want revenge. Bobby also knew that things ran much deeper than that for Jerry and Graham. They had never gotten along with the president.

After Bobby had pulled most of his money, he'd thought everything with the company had died off. Turned out, it was Jerry and Graham who ended up dead. From all Bobby gathered from his inside sources, the entire thing was tied back to terrorism. At first Bobby could hardly believe it—that was until the White House was attacked a year ago—the president being the main target—and Jerry and Graham both paid for their involvement with their lives. Ever since then, Bobby's life had been a whirlwind of fear and exhilaration.

The tidal wave of support to run against President

Williams came out of nowhere. The entire incident—even though the president had been cleared of wrongdoing—had scarred the presidency and left a bad taste in the American people's mouths. The problem for Bobby was he knew that when you ran for the highest office in the land, *all* of your skeletons would come out of the closet. That is why he hired Doug—to make sure those skeletons disappeared. The nastiest skeleton being his involvement with Everworld and, even worse, the few private meetings he had with the two now deceased senators.

Though Bobby knew he never invested in the company for anything other than a good return, Doug Chapman—the expert on such political matters—insisted that every measure needed to be taken to erase all doubt in the minds of Americans that he had anything to do with the terrorism-funding company. Doug told Bobby that *any* lingering suspicions about such involvement would be political suicide.

Yesterday morning Doug came to Bobby and assured him he could erase any chance that Bobby's name would ever be mentioned alongside the topic of terrorism. When Bobby asked Doug what that meant, he gave him the cliché answer that the less Bobby knew, the better. Plausible deniability, in other words, in case something went wrong. Doug said he would handle it discreetly, and then they would be in the clear.

As Bobby walked toward Doug, who was leaning against the inside wall of the shower, he could tell by the look on Doug's face that something terrible had happened.

Doug ushered him into the open shower room. The twelve-showerhead, white-tiled room smelled of soap, ironically mirroring Bobby's wish to wash all of this away. Doug poked his head back out to make sure nobody else was around.

"We have a problem," Doug said.

The words of every presidential hopeful's demise.

Bobby searched Doug's beady brown eyes for the depth of the problem. The salt-and-pepper-haired, skinny, middle-aged man was anything but physically intimidating. However, the power he wielded in political circles was the stuff of legend. He'd been with the CIA for fifteen years before beginning a career of political *fixing*. All of those covert operations he'd learned at the agency were very useful to powerful men like Bobby. Doug was someone he never would have hired if there'd been other viable options.

"Not really what I wanted to hear, Doug. How bad is it?"

Bobby watched Doug swallow hard. He knew right then that when a man as hard as Doug paused before bad news, it was *really* bad, and things would never be the same.

"Doug, what did you do?" Bobby folded his arms across his chest. He could feel his heart thudding.

"You heard about the explosion in London earlier today?"

"The car bomb some terrorists set off? Yeah, what about it?"

Doug was quiet.

"Doug?"

"I told you the less you knew, the better."

"I don't understand," Bobby said, moving his hands to his hips. "You brought me back here with an update on clearing me of the Everworld bullshit. Now, instead of updating me, you mention a terrorist attack in London and then tell me the less I know the better? What the hell is going on?"

"It was us," Doug said.

"What was us? What are you saying? Stop being vague and spit it out." Bobby's heart was beating so fast he was short of breath.

Doug's jaw was set as he squinted his eyes. "The attack, in London. That was us. And it didn't work."

9

London, UK

King turned off the shower and began toweling off. He bumped his knee against the toilet as he exited. Months spent in London and he still wasn't used to the small spaces. The cold tile beneath his feet gave him a chill as he limped over to the sink. The hot water had left a layer of steam on the mirror. He wiped it away with his hand, revealing his unbearded face in the cleared strip. He looked down at the bushy beard lying on the floor and smiled. He knew when he'd put it on earlier that it was a bit "*costume dramatic,*" but it had done the job. No camera in the city would be the wiser.

He stared at the stubble on his iron jaw. To shave or not to shave? He rattled his finger in his ear to clear some residual water—the same ear that was still ringing from being so close to the explosion. Other than the ringing, he'd come out unscathed. Many times in his career he hadn't been so lucky. He wiped another streak of steam away, and his torso came into view. There he saw the scars to prove other incidents had been a lot more painful. He rubbed the scar from a bullet wound on his right shoulder—a memento from Syria. Sam and his closest friend, Kyle, had been captured by Sanharib Khatib. It was a miracle they'd survived. His other friend, Sean, hadn't been so lucky that night.

King moved his hand from his shoulder to his stomach. A scar from a brutal shotgun blast to the solar plexus. The men had come for him on his boat. This time it was Sam and his former flame, Sarah Gilbright, who saved him. King was in a coma for two weeks after that.

He reached down for his calf muscle, another bullet wound scar.

He often wondered why he'd been lucky enough to survive those and countless other situations where there seemed no way out. Sam would often tell him it was because he was doing what he was meant to do. But it wasn't like this life was one he chose. Like most men in uniform, he supposed, this life had chosen him. He just happened to be particularly good at it. He asked Sam once what she would be doing if her life hadn't led her to MI6. She responded like she often did—telling him he was a fool for contemplating such things. When he asked her what she'd thought he'd be doing if the murder of his parents hadn't pushed him into the military, she just laughed, and mused that he and Kyle would probably be bartenders. Like the one Tom Cruise played in the movie *Cocktail*.

However, in the end, King supposed Sam was right. It was foolish to ponder things that never were or never would be. In a moment much like the one he was having in front of the mirror now, when he was flying to Los Angeles to try to save a young girl from a sex trafficking ring, he realized he was meant for nothing else. He was supposed to be the one they called when shit hit the fan. The man who could *fix* it. But things had changed in the past year. Ever since the day he faked his own death.

The thing that hadn't changed was his resolve to nail every last one of the bastards involved in the nanobot terrorist attack in March of 2019. Even though Sam, Kyle, his sister, and his niece, who'd all been implanted with one of the nanochips that could have killed them at the touch of a button, were now clear of the threat, it didn't lessen his desire to make all responsible parties pay. Pretending to be dead had been the only way to do that. No one responsible for the failed attack could know he was alive and preparing to come after them. The hardest part about all of it was that CIA Director Mary Hartsfield—one of only two people in the world who knew he was alive—couldn't know he was still going after them either.

Though King had promised Mary that he would let the CIA do the work to bring them all to justice, not for a single second had he planned to keep that promise. It was the entire reason he was living a lonely existence to that day. Not even his sister and niece, nor Kyle—who was like a brother—knew he was still alive. As a loner he could move and gather intel in a way an agency man never could. He didn't have to worry about rules. And he didn't have to worry about someone taking their anger out on his loved ones. That had happened far too many times in his life already.

King was now a ghost, a reality that had its perks, but as he realized with Bentley in the kitchen earlier—when he was happy just to have someone in his residence for the first time in a year—being a ghost also had some serious draw-backs. He knew it would all be worth it—at least that's what he'd convinced himself—when he found himself standing over the last person who almost killed what was left of his family. Then and *only* then would he be done with this mission.

There were a lot of things he had to figure out, though, to get there. In the meantime, he had to appease Director Hartsfield. And when his phone began vibrating on the nightstand in the bedroom, he knew it was Sam calling to let him know the drop had been made with info on his latest target. And this had nothing to do with what King had been up to with Bentley.

As he walked over to the phone, he couldn't help but laugh at the irony of his situation. A man who was supposed to be dead, he was not only alive but living two lives. A top secret counterterrorism assassin for the director of the CIA by day, vigilante justice seeker by night. He was exhausted just thinking about it. However, the revelation he'd had not long ago about who he was, and why he did what he did, helped him understand that he would never tire of going after those who meant his country harm. As long as there were people alive in the world wanting to take away his sister's and his niece's freedom, and jeopardize their safety and way of life, King would be there in the shadows to make sure they failed. *That* was what he was meant to do.

King answered the phone. "Hey, Sam. Miss me?" His brother-sister relationship with Sam had never wavered, even though they hadn't seen each other in so long.

"Not even for a moment," Sam said. Her sharp British accent had become less grating since he'd been living amongst the Brits for the past six months. But he would never tell her that.

"I love you too. I suppose the file is ready?"

"A courier just dropped a box at your flat. But that isn't why I'm calling."

He already knew what Sam was about to say.

She cleared her throat. "I suppose you heard about the terrorist attack just 'round the corner from you. Car bomb .. . dozen people injured . . ."

"I heard a lot of sirens, but I haven't had the TV on all day."

"Don't, X." Sam was stern. Ever since he *"died,"* she'd *made sure to call him X.* Just in case anyone was listening. "Not with me. Why didn't you tell me you were running this thing down with Bentley?"

"Let me guess, the agent said an American stopped his asset from dying, and you just assume it's me?"

Sam let out a sigh. "You may think you are different now, but I know you. Saving a woman is one of your favorite pastimes."

"She's just a girl, Sam. And we shouldn't be talking about this over the phone."

"Where is she?"

"I'll call you from the new burner phone."

"If you insist on doing this, at least let me help you. Things are about to get a lot more complicated for you. For everyone really."

King didn't like the sound of that.

"Why?"

Sam dodged the question. "I'm running into a meeting just outside of Athens. Let's continue this once you're up to speed."

"Why are things about to get more complicated, Sam?"

"You'll see when you get a look at your new target." Sam ended the call.

10

BOBBY'S STOMACH felt like it was turning inside out. Right after Doug told him that the attack in London was *their own people*, they were interrupted by his campaign manager. She told him that the media couldn't wait any longer and he needed to give them some sound bites on how the rally had gone. He knew this conversation with Doug wasn't going to be a quick one, so he was left with the pit in his stomach as he smiled for the cameras a moment ago, and played his role of the surefire pick for the next president of the United States.

He was wringing his hands in the back of the SUV when Doug finally opened the door and sat down.

"Tim, can you give us a few minutes?" Bobby said to his driver.

"Yes, sir." Tim got out of the car and left the two men alone.

Bobby's voice was shaky. "What the *hell* is going on,

Doug? I gave you the okay to make sure the last of the information tying me to McDonnell and Thomas in this whole Everworld debacle would stay quiet. How in the hell did this end up in a bombing? I would've never okayed anything like that. Are you nuts?"

Doug reached across the leather seat and took a handful of Bobby's shirt. Bobby couldn't believe what was happening.

"Let me tell you something, Bobby. You might as well quit your run for president right now 'cause you obviously don't have the stomach for it."

The fire in Doug's eyes was white-hot. Bobby had heard from the men who'd recommended Doug that he was an animal. But they had also said no one got things done like he could. That said, Bobby never thought for a second the man would lay his hands on him.

Bobby slapped away Doug's grip on his shirt. "Who do you think you are, Doug? Don't you ever touch me again. I'm a United States senator."

Doug looked Bobby right in the eyes. "You should remember who *I* am. If you think it matters to me that you're a senator, then whoever suggested you call me didn't explain my methods clearly enough. I'm trying to help you. But I'll just leave you holding the bag if that's what you want."

Bobby looked in the man's eyes and could suddenly see he was dealing with someone with no moral compass whatsoever. Whatever Bobby was able to do himself to rectify things, it would have to wait. Right now he was just going to have to play along with this savage. Maybe there was still a way out of this mess.

"Just tell me what happened," Bobby snapped back. The vein in his forehead nearly popped through his skin. "And don't question whether I have the balls for this position. Don't forget I'm a Marine. I've stared down many a long barrel."

That seemed to relax Doug. He loosened his tie and relayed the bad news.

"We're still operating under the less you know, the better, but I have to tell you this in case there's blowback."

"Just spit it out. How the hell could anything I'm doing necessitate a car bomb in London?"

"All I can tell you is that there is a girl—a financial mathematics prodigy—who knows everything that happened with the money in Everworld Solutions. She masterminded how to hide all of the money that was funneled from Everworld to the terrorists, who then used it to build the nanotechnology that almost killed the president last year."

"Doug, I told you, I didn't have anything to do with that. That was Jerry McDonnell and Graham Thomas."

"But you hired me to do a deep dive. And what I've found out is that the money you gave them to *invest* went directly into funding Gregor Maragos and the nanotech he built for this attack."

The pit in Bobby's stomach grew deeper. "How could you possibly know that?"

"It's what I do."

Bobby rubbed the corners of his eyes with his thumb and index finger. He could feel a migraine coming on. "So what could that—and this girl—have anything to do with a car bomb? I just don't get it."

"The bomb was meant to kill her, get her out of the picture so she couldn't link the money trail back to you," Doug said without emotion.

Bobby swallowed hard. "What? You can't kill someone

just because I might be in trouble!"

Doug leaned in. "You sure about that, Senator Gibbons? Mr. Presidential Hopeful?"

Bobby leaned in as well. "Yes, I'm damn sure of that. Under *no* circumstances would I have *ever* okayed that. Not even if I was guilty. Are you kidding me?!"

"Well, she didn't die, someone saved her. I'm back-channeling my CIA sources to see who it was. As of right now, nobody knows."

"You're telling me that someone knew about this, and saved the girl you were trying to kill with a car bomb? Who set the bomb, Doug? The news said it was men tied to a terrorist cell."

Doug smirked. "That's because I made sure that it was tied to a terrorist cell. Unfortunately, it was all for naught because we didn't get her. But don't worry, I will."

"You're out of your mind." Bobby reached across Doug and opened the SUV's door. "Get the hell out of my truck. You're fired."

Doug shook his head and pulled the door back shut. Then he pulled a pistol from his hip holster and shoved the barrel right beneath Bobby's chin so hard it made his teeth rattle. "You can't fire me, Bobby. That's not how this works. I'll see this through until you're a hundred percent in the clear. Then you'll get me the other half of my money. Then I'll move on to help someone else." He shoved the gun, snapping Bobby's head back. "You understand?"

"Yes. I—I understand. Now get that gun out of my face!"

Doug put the gun away, opened the door, and stepped out. He poked his head back inside. "Don't forget that I know your secrets. I didn't just find things out about you being tied to Everworld when I did my digging." The yellow interior light shone down on Doug's prideful smirk. "I know about that intern several years back too. You do your job, and I'll do mine. No one, including your pretty wife, has to know all your secrets. Good luck with the rally tomorrow night. I'll be in touch." The door slammed shut.

Bobby was shaking. Fifteen years as an active duty Marine and he'd never had a gun held to his head. He runs for president, and it happens in the back of his very own car. Maybe Doug was right. Maybe he wasn't cut out for this level of politics. He wanted to be the president of the United States but not if it meant people were going to die. Much less some innocent girl. This had spun out of control more quickly than he could have imagined. He was far worse off now than he had been before he hired Doug. He wasn't concerned about the intern. What Doug didn't know was that Bobby never lied to his wife. Bobby had made a mistake a decade ago, but he'd told Beth the next day. That was the least of his worries anyway, because a sex scandal paled in comparison to being an accessory to acts of terror.

Bobby shook his head and racked his brain. He had to handle this, but he had to treat it delicately. Doug was obviously connected, but so was Bobby. He just had to make sure whoever he contacted about this could be trusted absolutely. If Doug made this look like a terrorist cell was responsible, it meant he somehow had terrorist ties. Which, ironically, was the exact thing Bobby was trying to absolve himself of when he hired Doug.

The other major concern was the unidentified man who saved the girl in London from the car bomb. Who was this man and what did he know? If he was CIA, that means the CIA must know. If so, Doug could be tied back to Bobby, and that made the question of whom to call pretty simple. His old buddy Mary Hartsfield. Director of the whole damn agency.

Bobby picked up his phone and dialed her number.

"Senator Bobby Gibbons," Mary answered, "to what do I owe this pleasure? Aren't you on the campaign trail?"

"Hi, Mary. Just finished up a rally in Columbus this afternoon actually. How's the state of affairs in the world these days?"

"Bleak. But that's the job. Always has been, always will be. Please don't tell me it's about to get worse."

Bobby's wife got in the car. He held up a finger to let her know the call was important.

"I can trust you, right?"

"Shit," Mary said.

"I know. Sorry. But I didn't know who else to call."

"I get that a lot. You coming back to Washington?"

"I can."

"I'll be in my office all night. I'll let the front desk know you're coming."

"Thanks, Mary."

"Don't thank me yet. I've got a lot on my plate right now with this stuff in London. Everybody wants answers."

"Maybe I can help a little with that."

"Oh, Bobby. I sure hope not."

"I'll see you soon."

Bobby ended the call as his driver got back in.

"How bad is it?" Elizabeth said.

"We're in real trouble, Beth." Then to the driver he said, "Take us back to the hotel, please."

Beth took his hand. "I'm sure we've been through worse."

Bobby could tell by her tone that she was hoping to hear him say that they *had* been through worse. But they hadn't. He'd never lied to his wife, and he wasn't going to start now.

"Sweetheart, I'm not sure we have."

11

London, UK

KING OPENED THE CARDBOARD ENVELOPE LEFT BY THE courier in the lobby of his building. He removed the key and pocketed it, then took out his phone. Sam had texted him the address and the number of the locker where his new phone and assignment would be. He memorized it, then placed his phone inside the envelope. The envelope had a special interior lining. The lining was made of a material King had never heard of; all he knew was that it was indestructible. The reason for this special material involved the plastic tube at the bottom of the envelope. He snapped open the tube and placed it back inside the envelope beside his phone. He then sealed the envelope and tossed it in the bin beside him. The chemical in the tube would release and completely destroy the phone, as well as all evidence ever stored on it. Then he walked out into the cool night air.

It was just after dinner. London was bustling. As soon as he stepped onto the sidewalk, the city seemed to pour in all around him. People were talking and laughing as they walked by, car horns blared, the underground train announced its arrival at Piccadilly Circus, and police sirens wailed in the distance. King pulled his black ball cap down over his eyes and weaved in and out of people like a gust of wind. Felt maybe, but never really seen.

The mailbox where his files had been dropped wasn't far. He recognized the address from a previous use a month and a half ago. It was an N1 Mailbox store. Your basic PO Box and copy shop. Sam only used the same place a second time when the staff at the store had completely turned over. She was particular like that. It used to annoy him when they first got together—the two of them were constantly butting heads—but it wasn't long after her attention to detail saved his life for the first time that he began to appreciate it. Didn't mean he ever stopped giving her shit about it.

King rounded the corner, just away from the madness of Piccadilly. The mailbox store was just up ahead, only a couple of doors down from the bookstore where he'd become a regular. Just as he was about to reach for the door to the store, he popped the collar on his coat and strolled right on by. He had glanced across the street and noticed a woman shoot her glare away from him as soon as he looked in her direction. It ticked King's instincts and made him nervous.

King continued down the sidewalk. Who could possibly be watching him? He'd allowed no holes in the execution of his mission to retrieve Bentley. He'd painstakingly mapped out the entire thing. Every day that he had gone to watch Andonios Maragos at his lakeside home, he'd either shadowed Bentley before or after the fact. He'd staked out every corner outside her flat, and no one had ever followed or noticed him. Could this woman be CIA? King didn't think so, because Director Hartsfield would have had Sam tell him about any agency surveillance of a suspicious man in London.

King reached for his phone out of habit, but of course it was melting in the magic envelope back in the lobby of his flat at the moment. Sam would have been his call, but he knew she would know nothing about this either. This sort of thing had been the hardest part about not working with his team. Someone had always been there to bounce things off of. Now he had to solely rely on his gut, which had always been good, but it did need some sharpening after a year alone in the field. And right now his gut was telling him that he was sure no one had been onto him. So who was that woman? Could it just be his own paranoia? Was it just a woman attracted to a handsome man across the street? Something told him that wasn't the case either, so before this woman left the scene, he needed to find out what she was doing there. It wasn't what he wanted to do, because engaging with anyone when you were trying to avoid being seen was a bad idea. But a worse idea was letting someone get away who was in fact watching you.

King glanced back over his shoulder and noticed a bus coming his way. Just as it crossed in front of the woman's line of sight where she sat in her car, he jumped in front of it, then dashed across the street and ducked behind a parked car. He got a few stares from passersby, but he didn't draw too much attention. The good thing about taking cover in a big city like London is that the people who lived there were desensitized to crazy behaviors because they happened all the time.

King stayed low on the street side of the parked cars and

made his way back toward the passenger side of the woman's vehicle. He stopped a car behind her and could see her craning her neck in the rearview mirror to try to find him. She clearly wasn't a professional because she didn't drive away; not to mention, she'd parked right under a streetlamp that shone directly inside her car.

The woman started the car, and King surged forward. When he pulled his Glock and tapped the window with it, the woman—the girl—froze in fear. He ducked down to where she could see his face and told her to open the door, glancing at the pistol. She took the hint and unlocked the door. King opened it and slid inside.

"Who are you?" he said before getting a good look. If he had seen her face in the yellow glow of the car's interior light before opening his mouth, there would have been no need to ask.

The girl was Bentley Martin.

A cold wave rolled through King. It had been a while since he'd had the feeling of not knowing what was going on, and he didn't like it. Whoever the girl was that he saved from the car bomb was a dead ringer, but she was older. And up close, there was just enough difference in her nose that he could tell this was her. He should have remembered the shape of her nose being different than the girl in his apartment from the pictures he had of Bentley. But he'd missed it. And now the questions was what was it going to cost him.

It was clear she could tell that King knew who she was, but she still didn't say. So King did the talking. "Answer every single one of my questions, and maybe you'll make it out of this alive."

Bentley nodded.

"Who is the girl back at my apartment?"

"A friend." Bentley wasn't shaky, even in the face of such danger. "Ever since Karen and I met about a year ago, people have been telling us we look just like twins."

The interior light shut off.

"How did you know where to find me?"

"You're American." She sounded surprised.

King didn't react.

Bentley continued. "I put a tracking chip in her hat, just in case something happened."

King wasn't upset with himself because he didn't find the chip. There was no way he could have ever known. He needed to move the conversation forward.

"You almost got her killed."

This time it was she who gave no reaction.

He went on. "Why the swap? Why did you think someone was watching?"

"My father was murdered last night. It was only logical that I could be next."

So much for the theory that Bentley and Andonios had no communication. The direction this entire thing was taking wasn't sitting well. King didn't want to let on how much he knew; he wanted to keep Bentley talking.

"Who was your father?"

Bentley let out a sigh. "Look, I clearly have a lot of people after me, hence the car bomb that was meant for me, right? If you knew enough to be there to 'save me,' then you know who my father is. Don't treat me like a kid. I haven't been a kid in a very long time."

King was impressed. "Okay, fair enough. Why do you say 'a lot of people' are after you?"

Bentley turned to face him. "Obviously you don't mean

to kill me, so tell me, who are you? Why did you save me from an attack, only to hold me in your flat? It certainly seems as though you aren't just some random pervert. You know who I am, it's only fair I know the same."

Bentley was smart, but at least a little naive. That or the bravest girl King had ever met. Only time would let him know the difference. All he knew was that if he were seventeen and in her situation, he wouldn't be quite so bold.

"I saved you—saved your friend, that is—now I need something from you. Then I'll tell you everything I know if you promise to do the same."

"I'm not leaving this car, and I'm certainly not going anywhere with you."

"Smart, but you don't have a choice. Your friend is locked in my apartment, remember? I'm not here to play savior, I'm here to keep my country safe. I'm sure I don't have to tell you the length to which we Americans are willing to go to do just that."

For the first time, the light from the street showed a bit of fear in her eyes.

"What do you want?"

King nodded across the street and held up a key. "Mailbox 223. Get the envelope and bring it back here. Then I'll take you to your friend."

Bentley was quiet for a moment as she stared out the windshield. "I'll get the envelope. But I'm not going anywhere with you."

"You are."

"I'm not."

"You don't have a choice." King glanced down at the gun sitting in his lap.

Bentley snatched the key from his hand and exited the

car. As he watched her cross the street, his mind began to race about all the problems he'd just walked into. He would have to find a way to turn them into solutions.

Nothing good immediately came to mind. And *that* was a problem.

12

Saajid Hammoud finished a call with one of his senior generals in one of his several camps embedded in the United States. It was a good call. Everything was in place for the next step in delivering a message to the Americans. They just had to wait for the right moment. He walked back inside. Though he still hadn't heard from Andonios, it was time to sit with his children and teach them by reading from the Quran. It would help him settle his worry and clear his mind.

As soon as he stepped inside, his children and his attention were drawn to a pounding at the door.

"Are we expecting someone?" Saajid asked his wife.

"No. Not this late."

The pounding became more intense. Saajid went to the door. When he checked the peephole, he saw his brother. He immediately opened the door.

"Husaam? What is it?"

Husaam pushed his way inside. Saajid's younger brother looked frantic. His black cornrowed hair that was never out of place was a mess, and his long beard was disheveled in the same way. Husaam had always been the emotional one of the two, a hair-trigger temper as well, but Saajid wasn't used to seeing him look worried.

Saajid barely got the door shut before his brother began.

"He's dead. They killed him! Those bastards killed him!"

Saajid's stomach dropped, and he was confused, but the look on his children's face sobered him.

"Not here, Husaam." He gave his brother a shove.

"They killed him!"

Saajid pushed him through the living room and out the back door. Saajid knew exactly who Husaam was talking about, but he didn't want his children to hear. They too were close to Andonios. All of them called him Uncle.

Husaam continued what he was saying out the door. "The Americans have done it. I know it was them!"

Saajid made it outside and shut the door behind him. Husaam turned toward him. The look of worry he'd been wearing had been replaced with rage.

"They killed our brother. We need to hit them back immediately!"

"Calm down, Husaam. What happened?"

Saajid steeled himself for what he was about to hear.

"Ramaad kept trying to check in, but the gate guard hadn't been updated by the men at Andonios's house." Ramaad was the head of the security detail Saajid had sent to watch over Andonios in London. "Ramaad said he had to drive out to the lake to see what was going on because no one had checked in before shift change. The gate guard went to the house and found them all dead. The front door was wide open. How did the Americans find him? We have to send a message that this won't be tolerated. And we need to do it right now!"

Saajid felt sick. But thinking about another American agent taking the life of another one of Saajid's closest friends quickly transformed the nausea into anger. However, he was not like his little brother. Though he wanted the Americans to pay for what they'd done more than anything, he was patient. It had to be done right. This did change his plans, however. He *was* going to hit the Americans a little bit at a time with what they'd built in the US. Now he was thinking it would be best to give it to them all at once.

"Saajid!"

Saajid heard his brother, but he was so caught up in his thoughts it didn't register. The most important part of his long-term plan wouldn't be ready for a while in Washington, DC. It would be the game changer he'd been working on for years. No matter the damage they could do in the States with all the people they have put in place, it paled in comparison to his plans for Washington. So they were going to have to be patient for a while longer, no matter how difficult that would be.

"Saajid! Answer me!"

Saajid snapped out of his trance. He moved his blank stare to his brother's eyes. There was a fire inside them. The first step in the process would be managing his brother's anger. It had always been one of Saajid's biggest challenges. This time would be no different.

"You need to center yourself, brother," Saajid finally said.

"What? Center myself? Are you kidding me?"

"Husaam."

"They killed our father, Gregor, Anastasia, and now Andonios, and you want me to center myself? Father would be so disappointed in you."

Out of sheer reflex, Saajid shot his hand forward and slapped Husaam across the face. Husaam was shocked. Saajid may have been using violence as a tool to serve his religion, but he had never personally laid hands on his brother. Out of the corner of his eye, he saw his wife standing just outside; she was surprised as well.

Husaam was quiet for a moment, then began to nod his head. "I shouldn't be surprised that you aren't ready to act, Saajid. You're always too busy *planning* to carry out our father's work."

This cut Saajid to his core, but he didn't react.

Husaam continued. "Once again it will be me who follows through with retaliation. Who actually fights our enemy. Just like last year, when all of your planning with your technology came to nothing. It was me who struck the only blow, sending your message of death—against your will, mind you—to the Americans visiting Athens. While you are forever plotting, I am showing the Americans that we will not tolerate their ignorance. This, apparently, will be the same."

"You will wait until I have everything in place in Washington." Saajid was stern. His fists were clenched and his jaw was set. He couldn't let his brother's bravado and quick temper ruin the bigger picture. Not now.

"You will wait, brother. I will act."

"I have already acted, Husaam." Saajid said. "Did I not tell you how it would pay off to take down the American agent that had been in Athens tracking us for more than a year? Just be patient! The credentials and check-ins you got out of him will pay off. Just like waiting for me to get things together in Washington. What I am doing is bigger than just scaring the United States. We can control it!"

"Meanwhile, another of ours, Andonios, dies without retaliation? No. Like I said, you plan, I will act."

Husaam began to walk away, but Saajid stopped him with a palm to the chest. Husaam ripped his brother's arm away, then shoved him. The force caused Saajid to fall to the floor.

"Just stay out of my way, Saajid. I am going to the US myself to see this through. Nothing will stop me."

Husaam stormed off.

"Husaam!" Saajid shouted.

Saajid's wife, Aiza, hurried over and reached out her hand to help him up. Saajid slapped her hand away and rose to his feet. For the first time, he was going to have to go this alone. No Husaam and none of the Maragos family to assist him. He could finally do it his way.

"Saajid, Husaam has gone off like this before. It nearly got all of us killed."

Saajid swung his head in Aiza's direction. His blood was boiling. He slapped her across the face. "You will not speak to me in this way. I am not worried about my brother. If he goes and gets himself killed, it will be for the cause. But it will not interfere with my plans."

Aiza took a step back. "I'm just looking out for all of us. Please."

Saajid looked at her again. Her lip was bloodied. He was disappointed in himself for letting his temper get the best of him. He nodded for her to continue.

"The last time Husaam went off like this, he ruined your plans."

Saajid walked toward his wife, and she cowered as he came close. She jerked her head away as he brought his hand up to wipe the blood from her lip. Once she saw he meant no more harm, she let him caress her cheek.

"Last time Husaam ruined my plan, he actually knew my plan. This time, I have kept him mostly in the dark, for this very reason."

A fearful half smile crossed Aiza's face. He kissed her on the forehead. "Clean yourself up before the children see." Then he walked away.

As he ascended the stairs, he ignored his children's attempts at affection. His mind wasn't in a place for them. He was sad that his oldest friend, Andonios, was gone. But mostly, he was angry. Anger, unlike with his brother, focused Saajid. And he was extremely focused on taking the fight he'd been organizing for more than eleven years straight to the United States of America. They needed to feel what he was feeling. But most of all, they needed to see the error of their leaders' ways. And whoever killed Andonios would see their ways, their very lives, soon come to an end.

13

Bentley Martin emerged from the mailbox store and waited on the sidewalk for traffic to clear. King had spent the last couple of minutes digesting Bentley's story about her look-alike friend. He wondered how many times while he was surveilling Bentley that he had confused her for this other girl. The resemblance was uncanny.

As Bentley crossed the street, he shifted his focus from what had already happened to what he needed to do now, and what he needed to know. The reason he had been watching Bentley was because Sam had heard some chatter in Langley, through Director Hartsfield, that Bentley could be involved with a terrorist group in Athens. At the time, it was only in passing—a conversation Sam wasn't supposed to hear. Since King had been trying to get at Bentley's father, Andonios, from every angle, he started taking an interest for his own reasons. He'd wanted to know if she visited her father, and if so, how well did they know each

78

other? Most of all, he wanted to know if Bentley was a weakness for Andonios. King never felt as though she was; otherwise, he would have taken Bentley to get information out of Andonios about who was the true head of the terrorist cell.

Clearly, Bentley was more important than King had thought, what with attempts on her life and all, but he didn't really know the reason why. Why would another American want her dead, and why would the CIA have chosen to put an entire team in place to watch her?

Bentley opened the door, sat down, and handed him the envelope.

"What the hell am I supposed to do now?" she asked.

King hit the overhead light and began opening the envelope. "Good question."

Bentley turned toward him. "Good question? That's it? So what the hell was your plan when you took me to your flat, Mr. Secret Agent? You didn't have a next step?"

King pulled a manila folder from the envelope. The last thing he needed right now was another assignment. He was already knee-deep in need-to-figure-shit-out as it was. As far as Bentley's question of next step, he had one, but when the terrorist in the Tube told him that an American was responsible for calling for the bomb meant to kill her, that sort of threw a wrench in things.

"I was going to take you to a safe house not far from here, but seeing as how you are so popular, I don't feel like that's the best place for you."

Director Hartsfield had set up a safe house when King had moved into his flat a few months ago. A place to go if shit ever hit the fan. The problem now was if an American was after Bentley, King didn't feel like he could trust the safe house. Maybe no one knew about it, but clearly there was a leak somewhere in the States, so to King, the safe house in London was as good as burnt.

Bentley let out a sigh. "How did you know that car bomb was going to go off? How did you know to try to save me?"

"It's complicated."

King knew it wasn't the answer Bentley wanted to hear, but it was true. While Sam and Director Hartsfield were supposed to be the only two people who knew King was still alive, King knew when he had walked away from his previous life that he was going to need help to keep his loved ones safe, and an ace in the hole when he needed to change the cards he was dealt. Someone who could help him keep Sam safe, too, without her knowing it. Last year when King was running down the people responsible for the pending terrorist attack on the White House, he came across one of the sharpest individuals he'd ever met. Dbie Johnson had all but saved his friends and family with her ability to hack computers and, more importantly, recalibrate the nanobots built by the Marageses that were set to kill the president of the United States.

Not long after King turned himself into a ghost, he haunted Dbie one night at her home in Cincinnati, Ohio. Because of the way they had worked together, and the way King had also saved her life, she was willing to keep their relationship, and his existence, quiet. It was a risk for King to involve her. He didn't *really* know Dbie, but that's also what made her perfect for the job. He did trust her, but if for some reason she double-crossed him, it wouldn't be as painful for him to eliminate the problem. It was a callous thought, but the night he visited Dbie, he told her the same thing. She understood what was at stake for King, and even though her life could one day be in danger for knowing he was alive, she didn't hesitate to offer her services.

Those services had been a big help in gaining an advantage during some of King's CIA assignments during the past year. And Dbie was the sole reason he knew about the car bomb so he could save Bentley's life. Over the last week, King had put Dbie on the task of diving deep into the terror group growing rapidly somewhere near Athens, Greece. They had been increasing their presence in London, and Dbie had been able to hack the phone of one of the men she found entering London from Athens. Just this morning Dbie was able to get word to King that she found out there was a hit taking place on Oxford Street, the same street Bentley lived on. King put a plan in motion as quickly as he could.

In hindsight, he should have had Dbie tip off the CIA, but he believed it was only an attempt on Bentley's life, not a terrorist attack like it had ended up being disguised as. That's why he dove for Bentley when he saw her going out for a run. It was to shield her from a potential sniper; he had no idea the car was going to blow up. Pulling her away from that had been nothing but luck. Sometimes, like football, life and death is a violent game of inches.

What wasn't luck, however, was his escape route from Oxford Street. He'd been planning it for weeks, just in case someone made him while he was surveilling Bentley. The trick with shutting down the train and disconnecting cameras, well, that was King's secret weapon, Dbie.

So now, he needed to talk to Sam, to fill her in on everything that was going on, and to get her counsel on what to do next. He also needed to talk to Dbie, to get her started on figuring out just who in the hell the American could be that set off that bomb. But he couldn't do any of that until he knew what he was dealing with on his next *real* assignment.

"Hey man, are you okay?"

King snapped out of his trance. "What?"

"I've been talking to you for two minutes. You were on another planet."

"If you haven't noticed, there's kind of a lot going on."

King opened the manila folder and moved the briefing sheets so he could get a look at the picture of his next CIA-mandated job. He wanted to get right to it after Sam had told him things were about to get more complicated because of who this was. After one look at his assignment, he realized the word *complicated* was entirely inadequate.

As he stared down at a picture of Bentley Martin, he realized complicated now sounded like a vacation. This had just turned into an absolute clusterfuck.

14

"WHAT IS IT NOW?" BENTLEY BROKE THE SILENCE IN THE CAR. "You look like you've seen a ghost."

King pulled his Glock from his concealed holster and put it to Bentley's chin. She sucked in a lungful of air in shock, and for the first time, fear encompassed her.

"Please, whatever that envelope says I did, I didn't do it. I swear!"

"Sounds like something a guilty woman might say." There was no emotion in King's voice.

"Okay, okay. I promise I'll tell you everything I know. Just please take the gun off me."

King hesitated for a moment. She pleaded with her eyes. He put his gun away, then did something he should have done as soon as he got in the car. He patted her down for a weapon. Bentley didn't protest, she was just happy to no longer have a gun to her head. She was clean of any weapons, but he took her phone. He held down the button until he could power it off.

"Why would you do that?" she shouted.

"For your own good."

"How would taking my phone help anything?"

Kids and their precious phones.

King changed the subject.

"Why would the United States government want you dead?"

Bentley's eyes widened. She was no longer worried about her phone. "What? Is that what that is?" Her wide eyes glanced at the folder. "Your orders to kill me?"

King held up the picture of her as his answer.

"O . . . M . . . G . . . I don't understand!"

"Well, you'd better help *me* understand. I've never had a target get away."

Bentley searched his eyes. Seeing nothing but truth in them, her bottom lip began to quiver, and her hands were shaking—responses he had never seen from anyone his government deemed worthy of a death sentence. Something wasn't adding up.

Bentley took a deep breath. "I—I don't think that's me in that picture."

King shuffled back to the profile information. "Nope, says right here . . . Bentley Renea Martin."

"No, I mean I think they—your people—think it's me who's doing terrible things. But I think it's Karen. I think she's been doing it for a while now."

King's mind flashed back to the girl—woman—in his apartment. He knew exactly what Bentley was getting at, and his stomach dropped. Even though this Karen woman wouldn't be able to find anything in his place that would reveal his identity, she may have found a way to convey her location to whoever she was working for. *If* she could find a way out of his locked apartment door. But that lock wasn't made to keep a professional in. If Karen was a professional, if she wanted to she could always climb out the window. The lock on the door was more of a show to make her think she was trapped.

"Okay, Bentley. Elaborate. Are you saying you didn't put that chip in her hat in case something happened to her but to make sure she wasn't lying to you? You were planning to follow her, weren't you?"

"Yes."

Some confidence returned to Bentley's voice. Having King follow her logic meant he would probably keep her alive. Clearly someone in Director Hartsfield's world wanted her dead, but King wouldn't kill a seventeen-year-old girl unless she was about to blow up the White House itself. Bentley may be a lot of things, but his early read was that someone in the CIA had gotten this wrong.

"Start from the beginning, Bentley, but give me the Cliffs Notes version."

Bentley nodded as she interlocked her fingers, pushed them out away from her, and cracked her knuckles. "I met Karen at a pub one night a little less than a year ago. She bought me a beer because she ran into me and knocked me over. That night we got royally pissed drunk and had pretty much the time of our lives. The next few months, we were together all the time. She is a senior at Cambridge—well, so she says—and I study at Oxford, so days would go by that we didn't see each other, but we talked and texted all the time."

"I said the short version," King interrupted. He was scanning the profile on Bentley in the folder as she spoke.

"Right, well, things started to get . . . well, odd. She would say she was at school, but then we'd video chat and I would hear people around her speaking Greek. Obviously, I recognized it since I am half Greek myself."

Alarm bells went off when King heard Greek. "We'll get into that later."

"Whatever you want, I have nothing to hide."

Also spoken like a guilty person, but King was beginning to put some pieces together as Bentley was describing Karen and their relationship. He nodded for her to continue, but he really needed her to hurry. The more she spoke, the more a burning in his gut was urging him to get back to his apartment. There was no telling what he might find.

"Anyway, more and more things like that started to happen. I was already wondering why she was being more weird, but I just figured it might be to get to my money or something. But after I found out my father was killed, that's when I decided this morning that I would try to see what she was *really* up to."

"So many questions," King said. "First, why did you have a tracking device on hand to put in Karen's hat?"

Bentley half smiled. "Oh, it's standard-issue crazy from my mother. Ever since she and my father split, she'd been down a lot of rabbit holes thinking people were watching us. She used to make me carry that same chip to school every day. In case someone took me. She was always worried about someone trying to kidnap me for ransom."

"Got it. I actually understand, and she probably wasn't crazy. More importantly, how did you know Andonios—your father—was dead?"

'Cause I only just killed him last night, he thought.

"Because I overheard 'Karen,'" Bentley said, making air quotes with her fingers, "on the phone telling someone that he was dead. That they found him in some house by Bewl Water."

This time King's stomach turned. While it was good that Bentley maybe hadn't been in contact with her father after all, it also meant he had led a wolf, this Karen woman, right into his pasture for sure. The questions he had about Bentley helping her father with the shady accounting for Everworld Solutions like the CIA profile is saying, they would have to wait.

King pulled the phone he'd taken from Karen back at the apartment. Just as he suspected, it had been wiped clean. Probably a software installed on it that erased it automatically every hour or so. But technology was a funny thing. Though King would never be able to retrieve any information himself, his little secret weapon, Dbie Johnson, would be able to if it was at all possible.

"Okay, Bentley, we still have a lot to talk about, but I don't have time right now."

"You have to go make sure Karen doesn't figure out who you are, don't you?"

"Something like that."

"Who do you think she is?"

"I don't know," King said. "But I have a feeling she's been pretending to be you for a lot longer than you think."

Bentley nodded and moved her stare out the front windshield. "How did all this happen?" She was quiet for a moment. King put the folder back together and returned it to the envelope. She turned to him and waited until he found her eyes. "Are you going to kill me?"

King knew that he wasn't. He could tell that whatever information had led Director Hartsfield to choosing Bentley as his next target, obviously she was completely misled.

This wasn't the first time this kind of mix-up had happened either. The last time nearly got him and his entire team killed. King would be going into this with eyes wide open this time. However, he wasn't going to tell Bentley she was for sure off the hook yet. A little bit of fear for her life would compel her to dig even deeper for information that might help King reach the source of all this trouble.

"I won't kill you, as long as you're useful."

"Anything. Name it, I'll do it."

"Let's start with something simple." He took Karen's phone out, went to the notes section, and typed in Dbie's address. He handed Bentley Karen's phone. "Take this phone and overnight it to that address. Don't use your credit card."

"I don't have any cash."

King went back to his pocket and produced a key. "Mailbox 221. I keep a go bag there just for situations like this one. Inside—"

"Go bag?" she asked.

"Sorry—it's like a shit-hits-the-fan bag, if you will. Inside there are a lot of things, but in the first small pouch, there's a roll of cash. Use that. Keep the bag, get back to the car, and drive around until I call you."

"Okay, but I'll need my phone."

"Not happening."

"Okay, but if I mail Karen's phone, I won't have one."

"There will be a burner phone in the go bag. When you get it, just power it on."

Then he pulled the new burner phone from the envelope Sam had left him and powered it on. The number for it was taped to the top. He took the paper off and gave it to Bentley. "If you get into any trouble, just call me on this number."

"Why can't you just give me my phone back if you are going to give me a different one?"

"You know why, Bentley. If your mom was so crazy about tracking, you know good and well someone could be watching you by tracking your phone."

"All right, Mr. Secret Agent. Then you should know they can still track my phone even if it is powered off. That's Spy 101."

"That it is, smart-ass. The difference is, I *want* whoever is tracking your phone to follow me while I have it. It will save me the trouble of having to find them. Any other lessons you want to teach me?"

Bentley was quiet. King could tell she was used to being the smartest person in the room. Which made him a little nervous: maybe it *was* her who was helping her father hide his terrorist-funding money after all. That didn't mean she was guilty of anything. She wouldn't have known what it was for. But it did put her in a lot of danger if someone wanted to make sure all parties involved with that money and its intent went away. That would explain why someone was trying to kill her, but it didn't make sense as to why the CIA would want her dead. That's what really made him nervous.

Bentley rallied her thoughts. "Okay, you keep my phone, makes sense. But if you're giving me another phone, how do you know I won't call someone else?"

He knew she wouldn't because she clearly didn't know who she could trust. But instead of piling on to her already rough night, King kept it light.

"Because no one your age knows actual phone numbers. You just press the contact on your phone and it calls them. You probably don't even know your own mom's number, do you?"

Bentley gave him the side eye. Then she searched her mind to see if she did know any actual numbers. Her smirk when she looked back at him said it all.

"Right," he said. "Anyway, you're all set. When you get back to the car, just drive around until I call you on the phone in the bag. Got it?"

Bentley held up Karen's phone and repeated the instructions back to him. "Overnight this phone to the address in the notes, pay for it with the money from the grab-bag, or whatever you call it, in box 221, then get back to the car, power on the Bat-phone, and drive around until you call. Got it."

"Bentley, do *nothing* else but those things, do you understand?"

His tone brought a look of fear from her. She nodded.

"Nothing else, I mean it. And if you see anything suspicious, you call me, and you drive."

"How do you know I won't run from you? You're supposed to kill me, remember?"

King opened the door and got out of the car. Then he turned and ducked his head back in. "Because I'm also the only person who can keep you alive."

King watched as she swallowed hard. This time there was a quiver in her voice. "You're really scaring me."

That was exactly what he wanted to hear.

"Good."

King shut the car door and started back toward his apartment. The web was tangling all around him, but his mind stayed focused. When he was a Navy SEAL, they taught him that the only easy day was yesterday. With all that was swirling around him, he knew that tomorrow that saying would be more true than ever. But there was nothing easy about what he was walking into. When a man has been fighting battles for half his life, he develops a sort of foreboding ability to sense a battle coming on. And right now he felt like he was walking right back into the snake pit. For King that feeling was nothing new. In fact, it kind of felt like home.

15

KING ROUNDED THE FINAL CORNER ON THE WAY BACK TO HIS apartment. He couldn't stop to search for followers; that would be too obvious if someone was watching. Instead, he slowed his pace and pretended to take in the scenery as any tourist might. It was still early in the night, and the hustle and bustle all around him was heavy. Someone could come at him from any angle. Being exposed was a terrible feeling. Though he didn't know for sure that Karen had managed to get out of his apartment, he knew he needed to be fully ready for anything once he got back there.

He was just a block away now. The traffic was steady, and the neon glow of storefront lights were shining, beckoning potential shoppers like moths to a flame. The last couple of months he would watch these pedestrians from the window of a coffee shop, wondering what it would be like only to have to worry about the shirt they might purchase next. How it might feel to be so oblivious to the horrors of the world that constantly surrounded them. How they had no idea that the guy having a coffee next to them had killed before, and the only reason he had was because he and his government were determined to ensure that they could continue to worry only about that shirt and whether or not it made them look cute. It was an odd world, but just as the layperson could never imagine doing what King does, he could just as easily never imagine doing what they did to pass the time either. All because someone murdered his parents when he was young, he never had the chance to try a different sort of life. A *normal* life. And with the adrenaline beginning to leak into his veins as he approached the door to his building, and a possible deadly situation, he couldn't imagine wanting to live any other way.

He approached the door with a focused mind. He moved his right hand to his hip holster hidden beneath his coat as he punched in the door code with his left. The door buzzed as it unlocked, and King stepped into the empty lobby. There was no doorman, no building security either, part of his criteria when he was searching for a place in this part of the city. He bypassed the elevator, moved through the door beside it, and made his way up the stairs, his hand fixed to the grip on his gun.

The stairwell was quiet. So much so that the squeaks of his sneakers echoed through the entire space. While he wasn't sure what he would find when he made it back to his apartment, he was sure it wouldn't be Karen snuggled up on the couch with one of his books. Some people might kick themselves for not noticing that Karen wasn't Bentley, but they really did look a lot alike. And with Karen's hat pulled low, coupled with the fact that he'd never actually met Bentley in person, it was an easy miss. But King still didn't like misses. Even the smallest ones often meant the difference between living and dying—solving the puzzle and not solving it. However, the good fortune of catching Bentley's lingering stare on the street had erased that for him. It gave him the second chance to gain the upper hand. Though he might not know where Karen was at the moment, just to know to be more on edge made all the difference for a man as skilled as King.

He came to the door to the hallway on his floor. There was no window, so he had to open it to have a look. The hallway was empty to the right. He took out his phone, opened the camera, and edged it out around the doorframe. Just enough to snap a picture of the left side. The picture showed a couple making out against the wall but nothing else. He knew this couple well. She liked to be tied up, and he liked to play dress up. Oh, the joys of city living and thin walls.

King entered the hallway. The couple stopped kissing when they noticed him approaching.

"Hey guys, sorry to bother you," King said.

"He speaks!" The too-cool-for-school young man in the Ramones T-shirt was a walking hipster cliché. He held out his fist, and King gave it a bump. "I'm James, and this is Tish. Nice to finally meet you. You sure are a quiet one."

The two of you certainly aren't, he thought. King already knew James by name. He'd heard Tish scream it at least a thousand times.

King nodded to Tish. "Nice to meet you both. Listen, I don't mean to be short, but I can't seem to find my niece. Either one of you happen to see her leave a bit ago?"

"Dark hair, long legs?" James said.

Tish gave him a playful punch to the shoulder.

"What?" James laughed. "I did see her just a few minutes ago, is all." He looked back at King. "I said hello, but she just pulled her hat low and rushed down the hall."

"She take the elevator or the stairs?" King said.

"No, mate, she was going back to your place."

A chill ran down King's spine.

"How long ago was this?"

"Couldn't have been more than a couple of minutes. I was out here waiting for Tish 'cause I forgot my key."

"Thanks." King rushed toward his door.

"Everything okay, mate?"

He ignored the question as he pulled his gun. There was no reason to try to hide the weapon now; he was never coming back to this apartment complex again anyway. If Karen had left and come back, that meant she was not only a professional but most likely an assassin. An assassin in waiting.

King looked back down the hall at the couple. "Just do me a favor and both of you go grab a pint. It's not safe here right now." Then he glanced down at his gun.

The couple didn't need any more of a hint than that. The two of them scurried toward the stairwell and disappeared. King had no idea what he was about to walk into, but he didn't want them caught in the cross fire if they didn't have to be.

He reached for the door. It didn't surprise him that it was unlocked. Karen would want him to think that she had escaped and never come back. He let go of the knob and backed away from the door. She wanted him to walk in, that much was clear. But to what end? To kill him? She had to know, after what happened in the underground—the train stopping and King knowing the back way out of the tunnel —that he wasn't the type of guy who didn't think things through. That said, he knew she would still try to kill him if she got orders to do so, even if she thought it was too dangerous.

The thing King hated the most was not knowing anything about who he was dealing with. Having a CIA file on someone didn't mean you knew everything about them, but it at least gave you a glimpse into their tendencies and their actions. With "Karen," he was flying entirely blind. She could be a simple lower-level agent, sent in to mirror Bentley and learn about her, or she could be a high-level agent tasked with pinning terroristic acts on an innocent girl. Bentley is guilty by association having a father like Andonios Maragos. If King knew that, so did other people in the world. All of those musings collided with his initial hypothesis when he learned she'd left and come back. She may be any one of those things he considered, but coming back now meant she was there to kill him. Low-level agent or seasoned assassin, murder was what awaited him.

He couldn't just walk into the apartment guns blazing. This wasn't a Spaghetti Western. Bullets in real life don't just magically miss the good guy. Before he could begin to form a plan, he heard a click on the other side of the door, right at eye level. He knew it was the cover on the peephole, because the next thing he heard was Karen's footsteps as she bolted away from the door.

She wasn't ready for him to be home so quickly.

Big mistake.

He knew she was headed for the fire escape outside his bedroom window on the back side of the building.

King also knew that if he let her get away now, he would never see her again. And she might be the clue he'd been seeking for the past year. The clue that showed him the path all the way to the monster at the top of a global terrorist regime.

16

KING WAS GOING INTO HIS APARTMENT AFTER KAREN regardless, but the smell of smoke put an extra rush in his step. When he opened the door, a dark gray cloud was billowing from the kitchen on his left. It smelled like burnt cotton. With his gun extended, he raced for his bedroom door in front of him. The sheer window curtains were still blowing in the breeze from the woman who'd just escaped his apartment.

King surged forward, popping his head out the window. Karen was two floors below him, and moving fast. The metal fire escape and the people below on the sidewalk made it impossible to take a shot. Just as he threw his right leg over the windowsill, a blast behind him pushed him on through before he was ready. He didn't know if it was a small bomb Karen had left or the oven range exploding; either way, as he landed in a thud against the outside rail, he was too disoriented to care. His gun, however, was a casualty after it flew from his hand and landed inside a dumpster below.

Though he was thrown off by the explosion and loss of

his weapon, he didn't let it pull his focus. The burning apartment was behind him, and there was nothing he could do about the gun. Meanwhile, Karen had made it another two floors down before he could get to his feet and jump most of the stairs in front of him to the next level. He rounded the rail and sped down the crooked fire escape as fast as he could.

King was on the second floor when he watched Karen connect with the sidewalk. The woman could run. He was fortunate he had decided to go out with his sneakers on; it gave him a better chance at catching up. But if Karen made it a couple more blocks, the streets were so packed, there was a good chance he would lose her.

As he ran down the last of the fire escape, he threw his coat off and bounded forward. Because he was taller than average, King could still see over pedestrians well enough to keep an eye on the white hat weaving in and out of people on the sidewalk. As he made a similar pattern dodging people, he tried to think ahead. The direction she was going, she could hit the Tube at Piccadilly Circus in a few blocks. But there were dozens of shops to disappear into along the way. Not to mention a myriad of side streets, and that was if she wasn't already headed for a getaway vehicle.

King was making up ground, but not fast enough. He was losing her more and more in the crowd. The lights weren't as bright on this side of the street, and he couldn't help but think she was going to get away.

Then he lost sight of her completely. As best he could while he continued running, he craned his neck for a glimpse. But no white hat could be found. He ran up on an intersection, dodging a baby carriage and a Rolls Royce, missing both by inches. With another look forward, Karen was nowhere in sight. King had lost her.

A cell phone began to ring. It wasn't a ring he recognized, so he maintained his pace, thinking it was one of the many people he was passing on the street. When the same ring went off again, just as close as the last time, he realized it was his burner phone. Only two people had that number. His partner in crime, Sam, and Bentley Martin.

He pulled the phone from his pocket without slowing down. He wasn't going to give up. There was too much at stake. "Hello?"

"Everything okay? I could have sworn I just saw Karen in her white hat run out in front of a car."

"Where?!"

King's shout brought urgency to Bentley's voice. "Uh . . . I just passed the Whole Foods, so I guess it would be . . ."

"Brewer Street! She's headed toward Chinatown. Meet me there!"

King pocketed the phone, then turned left, sliding across the hood of a car. Horns erupted as he crossed without hesitation, which brought shouts from onlookers on the sidewalk. None of this registered to King. He was close, and he had found another gear as he moved onto Brewer Street.

This side street was less crowded than the last, and without having to do so much dodging, he could really turn on the jets. Chinatown was only two blocks away, but it would be easy for Karen to get lost there. He knew he couldn't focus on the white hat any longer; she would've been smart enough to lose it. He just hoped seeing her dark hair contrasted against the white MIND THE GAP T-shirt he'd given her earlier would be enough to draw his attention.

King crossed the street as he made a right on Berners Street. He sprinted forward, making a left just past St.

Anne's Churchyard. Just up the street and one more right turn, he found himself in the middle of what seemed a different city. Chinese lanterns hung in row after row above the street. King was familiar with this part of town, not only because he got to know everything about his surroundings in case something like tonight happened, but also because he'd found a tiny restaurant down there that had phenomenal pork dumplings.

Unfortunately, the heavy crowd was back, but out of the corner of his eye, he saw a white hat duck inside a storefront.

He had her.

King jogged forward and turned into a noodle restaurant that couldn't have been more than fifteen feet wide and thirty feet deep. A bell dinged above the door when he walked in. Tables on the left and right were full of patrons, and a line of people ordering filled the middle aisle. At the end of it, a dark-haired woman in a white T-shirt was acting like she was digging in her purse.

King stepped forward and put his hand on her right wrist and another on the back of her neck. He was ready for a fight. What he got instead was disappointment when he saw an Asian woman turn toward him with a look of fright. King threw up his hands and backed away. "I'm so sorry. My mistake."

He pushed the door open with his ass and backed out into the street. He was breathing hard. Not from the run but from the anger flooding him for letting Karen get away. This was going to come back and haunt him at some point. He knew that much for certain.

His phone began to ring. It was Bentley. He needed to get her to safety as soon as possible. He was going to have to regroup tonight and be ready with a plan of attack first thing in the morning.

"Where are you?" he answered.

His adrenaline jumped when Bentley's voice came through in a whisper. "You've got to help me. I'm hiding behind a tree! She saw me. She has a gun!"

"Where are you?"

Silence.

"Bentley!"

Doubt that he could help her in that moment began to seep in. Then he remembered turning Bentley's phone off and putting it in his pocket. He quickly got it out and powered it on. If he could find the app she was using to track the chip she'd placed in Karen's hat, it would lead him right to her. As soon as the Apple disappeared on her phone, so too did the hope of finding the tracking app. He didn't know Bentley's passcode.

King put the phone away and closed his eyes. He was going to have to find her using means other than technology. The only lead he had was that Bentley mentioned she was hiding behind a tree. Though that may have seemed vague, it actually narrowed things down quite a bit in the area surrounding Chinatown.

As he concentrated with his eyes still closed, people brushed past him on their way toward dinner or drinks. However, as the chatter from their conversations faded and the street noise behind him became muffled like a hand covering a speaker, King focused everything he had on the map of the area he'd pulled up in his imagination.

Behind the buildings to his left was a parking structure. No trees there.

Behind the buildings on his right was nothing but

restaurants, then the Picturehouse Central movie theater. No trees.

In his mental map, he moved across the street in front of him. There were rows of shops and restaurants, in particular the LEGO Store. This was burned into his memory because every time he passed it, he couldn't help but think of his niece, Kaley. She loved LEGO. But right now the best part about that LEGO store was that it was across the street from Leicester Square.

Leicester Square had trees.

17

As the Chinese lanterns above his head swayed in the breeze, King created his own wind as he sprinted for the next block. He ran around the row of buildings that housed more than a few Chinese eateries, then stormed down Leicester Street, past the Empire Casino, heading straight for the Square. Lights glowed from the buildings surrounding the small green courtyard, but they didn't much penetrate the trees. Under the canopy it was quite dark.

King dodged a line of traffic in the street and sidled up next to the first tree he could find. He knew there was a fountain in the middle of the Square, then a small ticket booth building on the other side. He searched the dimly lit park, looking for anything out of the ordinary more so than for Karen herself. Sure enough, on the right side of the fountain a group of people were running toward him. King moved toward a tree on his right that brought him a little closer.

While he was concerned about Karen and her gun, he was more worried about whether or not she had any help. If she had time to get out of his apartment and then come back, she had time to find a phone and call for help. But just like everything else about this mysterious woman, he had no idea if she was working alone or not.

His phone began to ring.

"Where are you?" he answered.

"The ticket booth in Leicester Square. Please help me. She saw me come in here!"

King pocketed the phone and ran for the fountain. He dove behind an oversized stone flower pot at the foot of the fountain when he saw a woman in a white hat approaching the ticket booth. She was moving for the right side, so he stayed low and ran around the left side of the fountain. He did a quick scan of the surrounding area, but it was too dark to detect any help nearby that Karen may have called in. He had no choice but to act as if she hadn't.

As Karen disappeared around the front of the ticket booth, King ran for the same place on the opposite side. When he rounded the ticket booth, he heard Bentley scream.

"Please, don't shoot!"

King hopped the short wrought iron fence that divided the park from the ticket booth, and the next thing he saw was Karen pointing her gun inside the window. There was nowhere for Bentley to hide inside that little building. King lowered his head and dove for Karen's waist. At the same time he made contact, he heard the gun go off. He landed on top of Karen, and a chorus of screams sounded from bystanders on the surrounding block.

King quickly moved into a mounted position over Karen's body. He sat his full weight down on her hips as he straddled her, lying forward to pin her upper body beneath him as he wrapped his right hand around her left wrist. He squeezed with great strength, and when he slammed the back of her hand against the concrete, the gun bounced a few feet down the sidewalk.

A crowd began to gather around them as Karen squirmed beneath him.

"MI5!" King shouted. "Back away!" He had about the furthest thing you could have from a British accent. He didn't exactly have a country twang, but Kentucky boys never sound as sophisticated as a Londoner.

The crowd didn't move away, but he hoped claiming to be British intelligence would at least keep anyone from trying to intervene.

Karen shrimped her legs up between his as she pushed his hip back with her right hand—a Brazilian Jiu Jitsu escape attempt. This wasn't high-level defense, but clearly Karen was trained. King countered the escape by pushing her legs back down between his, scooting up on her body, and digging his forearm under her chin. Once he got back to mount, he squeezed his legs together and put the rest of his weight on her neck with his forearm. There was only one move she could make now before he crushed her windpipe. She was going to have to give up her back.

When the pressure became too much for her to bear, she rolled underneath him, putting her stomach on the ground. It was always a person's last last-ditch survival effort in this situation, and King was ready for it. He slid his right arm under her chin and locked in a rear naked choke. She was unconscious five seconds later.

King rose up, put his knee on her back, and looked into the crowd.

"I lost my handcuffs a couple of blocks back. Anyone have a belt or a tie I can use? She's gonna wake up any second now."

"Sure, here ya go, mate." A man stepped forward undoing his tie.

Karen came back to life under his knee, gasping for breath. King sat back down, straddling her, as he took the tie.

"One more favor?" King said to the man.

"Sure."

"Grab her gun over there for me?" He pointed off to the right. "Just don't touch the trigger. Pick it up by the barrel."

The man did as King asked.

Karen found her voice. "Get off of me!"

King took the gun from the man and tucked it in his hip holster. It wasn't an exact fit, but it was close enough to stay put. He then took Karen's left arm and bent it back behind her. She screamed in pain.

"Are you all just going to stand there while this maniac assaults me?" Karen shouted.

"They all saw you with the gun." He grabbed her right arm, but she ripped it away from him. King looked up at the young man again. "You mind?"

The young man crouched down and began turning Karen's arm back toward King.

"What the hell are you doing?" she shouted. "Help me!"

The young man helped hold Karen's arm in place as King tied the tie around her wrists. Tight.

"One last thing, will you check on the girl in the ticket booth?"

King stood and brought Karen up with him. Before the young man could have a look, Bentley came crawling out of the window.

"I think he's dead!" Bentley shouted.

"Holy shit!" the young man said when he ducked his head through the window.

King knew Karen's bullet must have moved to the ticket attendant, away from Bentley, when he tackled Karen. They needed to get out of there. The police would be there any second. Before King could react, Bentley walked over and punched Karen in the face.

"We were supposed to be friends!"

"Bentley," King said. "We have to go. Go get the car."

Sirens sounded in the distance, but they weren't far. Bentley backed away. "I'm staying and going with the police."

"Bentley."

"This is the second time today someone has tried to kill me."

"And this is the second time today I didn't let it happen."

King could see that Bentley's wheels were turning. The sirens drew closer. The crowd didn't dissolve. King could *feel* the cell phone cameras watching and listening to everything they were saying. As he held Karen's arms tight, he pulled his hat lower with his free hand.

"Bentley, just listen to me. By now the police know that you were the target of the car bomb. When you tell them who you are, which you will have to do when you are telling them about how Karen here tried to kill you, they'll have no choice but to report it to MI5. Once they do that, the US will be notified as well. I don't think I have to mention what might happen if the people who tried to kill you find out where you are. And I won't be there to save you a third time."

Multiple police cars swerved around the Square. Their window to escape was closing. And Alexander King absolutely could not be brought in. Explaining how a dead man walked the streets of London would be extremely difficult. Not to mention the fact he was going to have to carry Karen.

They had to go right then, or he was going to have to let Karen go. And that wasn't an option.

Karen turned and managed to knee King in the groin. Though the pain was excruciating, he didn't let go of her wrists. Instead, when he doubled over, it pulled her closer, pretty much where he had been standing. That's why the bullet ripped right through her head instead of his. King didn't even know Karen had been shot until the report from the sniper rifle caught up to his ears and her blood began pouring onto his back as she wobbled dead on her feet before she fell.

The screams from the crowd erupted, and they finally all cleared out of the area. As they panicked, King focused, and he rushed forward, took Bentley over his shoulder, and turned to run back to Chinatown. The police all began searching for the sniper, giving King back that window he needed to get away.

King knew he was lucky to be running at all. As he crossed the street, he put Bentley down and made sure she began running with him. He knew he was going to make the most of this second chance. He was finished playing defense; it was time to take the fight to the enemy.

As soon as he found out who the enemy really was.

18

Bruges, Belgium

ALEXANDER KING AND BENTLEY MARTIN WERE ABLE TO MAKE it to Bentley's car and get out of London without another brush with the police. The sniper shooting Karen had drawn the attention of those officers away from them. And King couldn't help but think that Karen dying before he could question her really set him back in his chances of connecting the dots back to the man or woman pulling the terrorist strings.

Alexander King made the final turn of the drive and coasted toward the safe house.

"Where are we?" Bentley roused in the passenger seat with a yawn and a stretch.

"Bruges."

It wasn't visible at the moment because it was still dark, but at the end of the street there was water. King had only been there once, but the safe house was a little cottage on a corner, adjacent to the canal.

"Belgium?" She sat up and peered out the window. "How long have I been asleep?"

"About an hour and twenty. Been here before?"

"No, but I've heard about it. Doesn't it have a nickname because of its canals or something?"

"The Venice of the North," he said.

"Yes, that's it. I figured after we got out of the Channel Tunnel, you'd for sure be taking me to Paris. Is it safe here in Bruges?"

King glanced over at her as he turned into the driveway. "I think the only safe thing to do at this point is just assume that nowhere is safe. We won't be staying long."

Bentley was quiet.

"Why were you crying earlier?" he asked her. "When we first got in the car?"

"Karen was, well, I thought she was my friend. I've never seen anyone close to me get killed like that."

King nodded. He understood, a little, but the way she had been sobbing still seemed off to him. But she was a seventeen-year-old. No matter how mature and smart she was, she was still just a kid.

King shut off the engine and exited the car. There was a chill in the air and he could feel the dampness that surrounded them. Bentley got out and followed close behind. There were streetlamps behind them, but the yellow light barely made it to the front door of the cottage. King approached the keypad. He typed in the four digits, and the dead bolt released. King felt for his weapon. The grip on Karen's Beretta felt odd in his hand after being so used to carrying a Glock. But it would do the job all the same. He pulled it out and turned the doorknob with his other hand.

Inside, the cottage had an abandoned smell. Like no one had lived there in years. Probably because they hadn't. These types of places were maintained by a contracted agency, and they were rarely used.

"Wait here," King said. He flipped on the light. There were stairs directly in front of them. He remembered that straight down the hall was the kitchen.

He gave the house a thorough walk-through and decided it was safe. After he pulled the car into the garage, he suggested Bentley get some more rest.

"What about you? Don't you ever sleep?" she asked as he walked her into the only bedroom in the house.

"I'll sleep when I'm dead."

It was something his dad used to say. His mom hated when he said it. His father's point to Alexander at the time was that people who slept too much were getting outworked. His father was a relentless businessman. That was the side of his dad that King was trying his best to remember. Instead of what happened in Moscow. How he had betrayed his son and his entire family.

"Earth to Secret Agent Guy!" Bentley said loudly, snapping him out of his trance.

"Sorry, what?"

"I said, I don't even know your name. What do I call you?"

King opened the closet and pulled a pillow and a blanket from the top shelf. "Just call me X."

"Okay, X. Where are you going to sleep?"

"I'll take the couch. Try to get some sleep. Tomorrow's going to be a long day."

"What are we going to do?"

"I don't know." King walked out the door into the hallway.

"Then how do you know it's going to be a long day?"

"From experience. Every day is long when someone is trying to kill you."

Bentley frowned and folded her arms across her chest. "Oh, great. Sweet dreams to you too, X."

King smiled and turned to walk down the hall.

"Wait," Bentley said.

When he turned around, she was standing in the doorway, looking down at her feet.

"Thank you."

King watched as she ran her foot along the hardwood in a nervous motion. Then she looked up at him.

"Really, you saved my life."

King gave her a nod. "It's my job."

"No, your job was to kill me. Instead, you technically saved me twice. Why? Is it because you feel bad? Because you killed my father?"

King was shocked for a moment. That was about the last thing he expected to come out of her mouth. After a spilt second of panic, he realized she was speculating. Bentley was clearly a smart cookie, so he had to tread lightly.

"Partially."

Or not.

King learned long ago that when someone is smart and intuitive, as Bentley clearly was, it was best to lead with the truth. He immediately second-guessed himself when he watched her jaw nearly hit the floor.

"Wow." She cleared her throat and recovered from her shock. "For a secret agent, you aren't very good with secrets."

"I'm sorry you had to find out this way, Bentley."

"You kidding me? I was just shocked you admitted it. I'm actually doing my best not to run over there and hug you. That man made my mother's life miserable. And he for damn sure never cared about me."

King felt relieved. One of the reasons he was so quick to blurt out the truth was because of what he'd been through in the past. The way his father lied to his entire family made King strive to be straight up, always. Sometimes that was a bad thing—being overly honest—but at least people knew where you stood.

"So . . . partially?" she said.

"Excuse me?"

"I asked if you saved me because you killed my dad. And you said partially. What's the rest?"

Bentley's kill order report said she had been involved in managing the numbers for her father's company, which helped fund the terrorist organization King was trying to run down. It said she was some sort of mathematical genius. He needed to start there. He could just come out and ask her if she worked with her father, but asking it a different way would give him a more honest answer.

"You said you're studying at Oxford?"

"Right."

"What's your major?"

She folded her arms. "Are you changing the subject? I asked why you saved me. What does college have to do with that?"

"Just answer the question." It was King's turn to fold his arms across his chest.

"Okay . . . English. Well, technically creative writing."

This would be easy enough to check on, and Bentley would know that, so he didn't believe she was lying. It answered the question in his mind of whether she'd been the one running the numbers for her father. He followed another line of thought.

"Okay. Did Karen ever tell you what she was studying at Cambridge?"

"No. But I don't even think she was ever really going to any university. I think it was all a lie."

King agreed with her. He felt Karen's only job was to shadow Bentley. What he really wanted to know, though, was for whom.

"Girl was damn good with numbers, though. Like freakishly good. She could calculate huge numbers on the fly."

Alarm bells rang out everywhere in King's head. He needed to talk to Sam, and he needed to have a conversation with Director Hartsfield as well. Somebody somewhere inside the government had arranged for a target to be put on Bentley's back. These kinds of things didn't happen by mistake, and he had to get to the bottom of it.

"Well, I've got some phone calls to make," he told her. "If you need something, I'll be right downstairs."

"Seriously? You still didn't tell me why you saved me. I answered your questions. Can you give me that much?"

Once again he decided to go with the truth. "I thought you could be the key to bringing down one of the largest terrorist organizations in the world."

Bentley laughed as she shook her head in disbelief. "Me?"

"Yeah . . . you."

"And what did you discover?" she said.

"That you can't."

"Sorry to disappoint, but I could have told you that much, X."

"*You* can't," he said, staying on the subject, "but I think Karen can."

19

BOBBY GIBBONS WATCHED as his old friend and director of the CIA, Mary Hartsfield, poured him a coffee. It had been a while since he'd seen her. The stresses of the job had aged her in what seemed double time. She didn't look old; she just looked . . . tired. Her office looked more like a bedroom. Linens and pillows were strewn over the couch.

"I'm really sorry to bother you so late, Mary. But this just couldn't wait."

Mary took the carafe back over to the table. She put her shoulder-length, salt-and-pepper hair up in a ponytail. "Well, it's good to see you, Bobby. Looks like things are going well out on the campaign trail. I wish we could talk more in depth about it, but I can't say I have a lot of time. This second incident in London has everyone in a panic."

Bobby took a sip of coffee. It was hot on his lips, but drinkable. The thought of the CIA investigating what Doug had dragged him into in London made his stomach sour. "What do attacks in London have to do with CIA?"

"MI5 says someone with an American accent was claiming to be MI5 at the scene of the shooting. Videos of the incident are all over the internet now. We're just trying to get our arms around it."

Bobby glanced over at the linens on the couch. "Looks like you're pulling double duty."

She followed his eyes. "Oh, yeah, well . . . that's been a regular occurrence as of late, unfortunately. I just grab a nap whenever I can."

"You can always come work for me. Pay's just as good, and nowhere near the stress."

Mary sipped her coffee, then set it on her desk as she took a seat. "That why you're here, Bobby? To offer me a job?"

Bobby hung his head. "I wish. But I've got a real problem, Mary."

"What's the line from that movie? 'A friend in need is a pest'?" She gave him half a smile as she tried to lighten the mood. Her quip fell flat.

Though she smiled at him, Bobby knew there was some truth to it. She had so much on her plate as it was; he hated to add another helping.

"I'm afraid that's probably true. But you know I wouldn't ask if I didn't have to."

"All right then, let's have it."

He cleared his throat and stopped his right leg from fidgeting. "I can trust this stays between you and me?"

"Of course." Mary leaned forward, folded her hands together, and rested her elbows on her desk.

"You remember Everworld Solutions?"

Mary rolled her eyes. "How could I not? If it hadn't been

for my best operative, their money would have killed the president."

"Right, well . . ."

Bobby didn't know how to say it. No matter how he framed it, he sounded guilty. He was beginning to think coming to Mary had been a mistake. He thought maybe he should just stick to what was already in motion and let Doug get him out of his mess. Then he remembered Doug had custom ordered a "terrorist attack" to kill a young woman, and then held a gun to Bobby's head when he questioned him about it.

"You're starting to make me nervous, Bobby. What is this? How much trouble are you in?"

He felt some relief when she brought up him being in trouble. For some reason it made him feel as though he really was in a safe place with someone who could help him.

"Real trouble." His voice shook.

Mary stood and rounded her desk. She took the seat beside him and scooted it around to face him.

"Let's have it, then. I can't help you if you don't tell me everything."

Bobby nodded as he wiped the nervous sweat from his forehead.

"I was an investor in Everworld. Senators Thomas and McDonnell convinced me it was a good investment. I swear to you, I had no idea what they were plotting to do with the money."

Mary was quiet for a moment. She checked her watch. "So now that you're running for president, you're worried that it might come back to bite you if word gets out you were involved in the scandal."

"I *was* worried about that . . . and that's how I got in trouble."

"Let's stop beating around the bush, shall we? I really have to get back to work."

Bobby didn't mince words. "I hired Doug Chapman."

Mary's reaction was immediate. "Ah shit, Bobby. Why the hell would you go and do that?"

"So you know who he is?"

"Know who he is?" Mary stood and put her hands on her hips. "I was the reason the last director was forced to fire him from the CIA. Son of a bitch is lucky he's not in jail for treason. If Director Manning hadn't covered Doug's tracks, and his own, Doug would be rotting in a jail cell right now."

"God, Mary, I didn't know all that."

"What? Why not?" Mary was incensed. She walked over to the bar cart in the corner of the room. She picked up a decanter and poured two drinks of brown liquor. "Why would you hire him without vetting him?"

"I did vet him, Mary. But the people who recommended him didn't fill me in on all the gory details. They just said he'd get the job done."

"What's the job, Bobby?" She handed him a glass and took hers back in one shot. "You mentioned London on the phone. What don't I know?"

Bobby nosed his glass. He could smell the oak in the bourbon. He didn't have the stomach for it, so he set it on Mary's desk in front of him.

"After my rally, he told me he had orchestrated the car bomb in London."

"What?" Mary shouted. "Are you out of your mind?"

"I had no idea, Mary. You know me. When he pulled me aside a couple of hours ago and told me this is what happened, I had the same reaction you did. I told him he was fired—that I *never* would have okayed something like that!"

Mary began to pace the floor. "I can't contain this, Bobby. This is an international crime. There's no way this doesn't blow back on you. You just killed your shot at becoming president."

Bobby of course had already had the same thought. He had all but resigned himself to that fact. His focus was now more on staying alive.

"Yeah, I get that, Mary. I'm just trying to make sure Doug doesn't do something else. He has to be stopped."

"Where is he now?" Mary asked.

"I have no idea."

Mary walked over and downed the bourbon she'd poured for Bobby. "I know Doug, Bobby. If he finds out you're here . . ." She trailed off.

Bobby knew what she was about to say. "Try to kill me? Well, he already put a gun to my chin in the back of my own car. So I'm well aware of what's at stake. That's why I told you I didn't have a choice but to come to you."

Mary leaned against the edge of her desk and sighed as she stared up at the ceiling. "Bobby . . . listen carefully." She looked down and found his eyes. "Doug won't *try* to kill you if he wants you dead. He was an elite agent here for years. His job was to make people disappear. You've gotten yourself into a real mess."

Bobby stood. He had no idea it was this bad. "Then I'm glad I came to you."

"I'll get your Secret Service detail doubled. And I'll put the word out to look for him. But there isn't much else I can do. I have an agent in the wind in London and a lot of cleanup work to do there."

"Thank you, Mary."

Bobby stepped forward and gave her a hug.

Mary gave a quick squeeze, then pulled away. "When's your next public appearance?"

"They're every day. I'm running for president."

"You should consider bowing out of the race. For your safety and your wife's."

Bobby let out a sigh. There were a lot of people counting on him. He didn't want to let them down, but he had to consider what Mary was telling him.

"I'll think it through."

Mary's cell phone started ringing. "I have to take this. I'll keep you posted."

Bobby nodded and turned for the door.

"Bobby?"

He stopped and faced her.

She swiped her phone to accept the call and put it to her ear. "Be careful."

20

Bruges, Belgium

"This is Director Hartsfield."

King finished his glass of water as he took a seat on the couch. "Mary, it's X."

"Oh, thank God. I'm hearing from one of my agents about a man in a gray hoodie saving a girl from a car bomb. Then I'm seeing a guy in online videos who looks an awfully lot like you with a hat pulled really low, claiming to be MI5, when a woman gets shot by a sniper in the middle of the city. What the hell is going on over there?"

"I was just about to ask you the same thing, Mary."

King had a lot of time to think on the quiet four-hour drive to Bruges from London, and all the getting through the Channel Tunnel. And a whole lot of things weren't adding up. He knew he should be careful what he said to Mary, but he had never been good at holding his tongue.

"I'm not sure what you mean."

"I mean, the girl I saved—Bentley Martin, as you well know—showed up in my mailbox as my next target."

"What?"

King detected Mary's sharp inhale, something he'd been taught meant genuine surprise. But he still had to be guarded.

"You trying to tell me you didn't know who my target was?"

"I'm trying to tell you that I know exactly who your target was, and it was *not* Bentley Martin."

King's blood ran cold. There were only two people who were ever involved in sending him his next mission: Mary Hartsfield and his longtime partner, Sam Harrison. King knew that Sam would never lie to him. She would die for him. And almost had on several occasions. If Mary was telling the truth, that meant someone was able to circumvent the top secret file before it got to Sam. The first thing King had to do was decide whether or not he could trust Mary was telling him the truth. She had always gone to bat for him in the past, and they had actually become friends, but when your own father turns on you, it's possible *anyone* can turn on you. With Mary, though, it was the last thing King would expect.

"X?" Mary said.

"Just processing." His mind was flipping through the scenarios of how this could have happened.

"Have you talked to Sam?"

"I called her, she didn't answer. But it's the middle of the night in Greece."

"I know."

King was growing frustrated that Mary wasn't addressing the obvious problem. That there was a breakdown somewhere under her watch.

"Mary?"

"I already know what you're going to say, X."

"Then don't make me say it."

"Hold on, you're not going to try to lecture *me* here, are you?"

He didn't expect her defensive tone.

"I don't follow," King said.

"You think I don't know it was you who took out Andonios Maragos?"

King knew it was only a matter of time before this came up. Of course, he would never admit it, even though he was fully aware Mary knew it was him.

"I couldn't be happier he's dead, Mary. But it wasn't me."

"Bullshit."

King doubled down. "I don't understand what you're getting at. If I had killed Maragos, what does that have to do with you losing control of your organization to the point that an entire black op, which only you and Sam knew about, got hijacked? Am I burned? How bad is this?"

King rose from the couch to pace the room. His blood pressure was on the rise, and he needed to walk it off. Mary was quiet, and in those moments, he began to worry about Sam.

"You're not burned, X. No one knows about you."

"How do my target files get to me?"

"I can't tell you that. It would put you in danger."

"You're kidding, right? I almost got car-bombed, and a sniper's bullet flew half a foot from my head, but you telling me how I get a file will put me in danger? We have to cut the shit, Mary. This is *real* trouble!"

King's heart was pounding pretty heavy.

"Excuse me! Who do you think you're talking to?!"

King couldn't hold his tongue. "Right now? I think I'm

talking to the person who doesn't want to say that there is a leak somewhere beneath her. I think I'm talking to the person who might get me and my partner killed. Sam and I can do this on our own, Mary. We've done it before. Don't forget how we met!"

King was ready for Mary to strike back, but it didn't come. Instead, he heard her take a deep breath.

"All right. Calm down. I can manage this. I know perfectly well what you are capable of, and I want to work with you. But that doesn't mean you don't need me. Let's take a step back and start putting this together."

King took a deep breath himself and went to the sink for some water. "How do you get the files to me? The agent I met in the underground earlier today?"

"Special Agent Shawn Roberts. Yes, this time it was him. Whenever you get a file, I send Sam an encrypted digital file. It can only be opened twice—once when she opens it and again when she sends it to the agent that I tell her is working in your area. That agent doesn't know that it comes from Sam, and they also don't know that it is going to you. Both Sam and the agent are given an authentication code. Once the agent in your area sees that the code matches up, that agent puts together a file for you and leaves it in the place where the self-deleting, encrypted file tells them too. Like the place you picked up the file tonight."

"So it was agent Roberts who changed the file to Bentley Martin."

"We don't know that, X. I know Roberts. He wouldn't—"

"Don't say it. You and I have both been double-crossed enough to know better." King chugged another glass of water.

"You're right about that."

King decided to try the polite approach. "Can I tell you what I think we should do?"

"Please."

"I need to go see Agent Roberts. But I can't leave Bentley here by herself. I need an agent to come and stay with her, but I have to be able to trust them. I promised Bentley I'd keep her safe."

King could hear some typing in the background.

"Umm . . . let me see," Mary said. "I have four senior agents within two hundred miles of you."

"That doesn't mean anything to me. Can you trust them? Do I know any of them?"

"I also have a special agent in Brussels, actually. He's tracking a businessman, but it's not a high-level target—wait a minute—I think you—oh yeah, you know him. Agent John Karn. Helped you back in Washington with Anastasia Maragos."

"Agent Karn is in Brussels?" King couldn't believe it.

"Sure is."

"Karn saved my ass once. I'd definitely feel Bentley is safe with him here."

"That's only sixty miles or so. I can have him there before sunrise. But that just adds another person who knows you're not dead. You okay with that?"

"I don't have a choice. Send him. But before you go, I need something else."

"Name it."

"I need to know the real identity of the woman who got shot beside me in Leicester Square."

"Why were you after her, anyway?"

"Because I didn't save Bentley Martin from the car bomb, I saved Karen, her look-alike."

"What?"

"I'll get to it. Here's the short version. Bentley said this woman went by the name of Karen Panos. She said they'd met randomly at a bar, become close, but then things became strange."

"Strange. And you think that means she isn't really Karen Panos."

"I think she has been posing as Bentley." That made the explanation extra short.

"Wait, what?"

"Bottom line. This Karen was definitely not who she said she was. I'm certain she was an undercover agent for someone. She blew up my apartment trying to kill me. And she just moved and fought like she'd been professionally trained."

"I need more than this to go on, X. Why would an agent be posing as a billionaire's daughter?"

"The same reason someone switched my target to Bentley." King peeked through the shades of the living room window that overlooked the shimmering canal. "Someone is covering their tracks. Karen and Bentley look almost like twins. In the file, the reasoning for Bentley's kill order was because she was instrumental in moving money and cooking the books for her father's company. The one that helped Everworld fund the terrorist group that the Maragoses were involved with."

"But you don't think it was really Bentley?"

"She is an English major. Wants to be a writer. Nowhere near a math whiz."

Mary took a moment. "I still don't understand."

"Which part?" King said.

"Well, I understand why someone would want Bentley dead. If someone involved with Everworld thought Bentley had information damaging to them, that would make sense.

How they got the file to you is another disturbing story for another time. What I don't get is why would someone have this Karen person pose as Bentley? I don't see the logic or strategy in that."

"I don't either. But I really don't care. I just want to follow the trail from Karen to whoever hired her. I think that road will lead me to the person in charge of the entire terrorist organization."

"Okay, I'll put some people on it. In the meantime, Agent Karn is on his way to you. He just messaged and said he'll be there in an hour. And I've been trading messages with Agent Roberts in London. I told him I need him in Calais, France, as soon as he can get there. I figured you two could get there around the same time after you wait for Agent Karn to get to you. He'll be at a place called Total. It's a twenty-four-hour gas station with a small coffeehouse inside. You can decide how to handle Agent Roberts once you get there. I'll message you his cell number so you can coordinate. And you can also drill down on what happened with your target file that was switched to Bentley. We need to know if Roberts ever even received Sam's encrypted file, and if not, what happened. From the story he told me about the mysterious gray-hooded man in the underground who saved his ass, he owes you at least one favor."

"You did all that while we were talking?" King said.

"Who would have thought the director of the CIA could multitask, huh?"

"Sarcasm. Okay." King laughed. "I'll get things rolling with Agent Roberts on Karen since he's used to maneuvering in London—"

Mary interrupted. "And I'll work this Karen angle from my end, see if I can track down how the target file got swapped. That way we're coming at it from both ends. If we've got a hole, we need to plug it, STAT."

"Yeah, that *might* be a good idea. Listen, before I go, if Bentley wasn't my next target, then who was?"

Mary laughed. "Some lucky son of a bitch who gets to live a little bit longer than he would have."

"Touché."

"Stay in touch, X. And be careful. I've got an idea where some of our problems in London might be coming from."

"Oh yeah?"

King wasn't sure, but he thought he heard Mary take a sharp inhale. Either way, she didn't answer him.

"Mary?"

King pressed the phone against his ear, straining to hear what he thought sounded like someone's voice.

"What are you doing here—"

Two gunshots banged through the speaker of his phone.

King shot up from the couch. "Mary!"

He heard her moan, then some rustling around.

"Mary! Answer me!"

There was a little more shuffling with the phone; then he heard Mary's voice. She could hardly speak. Her voice was hoarse and labored. "Bobby . . . Gib . . . Gibbons."

Then he heard two more shots, and the phone clattered as it dropped to the floor.

21

KING'S EAR WAS STILL RINGING FROM THE FINAL TWO gunshots that blasted through the speaker of his phone. They were much closer than the first two, and his imagination, searching for clues to determine who had shot Mary, couldn't help but see her lying on the floor in her office and then being executed.

His chest was heaving. He couldn't believe what he'd just heard. He paced the room and listened intently to what was going on in Mary's office, which was almost four thousand miles away. In all his years in combat, of all the dangerous and deadly missions and situations he'd faced as a Navy SEAL then in Spec Ops, this . . . this was the most helpless he had ever felt. For a man who fixes things for a living, King couldn't bear the thought that this was going on —a friend just shot and probably killed—and there was absolutely nothing he could do about it.

"Pick up the phone, you coward!" he shouted into the phone. He was panting. Saliva shot from his mouth as he spoke. "Talk to me, you son of a bitch! I know you can hear me!"

Bentley came bounding down the stairs. "Is everything all right?" When she saw King seething, a wild look in his eyes, she backpedaled right back up the stairs.

That's when King heard breathing on the other end of the line.

A couple of seconds went by, and he was breathing heavily himself, trying to control his rage since he had nowhere to direct it.

Then a calm came over him.

He took a deep breath, and his heart rate began to slow. He could *feel* the negative energy of the person holding the phone, but somehow it brought him focus.

"I don't know who you are . . . but I will." King walked over to the front door and opened it, letting some cool air into the hot room. He was on fire. "And I may not know where you are going to run to . . . but I'll find you."

King's mind was racing down a rabbit hole. He was seeing the puzzle pieces of the entire situation moving together in front of him. He could feel that this person breathing into the phone, the person who'd likely just murdered the director of the CIA and his friend, Mary Hartsfield, was the same man responsible for what had happened in London.

Finally, a man's voice replaced the breaths from the other end of the phone. "I don't believe that *I* am the one who is running. Stay out of my way, or more loss will be coming to you."

King let those words wash over him. His mind flashed to his sister and his niece. It flashed to Sam, his friend Kyle, then to Sarah, and even to Natalie—his onetime love. His mind showed him his brother-in-arms, Sean Thompson, getting executed in Syria. Then the day his mother was gunned down in his driveway when he was just fifteen scrolled in his mind's eye. He knew loss. And every single time he'd lost someone, he'd always made someone else pay.

This would be no different.

King swallowed his anger and finished the call. "Everybody has to die someday . . . and your someday is coming soon."

22

KING COULDN'T SLEEP. HE COULDN'T LEAVE THE SAFE HOUSE before Agent Karn arrived, but he had so much pent-up aggression he was about to explode. Since he couldn't go for a run, he did his push-up, burpee, and squat routine until he couldn't even pick himself up off the floor. He lay there on the cool hardwood, with his mind racing.

He'd tried to call Sam several more times. Normally, her not answering wouldn't really worry him. She didn't sleep much, but when she did, she slept hard. After what happened to Mary, though, he couldn't help but feel the negative thoughts creeping in. He didn't like that Sam was alone in Greece, asking people questions about very dangerous people. He needed to be with her. And just as soon as he got a few answers from Agent Roberts in France, that was where he was going. Every instinct he had was telling him that was where he would find the head of the beast. He just didn't want Sam running into it without him.

The neighborhood they were in was quiet, so it was easy to hear the car coming. King rolled over to his knees and took the Glock from the coffee table. Having that familiar grip in his hand felt like home. Sam always left a spare in any go bag she kept for him at his drops. He felt just a little bit more invincible with his old friend on his hip.

King knew the timing matched up for it to be Karn coming from Brussels, but of course he had to be sure. He shut the front door that he'd had cracked, then sidled up to the window and separated the blinds. Sure enough, Agent Karn came walking around the corner. King was caught off guard by how relieved he was to see a familiar face. Even though he and Karn barely knew each other, it had been over a year since he'd seen someone he knew in person at all. He was glad to see that Karn was as paranoid as he was as he approached the door with his own gun drawn.

King let go of the shade and stepped back. "It's open."

King turned on the couch-side lamp as Karn stepped through the door. When Karn raised his gun out of shock, his face looked like he'd seen a ghost. Probably because in his mind he had.

Karn lowered his gun. "Ho-ly shit. Xander? I thought you were dead!"

King put his index finger to his lips, then pointed upstairs. "Call me X," he whispered.

Karn nodded, then came forward for a hug.

"It's good to see a familiar face," King said. "Sorry I can't stick around."

"No, I totally understand." Karn hadn't changed a bit. He was still well put together, and from the looks of things, the job had yet to age him. "How are you here?"

"Long story." King debated whether or not to tell Karn about what just happened to Mary. He decided it could wait. "Listen, things are heavy right now. I just need you to make sure Bentley stays safe."

"You got it. How long are you going to be?"

"Couple of hours. I have to meet someone in France, then I'll be coming right back. If you don't have a real important assignment, I could use you for the next couple of days."

"You got it. Director Hartsfield said I'm at the agent's disposal. Though I wish she would've given me the heads-up that the agent was you."

"What fun would that have been?" Through all the emotion, King forced a smile.

"Glad to see you haven't changed."

"I've got to get going. Don't go to sleep. I need you aware and alert at all times."

"Of course. You got it."

King nodded and stepped toward the door.

"Oh, hey," Karn said as he reached inside his trench coat, "Hartsfield said you might be hungry, so I picked you up a sandwich."

King turned and took it from him. It was like a dagger in the heart to know that the last thing Mary had done was make sure King was fed.

"Quark sandwich," Karn said. "I have no idea what it is, but the attendant said it's a Belgium specialty. They make good waffles, so I figured what the hell."

King unwrapped the sandwich, took half of it out, and wrapped it back up. He wasn't hungry. How could he be? But he knew he needed to eat. He handed the other half of the sandwich back to Karn. "For Bentley when she wakes up. Thank you."

Karn nodded.

"I'll be right back." King walked up the stairs.

When he got to Bentley's room, he nudged open the door. She was sitting up in the bed, staring at the water out the window. "I heard."

134

"I won't be gone long."

"Please just take me with you." She turned her eyes to his. The light was off, but the glow of a streetlight was enough for King to see her worried look.

If King wasn't concerned about Agent Roberts's potential involvement in switching the files, he would take Bentley with him. But Roberts could be waiting in Calais to kill him. He couldn't put Bentley in that situation.

"It's too dangerous."

"Obviously it's dangerous here, too, or you wouldn't have brought another agent here to watch me."

"It's just a safety precaution. No one knows about this place."

"You did," she said. "Aren't there others like you? Couldn't they be part of whatever the hell is going on?"

That was exactly why King brought Karn here to stay with her. It was unlikely but not impossible that others knew about the safe house. But he couldn't tell her that.

"You're safe with Agent Karn. He saved my life about a year ago. He knows what he's doing."

Bentley returned to looking out the window. She clearly wasn't convinced. King took Karen's Beretta out of his pocket. "You know how to use one of these?"

She stared at the gun. "I do. It's not easy to practice in London where they are banned, but my mother insisted I learn. Seeing as how my father wasn't what you would call one of the good guys."

King walked forward and handed her the gun. She took it and laid it on the bed. Then she buried her face in her hands. Her shoulders were heaving, she was crying so hard. King had never been good with this sort of thing, but over the last couple of years he'd been through enough of these situations to know what to do. The young girl he saved in the basement of the drug house in San Diego. The teenager he saved on the pier in Santa Monica. And of course his relationship with his niece, Kaley, whom he missed immensely. He thought about what he would do if this was Kaley, scared for her life, separated from her mother. Then he put his arm around Bentley's shoulder and pulled her close.

"It's going to be okay, Bentley. I won't let anything happen to you."

That's when she threw her arms around him. It caught him off guard. His mind was still in the space of imagining Bentley was his niece, and the emotion swelled inside him. Though Bentley acted tough, she was still just a teen. King couldn't imagine her fear with people coming after her and not having any of her normal comforts around her.

"I need to talk to my mom," she said in between sobs. "She's in Barcelona for work. What if they want her too?"

King hadn't thought about this, but she could well be in danger too. "Where is she staying? I'll have someone check on her?"

"I-I don't know. I mean, I don't remember. She sent me an email, but I have no way of checking it."

"Okay, we'll find her. It's what we do."

Bentley pulled back and looked up at him. "Thank you for saving me. And for not doing what your file said and killing me."

King checked his watch. Then he looked at Bentley with a wry smile. "It's only four in the morning, the day is still young."

Bentley smiled and nodded as she wrapped the blanket around her.

"Try to get some sleep," he said. "I won't be long."

"Please don't be."

King walked back downstairs and headed toward the door. "I'll be back soon."

Agent Karn stood from the couch. "We'll be here . . . Damn good to see you, X."

King gave a half smile and opened the door. The questions he had for Agent Roberts were already swimming in his head.

23

KING WALKED OUT INTO THE COOL NIGHT AIR. IT FELT GOOD. The lactic acid in his muscles still had him feeling tight, and the sweat at his lower back from the workout gave him a chill. He got into the car and started on his way. He punched the address of the gas station into the GPS. It told him politely that he had an hour and twenty minutes of driving. He knew he could get there in an hour at this time of the morning and with a heavy foot.

As he pulled out onto the highway, the dark road stretched out in front of him, but the only thing he could see was Mary Hartsfield lying dead in her office. This would have far-reaching effects. Not the least of which was the fact that at the time of Mary's last breath, he effectively no longer existed. Not for his government at least. What he had been doing might as well have been vigilante work anyway, because if he'd ever been caught, the CIA would have denied knowing he ever existed. But he supposed somewhere in the back of his mind that he thought he would be able to come back in at some point. That maybe once he finished off the last of the terrorists who tried to use his family and friends against him, he could actually get some sort of normal existence back. But with Mary gone, he couldn't help but think that hope was dead and buried. Now he truly was in this thing alone. Except for tried-and-true Sam herself.

The phone in his pocket vibrated and jangled his nerves as it shook him out of his deep thoughts. Speak of the devil, it was Sam. And he couldn't have been happier.

"Sam, thank God."

Though it was four in the morning, her voice was sprightly. "I must have the wrong number. The X I know would never say my name and the words *thank God* in the same sentence."

"Mary is dead."

"What?" Sam's voice went up an octave. "Mary Hartsfield?"

"No, Mary Poppins." King looked over at the sandwich on the console. Maybe he should eat.

Sam had no words.

"I was on the phone with her. Someone shot her dead."

"My God."

King pushed the pedal down a little further. The shock in Sam's tone leaked adrenaline into his system. He was ready to run through fire to find whoever killed Mary. Sam was not an emotional person when it came to work, but since King had faked his death, he knew that Mary and Sam had worked together a lot in his absence. And surely they'd grown pretty close.

Still, in typical Sam fashion, she plowed right ahead. "What do we know?"

"Mary managed to get the name Bobby Gibbons out before she was executed."

"The senator running for president?"

"Yeah." King swerved around the first car he'd seen on the road since he left the safe house. "Listen, Sam. Things have gone to shit here. I've got Bentley in a safe house, with Agent John Karn watching her."

"Karn? The agent who helped you in Washington? How did you get connected with him?"

"Mary."

"So you didn't kill Bentley like the file said to do," Sam said. "I knew you wouldn't, I just wanted you to see for yourself before we talked about it."

"It wasn't Bentley."

"I saw the file, X. It was Bentley and you know it."

"No, Sam. Just let me try to make sense of this entire thing, then we can talk about it."

"By all means."

"What I meant was, the girl I saved from the car bomb, that wasn't Bentley Martin. Long story short, it was a woman who called herself Karen Panos. Bentley's doppelgänger. Almost like twins. I believe she's been posing as Bentley, and maybe even been doing it for years. I think Karen was the one involved with fixing the numbers at Everworld, not Bentley. And that's why whoever ordered this hit thought it was Bentley who needed to be taken care of."

"What do you mean *whoever ordered this hit*?" Sam said. "You know Mary gives—*gave* us your targets exclusively."

"She said Bentley was not the file she sent you, Sam. Somewhere between you sending it to the agent in place in London and me receiving it, the file was changed."

"No, X. That can't be."

King suddenly realized he had thought of the timeline wrong. And so had Mary. He couldn't believe he'd missed this earlier.

"Shit, you're right," he said. "If you saw that it was a file targeting Bentley, it had been changed before it got to you."

Both of them were quiet. The small engine of Bentley's car screamed as King pushed its limits. He cracked the window to get some air. He was burning up, inside and out.

"How could that be, Sam?" he asked. "How could someone possibly know, not only *when* Mary was sending you a target, but how to intercept it, *and* change it?"

"I don't know, X."

"Would that sort of thing leave a digital trail?"

"Again, I have no idea. I'm not a techie."

"But Dbie Johnson is."

"Yes," Sam said. "She could probably help us. But I would have to give her secret CIA credentials to look into it."

"Then do it, Sam. I'm in the wind here. I don't exist. We have to run this thing down or I can forget ever having a real life again. Moreover, we are the only people who can figure this out . . . and make it right. Bring Dbie in on this all the way. I already sent her Karen's cell phone to go through. Maybe there will be something there that will help."

"What do you mean *you* sent it to Dbie?" Sam said. "You sent it as yourself?"

King instantly regretted the decision not to tell Sam he'd been in contact with Dbie in the first place. He'd only kept it from her to save himself a lecture about the fewer people who know he's alive, the better. Now he knew this was much worse. This would hurt Sam. But hopefully not her trust.

"I'm sorry, Sam. I should have told you. I just didn't want to hear your speech as to why I shouldn't contact her."

"Okay."

"That's it?"

"I'll see if I can get in touch with Bobby Gibbons," Sam said, changing the subject. "Hopefully he knows exactly why Mary said his name to you before she died. I hear a car engine. Where are you going?"

"To see the agent in London that I spoke with in the tunnel before getting away with Bentley, or Karen, I mean. Mary set it up. She thinks he can help in getting more information on Karen Panos. Or whoever she really is."

"Then what?" Sam said.

"Then I'm going to take the information you get from Bobby Gibbons, and go get the son of a bitch who killed Mary. I have a feeling it's the same person who changed the file to Bentley Martin."

"You're probably right . . . but you can't do that. Not now anyway."

"What? Why?" King slowed for the upcoming intersection.

"Because I need you here."

"In Greece?"

"X," Sam said. Her voice quieted a bit. He rolled the window up to hear her. "I know who the Maragoses were funneling their money to, and who they were working with."

Out of reflex, King let off the gas. "You don't mean . . ."

"Yes. I found the people who taught the Maragoses to hate the United States. The head of the snake. The people who tried to kill everyone you love."

24

King did as the GPS prompted and turned right into the Total gas station and coffeehouse. He parked the car and stared out the window. The lights of the rectangular building were bright against the still darkened sky, and steam was rising into the cool air from a couple of exhaust fans. It was hard for him to focus on the conversation he was about to have with Agent Roberts. The only reason he was still going through with it was because there was a chance he could still be of help. The bombshell news that Sam had just dropped on him wasn't complete. They knew *who* the man was at the head of the terrorist organization, but they didn't know the *where*. Finding out exactly who Karen really was could still help in some way. King figured she had to be connected, for a couple of reasons, not the least of which was that before King could question her, someone shot her in the head to keep her from talking. She knew something important. King needed to know what.

He grabbed his hat from the dash, pulled it on low, and exited the vehicle. It was now five in the morning. People in

Calais would be rousing soon. Through the window of the building, King saw a row of booths down the left side of the coffeehouse section. Only one man occupied one of the booths. He too wore a hat pulled low.

King walked inside. Agent Roberts didn't look up. He didn't have to. King knew Roberts had already spotted him when he pulled his car into the parking lot. He walked over and sat opposite of Roberts.

"Twice in one day," Roberts said. "For a ghost, you sure get out a lot."

King removed his hat.

The way Roberts's jaw gaped open, King knew the word *ghost* had merely been a coincidence.

"Xander King? But you're dead. Full twenty-one-gun salute. I saw the coverage of your funeral."

King smirked. "You should know better than most not to believe everything you hear or see."

"Damn. And that was you back in the underground. No wonder you thought my team was sloppy. You're the gold standard."

"Hardly. Sam is the standard."

"Either way, it's an honor. Thank you for your service. All of this is probably a cakewalk for you after the Navy SEALs."

"Different set of skills. Not sure I'm suited for espionage."

"Well, Director Hartsfield left the little tidbit out that I'd be meeting *you* when she told me to come here."

King looked away. When he heard Mary's name, the word *ghost* came back to mind. He wished her death had been as fake as his.

"Thank you, by the way."

King looked back at him.

"You saved my life," Roberts said. "Maybe my guys too."

King skipped the pleasantries. "Did Mary tell you what I need to know?"

Roberts sipped his coffee. "Yes and no. She just told me to look into the woman who was shot in Leicester Square. But I was already doing that. I screwed things up with the car bombing, so I wanted to get a head start. When the shooting came in over the wire, I called a contact I have in MI5."

"How good of a contact?" King said.

"We share a bed."

King was quiet. Roberts looked like he was awaiting a reaction to that statement. "So, you want a high five or what?"

Roberts shook his head and moved on. "She just called me back on the way over here. They're getting the coroner to rush the autopsy."

"What about the shooter?" King said.

King watched Roberts's mouth form a small circle, and he took a quick inhale. "You were the man in the hat claiming MI5?" Roberts said.

King gave no answer.

"Uh . . . a man was spotted with a long hard-case, something resembling a rifle at least, entering the casino that overlooks the Square. The timeline matches up for when you would have been there. That's all I have so far, but my team is going over all the area surveillance. We'll find him."

King knew Roberts wouldn't have much information on either of these topics. The shooting had only been a few hours ago. He was just hoping for some little nugget to help point him in the right direction. "What led to you being put on Bentley Martin watch?"

Roberts opened the lid on his coffee for ventilation.

"We've been trying to track down those responsible for the growing terrorist activity coming out of Athens, Greece."

"It's not Abdullah? His faction has claimed more than one attack."

"No. Well, yes, but we know he's not the one pulling the strings. We'd love to get our hands on him too, but I can tell you, he isn't the person at the top."

After talking to Sam, King of course knew that, but he wanted to see what Roberts had discovered before he told him Husaam Hammoud was the key player. If he told him this at all.

Roberts continued. "We've been trying to find out who is actually in control, but there's been little information from the top. Whoever's been spearheading the attacks is smarter than most of these terrorist freaks. He or she doesn't want to be known—they just want to keep quiet as their minions take the fall. Which is smart, just not the usual tactics of guys like bin Laden who want the credit for coming after our way of life."

So far, Roberts had proven to be no help at all.

King put his hat back on. "And the part about Bentley?"

"Oh, yes. A while back there had been some information intercepted that Bentley was somehow involved with the terror group from Athens. I always thought it was odd, but her biological father, Andonios Maragos, as you know firsthand, was also linked to this terror group when his sister and brother were killed during their attack on the White House last year. So, when a call from one of the low-level men in the terror group mentioning Bentley's name was intercepted, we were posted to watch the spot you saved her at today."

"Except I didn't save her. I saved the woman who was shot in Leicester Square."

Agent Roberts paused before his coffee cup reached his mouth. "What?"

"Listen, I have Bentley at a safe house. I need everything you can get me on Karen Panos, and the person who shot her. I know who is pulling the terrorist strings from Greece. I just don't know where to find them. But I will, with your help."

As Roberts was taking in the entirety of that statement, King produced the burner phone that he'd given Bentley earlier. "You report to me now. My number is the only one programmed in that phone. Call me as soon as you learn anything. Got it?"

King stood.

"What about Director Hartsfield? She didn't give me any instructions that—"

"Director Hartsfield is dead."

Roberts laughed. "I just spoke with her—"

"About an hour and a half ago. I know. She's dead now. And if you want to help me find who is behind all of this, you'll find the information I need and get it to me."

Roberts was speechless.

King began walking backward toward the door. "I'll check in if I don't hear from you in an hour. And every hour after that. I don't know what's going to happen when they find Mary and put someone else in charge. And I don't have time to care. Because I don't—"

"You don't exist." Roberts finished King's sentence, but it was clear his mind was elsewhere.

"Roberts. I need to know you're with me. There is too much at stake to freeze up on me. I need you."

Roberts literally shook himself out of his trance. "I've got you. Mary was a great leader. I want these guys as bad as you do."

King knew that absolutely wasn't true, but there was nothing wrong with letting Roberts believe it. Without a contact in Washington, King and Sam were going to need all the help they could get.

25

THE SUN WAS FINALLY ON THE RISE WHEN KING TURNED DOWN the road that led to the safe house on the canal. With how tired he suddenly felt after the last of the adrenaline had left his body, and the time of morning it was, he was reminded of his lifelong friend Kyle Hamilton. More specifically, he was reminded of coming in from the bars, the sun rising in the sky, as they so often used to, not all that long ago. Something about the light returning before you made it home from a night of partying was both a sickening feeling and one of satisfaction with a well-wasted night. Either way, Kyle came to mind, and he desperately missed the son of a bitch.

Despite the fog of going without sleep for over twenty-four hours, King was able, as he drove back from Calais, to think through to his next move. He had to get Bentley to safety. Every minute she remained close to the situation, the more danger she was in. King would have Agent Karn fly back to the United States with Bentley. He called Sam and had her set the entire thing up.

Next, King was going to Greece.

It was time to start chopping away at the root of the growing evil there. It was time to end the threat coming out of that region, the same one that involved King and his people a year ago. They had to pay for endangering his loved ones, and for the death they have brought to innocent people throughout the world in the name of what they believe. This had been happening for more than a decade, according to some reports.

As King approached the driveway, his phone began to ring. It was Sam.

"You have their plane tickets reserved?" King answered.

"Are you near a television?" Sam said.

"I'm walking into the safe house. Not sure there is a working one. Besides, I don't really have time for a *Game of Thrones* watch party."

"Mary's death is all over the news."

King hit the brakes. It had only been a couple of hours. There was no way reports should already be coming out. Even if Mary was discovered right away. The CIA would never let something like this out so fast. If ever.

"X?"

Just as King was trying to process what Sam had said, he dropped the phone and pulled his pistol. When he rolled up to the safe house, Agent Karn's vehicle was gone. At first he couldn't believe his eyes. There would be no reason for Karn to leave. A grim feeling washed over him. He knew something was terribly wrong. If Karn had been forced to leave because of an intruder, he would have called, or at least tried. King put his car in park, quietly stepped out, and walked toward the front door. When he peeked around the corner at the door, the rising sun behind him was reflecting on the side-panel window frame. It was absolutely glowing. But just below it lay pieces of splintered wood, right in front of the partially opened door.

King jerked his head back, out of sight of the front door. He took in his surroundings, the way he would have on instinct earlier if he hadn't been on a call with Sam. There was nothing out of the ordinary, except of course that Karn's car was gone.

Not good. King did not want to see what was inside that house. Whether it was empty or someone was dead, it was going to be bad.

Instead of rushing the front door, he went the opposite way, down the side of the house, then along the back. The sliding glass door was open, and partially shattered. Shards of white and unpainted wood lay at the foot of the entryway. Pieces of the door trim. It had been kicked in as well, which King felt was a bit odd. Why would both the front *and* back door be busted?

The neighborhood was intensely quiet. Wind chimes jangled in the breeze a couple of houses away, but that was the only sound. His ears were pricked as he crossed the threshold. Broken glass crunched under his sneakers. The lights were off, so once he was fully inside the kitchen, visibility dropped off. He didn't have to go far to see what had happened to Agent Karn. Once he turned the corner to go down the hall, King saw him lying face up on the living room couch.

King jogged over to Karn and found a gaping wound on the side of his neck, the source of all the blood beneath him. He was dead, but he hadn't been dead long. King remained quiet as he looked around for clues. He listened intently for a moment, though he figured there would be nothing to hear. Whoever had come for Bentley was already gone; he just hoped he wasn't going to find her dead as well.

King swept the rest of the first floor. All clear.

When he came back into the living room, he noticed a piece of paper tucked into the shoestring of Karn's boot. He knew right away Bentley wasn't going to be in her bed—dead or alive.

He rushed up the stairs. Her room was empty at first glance, but he moved to his right to check the other bedroom. It was empty also. Returning to her room, he found her purse still lying on the nightstand. As was the gun he had given her. She must have been asleep when the intruder entered. How did Karn not hear the doors being kicked in? He could see how Bentley may not have been able to hear, if her door was closed and she was sound asleep. But Karn? He should have heard the doors. Maybe he did, and when he went to investigate, the person who kicked in the second door was a distraction and he was killed from behind, then moved to the couch? So many things were flying through King's mind.

He paused for a second to take a breath, unsure what he was feeling. No one emotion stood out more than any others. Probably because he was feeling several at the same time. The last thirty-six hours had been a complete whirlwind, from the high of avenging his loved ones by killing Maragos to the low of standing in the situation he was in now—two colleagues dead who were also friends, and an innocent girl missing. A girl he was supposed to protect. The man who'd saved him before was lying dead on the couch, all because King had requested that he come and help him again.

Anger, sadness . . . helplessness. Whom could he turn to now?

King took a deep breath. He knew that panic and worry would do no good. He couldn't call Mary Hartsfield. But he still had Sam. She was all he needed to put these pieces together. They'd done it *many* times over the years. And since Mary had given him the gift of a name before her last breath, he and Sam would use it to pick themselves up off the mat. But there was a lot of work to be done.

Of all the unknowns, it was more clear than ever that whoever killed Mary in her office in Langley was an inside man. There was no way he and Bentley would've been found at this house otherwise. And because this person had also intercepted the most top secret of files, it was likely someone very high up, whether now or in the past, someone who knew how to use the system to get the information he or she desired.

Either way, standing in an empty bedroom wasn't going to get a single thing accomplished.

He had no idea where Bentley was, but he had a feeling he would be getting a call about it very soon.

King descended the stairs. He walked back over to Karn, took his two fingers and closed Karn's eyelids. Then he removed the paper from his boot. There were no words. There was only a telephone number.

An American telephone number.

One thing was clear: the individual responsible for everything that had happened since yesterday was one of their own. Unfortunately, this didn't faze King. This was nothing new. Some of the more corrupt people he'd faced, whether at home or on foreign soil, were once on his team. However, two major questions remained. Was this traitor the person Mary had named, Senator Bobby Gibbons, the man clearly ahead in the polls to become the next president of the United States? Or was Gibbons just someone who could help with answers? And finally, he wondered, as a sick feeling washed over him, was it possible this traitor was also connected to Husaam Hammoud? If not, there was an awful lot of overlap tying together all these recent events.

Either way, it was time to find out.

26

RAFINA, GREECE

SAAJID HADN'T BOTHERED TRYING to sleep. In fact, he never even went to bed. Instead, he walked down the street of the little village he'd built in the middle of nowhere. The reason he had been able to keep the Grecian government away was because he built the community under the guise of the church. He'd found some loopholes in the language of some of the laws, and as long as they weren't breaking any rules as far as the law was concerned, the government left him alone. And Saajid had made sure that he and his people appeared as much like model citizens as they could. In fact, no outsiders had been to the commune in over seven years. Saajid assumed that the government, and anyone else who might've known about the commune, had forgotten about it a long time ago. Which was exactly how Saajid wanted it.

He walked along the short dirt road that separated the small houses he'd built, and into the produce stand where they all brought their food and shared it as a community. He moved the baskets of fruit over as he'd done a thousand times, then lifted the door that blended into the wood of the floor and walked down, deep into the bunker he and Husaam had built for them and their officers to do business without being bothered. It was also a place where his family could go if someone ever found out about their little operation.

The underground bunker was a fully serviceable six-room facility. With everything a modern house could provide. Saajid entered the office, which was much like the one he'd had in Athens, and settled in to study and clear his mind. Despite his hatred for Western culture, he loved the aesthetics of Western workplaces. He was surrounded by cherry stained oak cabinets, shelving, and desk. The decor was right out of an early nineties *GQ* magazine exposé. For whatever reason, it helped him relax in turbulent times.

It had been a horrific thirty-six hours. Not only had he lost his childhood friend, Andonios, at the hands of another American assassin, but he had also lost his beloved niece, Althea Salameh. His sister had lost not only her lifetime love in Andonios the night before but also the daughter they'd had together. Though his sister and Andonios hadn't been with each other for years, it was one of those loves that was everlasting. Especially for Saajid's sister. And even though her daughter Althea had done what she was called to do in serving her god, it didn't mean accepting her loss was easy. It made it even harder that Althea was such a brilliant young woman. She could have been extremely useful once things were in place in the United States. But she knew the risks in getting involved, and she paid the ultimate price. Only the strong survive, and apparently she was not strong enough.

At first, Saajid had warned Andonios several times not to involve Althea in the game he was playing to try to get his other daughter, Bentley, away from her mother and back in Andonios's life. But Andonios hadn't listened. Althea eventually became so embroiled in his affairs, he lost her too. The only good thing about Andonios dying was that he didn't have to endure the death of his daughter. Saajid and Andonios had both experienced so much loss over the last two years. Sometimes it was hard to understand how all this tragedy could befall such loyal followers of Allah. But every time he picked up the good book and read it, it refueled his purpose and his willingness to give everything he loved if that is what his god commanded.

Saajid knew all the loss and pain would be worth it if he and Husaam just stayed the course. As soon as he refocused his mind, the good news started coming in. He could feel that things were about to change. The best decision he'd made was to call the CIA agent who'd lost his job after bungling a violent mission. Three years ago Saajid wasn't sure how he would use him, but over the last couple of hours, it was clear that the millions he'd sent him had been worth it. Saajid was right where he wanted to be: in position to be pulling the strings of an entire US presidential election. They were so close now, he could taste it. But he needed to keep his brother calm. He understood Husaam's frustration in having to wait until the end of the year for retaliation, but establishing power over the American presidential election would be well worth it. The possibilities would be endless.

Saajid's satellite phone began to ring. It was his American asset.

"Mr. Chapman," Saajid answered.

"My man in Belgium was able to secure the girl."

"Excellent," Saajid stood and paced the room. "What about the agent in the videos online, the one who was after Althea?"

"Dead. I had my guy gut him and leave him inside the house."

"Are you sure it's the same man?"

"No, but I had my guy leave a number on the body in case someone else was involved."

This Doug Chapman was smart. One of the finest agents in America before they tossed him to the wolves. When Saajid told Doug three years ago that he wanted to control an American election, not only had Doug not laughed but he also had great ideas. Saajid knew connecting with Doug would pay off. It was Doug's idea to become a political fixer. And it was working. Bobby Gibbons was the clear favorite in the upcoming election, but now he would be able to change that in favor of his man. With all the mess that Doug had involved Bobby Gibbons in now, Saajid could sink him like a stone. But Saajid wanted to hear Doug say it.

"Will you be able to tie what's happened to Bentley back to Senator Gibbons?" Saajid asked. "I sacrificed a family member in order to set this up."

"It will work." Confidence was not a problem for Doug. "Especially with the director of the CIA out of the way so she can't push any of her agents into continuing to look around. Any agent that was on Bentley's case will be pushed off of it now without Director Hartsfield in the picture. It has all come together perfectly. Now that the man who was after your look-alike niece is dead, there is nothing in our way. I'm sorry you lost her in the cross fire, but it was genius to play her off as Bentley and muddy the waters on who was really involved in moving the money from Everworld."

"Like I said, Mr. Chapman, it had better work. Your life

depends on it. Althea was my sister's daughter. I spent many years grooming her."

"Time well spent. I can't assure you what will happen once Bobby Gibbons is out of the race, but he will be. He was the last to visit the CIA director before she was shot. I had the best tech hacker in the world erase me from entry. He was even able to recharge my old ID to get me in, then erase it from the entry log. It's like I was never there."

"What about the security there? Didn't someone else see you?" Saajid said.

"Yes. Three men. But dead men can't talk. And as for Gibbons, he'll have an entire world coming down on him. Running for president will be a distant memory, I assure you."

"Good." Saajid took a seat, satisfied.

"Only question now is, do you really control the puppet who will now most likely win the election?" Doug said.

"That is none of your concern. Just make sure all of this business with Althea, Bentley, and any other agent involved is all tied off."

"Not a problem," Chapman said. "The last agent involved in the car bomb incident is already as good as dead. You'll have your scandal all served up on a silver platter."

"Good work," Saajid said. "Call me when the agent is dead."

"What about Bentley Martin?"

"She is very special to me. Her father was like a brother. Just make sure she stays safe."

"No problem."

"Your bonus, Mr. Chapman, is on its way."

Saajid ended the call. He sat back in his chair and took the moment in. He couldn't help but feel pride. Andonios,

Anastasia, and Gregor Maragos, along with Husaam, had all bought into the nanobot technology they thought would be the key to putting them in power. But Saajid had known better, that the long game he had in mind would be much more fruitful. He knew the way to true power wasn't to fight the most powerful nation in the world, it was to control it. The Maragoses and Husaam never believed it was possible to put their own man in power in America. But now, here Saajid was, incomprehensibly close to making a *real* difference for his religion and his people.

Saajid's father had been a great man. But like Husaam and the Maragoses, he had been shortsighted. Killing people off, whether in small acts of terror or massive acts of violence, wasn't the way to change the world. The Americans had been teaching the world that for years. The only way to make a difference wasn't to blow everything up but to control it.

If Saajid could keep Husaam on board, they would be controlling the largest, most powerful country in the world, in no time.

27

Bruges, Belgium

"For the last time, X, we can't call the number. All it is, is a way to know if someone is still out here trying to find them. That's why they left it on Karn. It's their way of making sure Karn was the agent they needed dead. We don't call, they'll believe they tied it all off."

King heard Sam, and could tell she was adamant. But it wasn't what he wanted to hear. He wanted to do what he always used to do: plow ahead and, through sheer force of will, make things happen. This new underground espionage world didn't lend itself well to that tactic. Sam was a lot better at it; it's what she did for so long with MI6 before she paired up with him. He had no choice but to listen to her, no matter how much he hated it.

"Mr. Kimball, your plane is ready." A brunette in a navy-blue flight attendant suit got King's attention. Jeremy Kimball was one of his US passport IDs. A businessman from Atlanta, Georgia, coming out with a new whiskey. Sam always said it was best, when creating fake backgrounds, to stay as close to the truth as possible. Less margin for error if a question about what he did for a living ever came up. King was as versed in the world of distilling the beautiful brown liquor as anyone, so this fake identity was good and solid.

King gave the flight attendant a nod. "The plane you chartered is ready for me, Sam. I'll be there in a couple of hours. Have you been able to get a hold of Bobby Gibbons?"

"Not yet." Sam's voice hollowed out. "But I'll keep trying."

Gibbons not answering Sam's calls was making King nervous. Though it was still the middle of the night in the States, a man like Gibbons, who was running for president, wasn't the type to keep his phone on silent. However, there was nothing King could do about it, so he needed to focus on what he could control.

"All right," King said to Sam as he followed the flight attendant out onto the tarmac. "I need to call Agent Roberts back before I take off. I'll see you in a couple of hours."

"There'll be a white Mercedes-Benz waiting there for you in Athens. If it's any other car, do not get in."

"Roger that. See you soon."

King ended the call and immediately dialed Agent Roberts.

"We've got a problem," Agent Roberts answered.

Not the way King had hoped Roberts would answer. He froze before following the flight attendant up the plane's stairs, holding up his finger to let her know it would be a moment.

"Don't sugarcoat it," King said.

"I just lost a tail."

"Shit!" King felt like they couldn't catch a break.

Whoever was pulling the strings on the other side of this was somehow staying one step ahead. He couldn't help but think that if Sam had been in London with him this entire time, she would've already run this thing down. She was the best at putting things together. King was like a wrecking ball. Sam was more of a fox. Regardless, she had made progress on what King thought was the bigger picture in Athens. Now that Mary and Agent Karn were dead, and Bentley was missing, he realized maybe the big picture was actually the problems he never saw coming. They usually were.

"You sure you lost them?" King said.

"They're gone, but I can't go back to my hotel. I'm heading to Alice's place now."

"Alice?"

"The MI5 agent I'm sleeping with, remember?"

"Got it," King said as he walked up the stairs and into the jet. "Good, maybe she can help you find Bentley."

"I'm sorry about your friend," Roberts said. "I didn't know him, but I heard he was a good agent."

King had messaged Roberts earlier to send a cleaner to the safe house. He wanted to keep everything quiet.

"Listen," King said, changing the subject, "whoever is in charge of this thing with Bentley is a professional. Don't mess around, or you'll end up like Karn."

Roberts didn't respond.

King continued. "On second thought, don't bother your MI5 friend about Bentley. Just let her focus on Karen Panos. I *need* to know if she can be traced back to Husaam Hammoud in any way."

"Husaam Hammoud? Son of the old terrorist the SEALs took down years ago?"

"Apple apparently doesn't fall far. Anyway, I need that

info yesterday. It could mean nothing, could mean everything."

"On it," Roberts said.

"I'm on my way to Greece. Before I find Hammoud, I want that info."

"I'll do all that I can. I can promise you that."

"I'll be in touch."

King put his phone away and took a seat. The jet was a Cessna Citation II. His father used to have one a lot like it when King was growing up. The interior was dated in this one, and a lot of memories of the fun times he and his father shared flooded back to him. It was the first time in a long time he'd thought of any good memories of his father. And it was almost enough to make him sick. The day his mom and dad were gunned down in front of him changed his life forever. It was the reason he joined the military at all. But it wasn't the worst day of his life. That day came not so long ago when he found out his father was still alive. Not only alive, but also the reason his mother was dead. It soured every memory he'd ever had of dear ole dad.

He closed his eyes to help keep the jet's interior from further reminding him of days that never meant what he'd thought they meant.

The next thing King knew, the tires were screeching against the runway. The force threw him forward as they landed in Athens. Somehow he'd managed not only to fall asleep but to remain completely passed out the entire flight. He hadn't realized how much his body needed it.

The plane slowed to taxi speed, and the flight attendant approached. "I'm sorry I couldn't be of any service to you, Mr. Kimball. You just looked like you really needed the rest."

"Yes, thank you," King said as he sat up. "It's been a long few days."

"Well, you're awake now. Would you like a drink for the road?"

For some reason King's father was still lingering in his mind. He remembered something his dad told a colleague on one of the rare occasions King had attended a work function with him. His dad told an old, balding fat man in a ritzy-looking suit to *never turn down a dollar, a drink, or a damsel in distress.* King never forgot the proud smile his dad wore when he turned to him and told Alexander not to forget it either. He hadn't realized it, but King didn't suppose he had turned down any of those things over the years. Not even once. And he wasn't about to start now.

"Bourbon, neat. And don't go gentle."

"You've got it." She winked and turned to go pour his drink.

As excited as King was to see Sam—it was by far the longest they'd gone since they met six years earlier—he was even happier to see the missed call from Agent Roberts and the subsequent text that read, *Call me. I know who Karen really is.*

Sometimes two hours is a lifetime when it comes to such high-stakes matters. When he looked at the time and did the math in his head, the sun was about to come up back on the East Coast. More answers, good or bad, would be coming in about Bobby Gibbons soon too.

He couldn't help but feel that was when the *real* work would begin.

28

"Bobby!"

Bobby Gibbons was in a deep sleep when he felt someone shaking him.

"Bobby!"

Registering his wife's voice, his eyes shot open, and she was standing over him. The light from their master bathroom shone behind her.

"Christ, Beth. What is it?"

"I just woke up, and on my way back from the restroom I saw that your phone had just stopped ringing."

Bobby sat up. He didn't understand the urgency. "Yeah, okay. So what? My phone must have been on silent."

"Bobby, there must be twenty-some calls you've missed tonight!"

That got his attention. He shot his hand over to his right, fumbled on the nightstand for his phone, then his reading glasses. The screen was bright to his unadjusted eyes. Sure enough, there were dozens of missed calls. The majority from the same number—one he'd never seen before. Bobby had been in a lot of tight spots in his life. Marines often seek out those spots. But the pit that formed in his stomach at the sight of all those missed calls was a black hole big enough for his entire world to fall through. Something was desperately wrong.

Just as he glanced at his phone, noticing it was five in the morning, an incoming call flashed on the screen. Same number that had been attempting all night long. His first thought was to ignore it. He should run the number by Mary and see if any of her CIA tricks could find out who the caller was before he answered their call. If he would even want to. But the overwhelming curiosity wouldn't let him wait. He was about to be very happy it didn't.

"Hello?" Bobby answered. His wife was wringing her hands as she sat on the edge of the bed next to him.

"Bobby Gibbons?" It was a woman with a British accent.

The scene of the London car bombing, which according to Doug he was ultimately responsible for, flashed in his mind. "Who wants to know?"

"You *really* ought to leave your ringer on when you sleep. Especially when you're wanted for the murder of the director of the CIA."

Bobby threw the covers off him and sprang out of bed so fast that he knocked Beth onto the floor. He had to take a deep breath before he could answer because this woman's words had stolen his air entirely.

"The CIA director is just fine. I just spoke with her last night."

"That's exactly why the CIA and probably the police are on their way to your house right now. To bring you in for questioning."

"Who the hell is this?"

"Mr. Gibbons, we need to be able to trust each other right now."

"Trust each other? I don't know who the hell you are. And you're calling me telling me my friend is dead, when I know better because I was just with her."

"Are they there yet?" the woman asked.

"Who? Is who here?"

Yellow lights glowed through the shades on the windows at the front of the house. Beth walked over, peeked between two of them, then turned back to Bobby. "Two black SUVs."

"What's going on? How did you know someone was coming to my home?"

"Like I said, it's the CIA coming to take you in. Mary Hartsfield and three security agents were gunned down just after you visited her at her office last night. Your name was the last thing she said to an agent over the phone. I can help you, but I need you to help me too. And you're going to have to decide right now, or I won't be able to help at all."

"Some men are getting out of the SUVs, Bobby," Beth told him from the window.

"That should help your decision," the woman said.

Then his phone vibrated. It was a text message from the same number the woman was calling from. He opened it and saw a link to a news story by the *Washington Post Online*. The headline read, "*CIA Director Shot and Killed.*"

Bobby felt as if something was squeezing tightly around his chest. He couldn't believe his eyes.

"Mr. Gibbons, if you don't move right now, I can't help you."

His breath caught; then he made the only decision he thought he could make in the moment. All he could think of was being the last one to see Mary; then for some reason he saw Doug's face. He couldn't help but feel as though he had been set up.

"Okay, who are you?"

"My name is Sam Harrison. I'm a CIA special agent, but more importantly for you, I am part of a secret program called Phoenix. Mary Hartsfield was the *only other* person who knew about the program. If you help me, I can keep you safe until we figure out exactly what is going on."

"You think I'm in danger?"

He knew it was a stupid question as soon as he asked it.

"Did you kill Mary Hartsfield?" the woman said.

"Of course not. She is—was a dear friend."

"All right. Then don't you think whoever did might want you next?"

Again, though he had no idea who murdered Mary, Doug Chapman's face flashed in his mind.

His doorbell rang downstairs. Bobby knew his secret service men at the front door wouldn't let the men pass without his okay. Unless it really was the CIA.

"Time's up, Bobby. If they take you into custody, you can't help me. If you can't help me, I have no need for you."

"What do I do?" he said.

"Take your wife and go out your back door. If you have men at the back, tell them to go and help stall the agents who have come for you." Bobby grabbed Beth by the sleeve of her robe and pulled her toward the bedroom door as Sam spoke. "Then hop your fence, go around your neighbor's house behind yours." He pulled Beth down the stairs. She didn't fight him; it was clear to her how urgent this was. "There will be a black Toyota Camry waiting for you there. Keep your heads down until you are clear of the neighborhood."

When Bobby reached the bottom of the stairs, he could see movement through the frosted glass that surrounded his front door. Their voices suggested things were getting heated. So far, going along with this Sam stranger seemed to be a good decision. He approached the two men guarding the back door. They didn't question him. Then he and Beth jogged toward the fence at the back of their yard.

"Where will the car take us?" Bobby asked.

"Kentucky."

"Kentucky? What the hell is in Kentucky?"

"A safe place to hide," Sam said. "And an important document I need you to retrieve."

Bobby pulled himself up and over the fence, then reached back and helped Beth over. They continued their jog past their neighbor's house.

"Okay. Where in Kentucky, exactly?" he asked, short of breath, mostly due to the excitement but also because of a lack of sufficient exercise on the campaign trail.

"We're in this together now, right?"

"Till the bitter end. I just ran from the CIA. Whether I did it or not, I look guilty as hell now."

"I have someone who will be able to fix that. You're going to his home. No one will go looking for you there."

"I don't understand."

Bobby spotted the black Camry Sam had told him would be there waiting. There was a woman in the driver's seat.

"Remember the attack on the White House a year ago?" Sam said.

"Yeah, of course. That King fella that used to be a Navy SEAL—the guy who had the racehorses, he died saving the president."

Sam didn't answer right away, and it clicked for Bobby.

"Phoenix . . ." Its definition—rising from the ashes—registered in his head.

"Yeah, he's not dead," Sam said.

"But now that Mary is"—Bobby's wheels were turning—"he's got no home. No allies at the agency. I understand. I'll do everything I can."

"And so will we. But before I let you go, I just need to know one thing."

Bobby opened the back door of the Camry and ushered Beth inside. "Anything."

"Why did Mary say your name right before she was murdered?"

29

ATHENS, GREECE

THE WHITE MERCEDES that Sam had waiting for King at the Athens airport pulled away, headed for the city center. The Hotel Grande Bretagne where Sam was staying was about a half an hour drive—plenty of time for King to return the call he'd missed from Agent Roberts. And he was more than anxious to do so.

"You're not going to believe this," Roberts answered.

"You'd be surprised, but go ahead."

"Alice rushed the dental on Karen Panos. Her real name was Althea Salameh."

"So she looks Greek but has a Muslim surname," King said.

"Crazy, right?"

"I'm not sure *crazy* is the right word, but I see what you're saying. The Maragoses are Greek and known for funding terrorists. But it would have been a little crazier if her last name had been Hammoud."

"Maybe there's still something there," Roberts said. "If you could somehow connect this Althea Salameh to Maragos *and* Husaam Hammoud, you've found what you're looking for, right?"

Roberts was right. This was what King wanted: to confirm without a doubt who the terrorists were who'd been working with the Maragos family. To tie the entire thing off with a nice, neat little bow. But the Greek and Muslim connection with Althea Salameh could just be a coincidence. Though his gut was telling him otherwise, he couldn't yet see the connection.

"Nice work, Roberts. I'll try to run it down."

"Be careful over there. This thing looks like it's getting complicated."

"Will do. Just focus on finding Bentley. Call me when you hear anything."

King ended the call and texted Sam. *I've got the real name of the woman posing as Bentley Martin. Be there in ten.*

Sam replied, *Now we're getting somewhere. I also talked to Gibbons. We can download when you get here.*

At least Gibbons was alive. As the Mercedes moved into the city, King couldn't help but think about Bentley. How scared she must be. He had promised her he'd keep her safe, and he had been unable to do that. The hardest part about it was not being able to stay in Belgium to find her. It was eating away at his gut. He never left anyone behind. But he justified going to Athens because he knew in his bones that whoever had Bentley was absolutely connected to the person he was looking for in Greece. One would reveal the other, but that didn't mean she would survive. The other thing that helped him move to the chase in Athens was that Agent Roberts was there in London, and seemed more than committed to finding Bentley.

"The Grande Bretagne, sir."

King reached in his pocket for money to tip with. An old habit from a former life. Instead, it was in his bag. He handed the man a twenty and stepped out into the warming Athens heat—and to the most beautiful sight he'd seen in more than a year.

Sam.

Neither Sam nor King said a word. They just moved toward each other and he wrapped her in a hug, lifting her off her feet. Her long black hair was tied back in a ponytail; her sharp cheekbones and almond-shaped eyes hadn't aged a bit. Holding her was like holding a piece of home. A home he'd been missing more than he knew.

Sam pulled back. "You look like shit." A smile crept up one side of her mouth.

"And you look ten years older. And pale. Couldn't you have at least laid by the pool for a few minutes?"

Brother and sister till the day they die. Yet blood played no part.

They hugged again.

"Come on," she said. "Let's get upstairs and dig in. We've got some real problems."

"What else is new?"

King followed her through the lavish hotel. Through the glass on the opposite side of the lobby, he could see the Acropolis in the distance. A relic from a former world stuck right in the middle of a new one. King could certainly relate. He and Sam entered the elevator and turned back toward the lobby. Just as the elevator doors began to close, two men walked around the corner. With intent. So much so that King noticed Sam reaching for her gun at the same time he went for his own.

The doors shut.

"Who are they?" King said.

Sam reached for the floor buttons and tapped one.

"If they got to our agent here who's been tracking them, most likely it's Hammoud's men."

"Great." Out of habit, King ejected the magazine in his Glock, checked the rounds, then slid it back in. "Welcome to Greece. What's your secondary exit plan?"

"In case they've been watching, I got a second room."

"Adjoining," King said knowingly.

"It's the only play. If they're on to us, there is no way out of here without shooting our way out."

"Is there anyone we can trust?"

"Yeah," Sam said. "You and me."

"If Hammoud flipped our agent here, he knows the United States is on to him."

Sam readied her stance for the elevator doors to open. "Which means whatever timeline Husaam had on the button he was going to push for an attack just got moved up."

"What the hell does all of this have to do with Bentley Martin, Mary Hartsfield, and Bobby Gibbons?"

"I have some ideas, but right now let's try to stay alive long enough to talk about it."

"I'll take left side," King said as the elevator door opened.

Sam moved at the same time and covered his right. The two of them fell right back into the rhythm that had gotten them out of so many jams in the past.

King just hoped this time would turn out like all the others.

30

When King and Sam checked the hallway from the elevator, it had been clear. They bypassed the room Sam had been staying in and entered the adjacent one. Once inside, they opened the adjoining door on their side, leaving only the one adjoining door closed that led to the next room. King and Sam were in enemy territory, so it was impossible to know how well-canvassed the hotel was. All they could do was take one step at a time. And the first step, the first sign of Hammoud's men, had just opened the hotel door adjacent to them.

"They had a key," Sam whispered.

She grabbed an empty glass sitting on the dresser beside the adjoining room door. She moved a few feet to her left toward the hotel room door. King shook his head at her. She gave a confident nod. He couldn't help but smile. He had missed her, quirks and all. He knew what she was trying to do; he'd heard the same thing about using a glass to hear through walls. He'd just figured it was total bullshit. Either way, he readied his gun and stood in front of the closed adjoining door, awaiting her signal.

She placed the rim of the glass against the wall, then put her ear to the bottom. She nodded at him. Then she began moving slowly his way along the wall, as if she was mirroring the enemy's position in the adjacent room. King couldn't hear a thing coming from the other room, but Sam nodded again. Then she held up two fingers.

Two men.

She pointed ahead to the door he was standing in front of. Then she kicked her foot out, showing him what she wanted him to do. He knew to wait for her signal. They'd been doing this long enough, communicating without words. He just hoped her glass-to-the-wall trick didn't get them both killed. No matter how silly he felt it was, he'd follow her down any rabbit hole.

Just as she reached the door, she pointed at it and held up one finger. Then she thumbed behind her and held up two fingers. She was giving him the position of the two men. Then she gave the stern nod he was waiting for.

King took a step forward with his left leg, planted, then used his right to front-kick the adjoining door as hard as he could. The door busted off the lock and hit an obstacle as it swung left. King followed the door's motion and slid on his knees across the threshold. His first two shots were low, the second of the two connecting with the leg of the man who'd been hit by the door. He quickly located man number two bolting out of the bathroom on his right. He moved his pistol up and to the right, squeezed twice more, hitting the man in the neck and shoulder area. The man collapsed to the floor and grasped at his throat.

The man who'd been hit in the leg was shouting. Sam rushed around King, grabbed a pillow from the bed, and held it over the man's face.

"Stop screaming or I'll put you out of your misery," she told him.

The man did as asked. Sam removed the pillow, stood on his bleeding leg, and put her gun to his head. "Who is after us, and how many of you are there?"

The man shouted in pain from the pressure on his wounded leg.

King was on his feet and moved around the two of them to make sure the second gunman was dead. He was staring blankly up at King, blood pooling beside his neck.

King went through the man's pockets as Sam continued her interrogation.

"Last time. Who are you working for, and how many of you are there?"

King didn't find anything of interest, so he took the man's phone and joined Sam standing over the first man. She was holding her foot over the bullet wound in his leg, ready to press. King reached over and pushed down on her knee. The man let out another groan. King crouched down and placed his gun under the man's chin.

"She asked you a question."

"Husaam. Husaam Hammoud."

King looked up at Sam. She nodded in confirmation. Now they knew their target for sure. There was no question. But they were going to have to survive this attack, then find a place to regroup. Neither would be easy.

"Okay, and how many?"

"I-I don't know. Ten? Twelve?"

"Good," King said. "Now one more and you live. I promise you that."

The man's dark eyes showed worry. King felt like he must have a family. He hoped the man just answered the question.

"Where can I find Husaam?"

To King's surprise, the man brightened—almost happy to hear that was the question. "He's . . . he's here."

"He's here now?" Sam said. "At the hotel?"

"Yes, please don't kill me."

"No way," Sam said. "A man like him doesn't fight, he gets people like you to do it for him."

"No, please! Husaam is different. He has trained many years for something like this. Please! I have a daughter."

"We have to move," Sam said to King.

King went through the man's pockets, took his phone, then lifted his leg to intensify the pressure. Sam had already moved through to the adjoining room to scout a way out. King extended the man's phone back to him.

"Call him."

Sam popped back in from the other room. "What? X, we don't have time for this."

King shot her a look, then turned back to the man. "Call Husaam right now. Tell him we are on the top floor. If you don't, not only will you end up like your friend"—King nodded toward the dead man by the bathroom door—"but I'll find your daughter too. Please don't test me."

Telling this man that he would find his daughter made King's skin crawl, because it was something he would never do, but it was important that this man *believed* that he would.

The man took the phone and dialed.

"Tell him you have us pinned," Sam said.

"We have them cornered," the man said into the phone. "Top floor."

The man handed King the phone. King pocketed it. Then he took the man's leg in his hands.

"I'll check the door," Sam said.

"Please," the man said, looking up at King. "You said you wouldn't kill me!"

"I won't, but you did try to kill me. Don't forget that. And I won't have you coming back to do it again. Not today."

King pulled the man's leg straight.

"Please!"

King stomped down through the man's kneecap. It would be severely painful, but the man would heal and be able to play with his daughter again. He just wouldn't be coming after King and Sam. Not today anyway.

As the man screamed, King moved into the other room and joined Sam at the door.

"I would have killed him," she said.

"I know, but you're heartless. Always have been."

Sam shrugged and opened the door to the hallway. "We're going to need a lot more *heartless* to get ourselves out of this hotel."

King knew she was a 100 percent right about that. But there was no way he was leaving that hotel. And she knew it. Not with the man King had been hunting for so long being so close. In the same building.

"You know this isn't the right time. We aren't prepared for this," Sam said.

"You have an extra magazine?" King said.

Sam felt down by her hip. "Always."

King nodded. "Then we're prepared."

31

SAM STEPPED OUT INTO THE HALLWAY AND KING MOVED IN behind her. She knew the hotel, so he had to follow her lead. She jogged to the end of the hallway and through the door to the stairwell.

"What do you know about Husaam Hammoud?" King said.

"His family grew up here. Dad was an Islamic extremist. It's been rumored that he has been involved in some plots of terror, but never anything concrete." They both started down the stairs. Sam spoke quietly to avoid an echo. "His brother, Saajid Hammoud, disappeared several years ago. Our agent here said no one has seen or heard from him in years, but obviously we can't trust that. We're in this situation right here because of him. However, according to my agent, out of the three Hammoud siblings, their sister, Jamila Salameh, is by far the most involved in terrorism."

King stopped in his tracks.

Sam looked back. "What are you doing? We have to move!"

"Did you say Salameh? Jamila Salameh?"

"Yes, so what?"

"Althea Salameh. That's Karen Panos's real name."

Sam started moving back down the stairs. "We have to beat Husaam to the lobby. He'll be on the move once he realizes we're not actually on the top floor. We can worry about the incestuous relationships of Greek gods and Islamic terrorists once we've left here without being in body bags."

King raced down after her. She was right. He just couldn't believe how closely tied together all of this seemed. He still didn't really understand how it all came together, but it was clear that somehow the Maragoses and the Hammouds had joined forces. Figuring out the when and why would have to wait. It didn't really matter to King as long as he made sure Husaam paid for putting his loved ones in danger.

Sam stopped at the door leading out to the lobby. She took her sunglasses from her pocket and put them on quickly. Then she removed her black leather jacket and tossed it to the floor, then tucked her pistol at the small of her back inside her jeans—trying her best to conceal it under her white tank top.

"They'll be looking for a man and a woman," Sam said. "Go to the concierge and ask about dinner. The desk faces the elevators. I'll make a coffee at the stand across the room."

"I've missed this," King said, tucking his pistol at his lower back, under his coat.

"I haven't missed it for a second."

Sam turned and walked straight for the coffee stand. King waited back for a second. She looked back and gave him a wry smile. Sam wasn't good with sharing feelings. This was the best he was going to get, and it was enough.

As the lobby door closed, his focus returned. He had to forget trying to connect Althea Salameh, he had to forget Bentley Martin, and he had to put out of his mind the American who was a step ahead of him at every turn. This was about Husaam Hammoud and finally putting the events of last year behind him. Once and for all.

King dropped his go bag with Sam's leather jacket in the hallway. He didn't want to leave it, but he didn't have a choice. He needed to be able to move freely. He walked through the door and spotted the concierge desk, but he never made it there. Shots rang out from across the lobby. Sam hadn't made it to the coffee stand before Husaam and three of his men had walked out of the elevator. Sam had taken out the one in front before they knew what hit them. The other two men brought up semiautomatic rifles and laid down suppressive fire as the man behind them bolted for the hotel entrance.

Husaam.

King saw that Sam had dived behind the couches in the coffee area. She was taking fire. But he couldn't let Husaam get away. He knew if he did, they might never see him again. King sprinted for the front door and pulled his pistol. He fired in the direction of the two men. He wasn't concerned with hitting them; he just hoped it would be enough to give Sam the upper hand. Once he reached the massive glass doors, he focused everything he had on the man driving away from the valet in a Lamborghini. King looked around. It was a massive luxury hotel, but all the rest of the vehicles surrounding the entrance were SUVs. He would never catch Husaam in those.

Then one of the SUVs moved, and hiding behind it was a man unstraddling what King instantly recognized was a brand-new Ducati Superleggera—the fastest production bike ever made. The gunshots from inside were just making themselves known outside. King swiped the keys to the bike from the frightened man who'd just ducked behind a delivery truck. A second later the engine roared to life and King was spinning the rear tire as he pulled back the throttle with his right hand, and catapulted out of the valet circle.

Fortunately, the Lamborghini Husaam drove away in was orange, so it stood out like a pimple on the tip of a nose. King shifted to third gear and weaved around a few slower-moving cars. It didn't matter what that Lamborghini had in it, there was no way it could outrun King on that super bike. Husaam's only chance was his familiarity with the back roads.

Husaam made a right and whipped the Lambo off the main road. King had to check his rearview before he could make the move. Two more motorcycles came into his view, and they were not out for a leisurely stroll. He could see an AK-47 dangling from the shoulder strap of the man on the right. King downshifted as he squeezed his back brake. The back tire slid wide as he turned right, but the traction control kicked in and put him on the straight path. He pulled back the throttle, and the bike was so powerful it almost put him on his back. He tampered it just enough to ride out the wheelie until he could set the front tire down and accelerate normally. Husaam then turned again, this time to the left, and King had to cut across oncoming traffic to make the turn himself. A pickup truck slammed on its brakes just enough to miss King's back tire. He was lucky.

Husaam was not.

He must not have been ready for the power of the Lamborghini when he stomped on the gas out of the turn, because he lost control of the back end and slammed into a truck that was parked on the side of the road. King skidded to a stop across the street and turned around just in time to see one of the motorcyclists get smacked by a delivery truck. The second rider was able to avoid it, but it put him out of control. He began sliding sideways, then laid the bike down twenty-five yards from King.

King pulled his Glock, walked forward, and put two in the man's back before he could even roll over to take a shot back. When King looked back to the Lamborghini, Husaam was on his way out through the passenger-side door.

King turned back to the motorcycle and motioned toward two bystanders. "Grab his gun and call the police! Now!"

He didn't wait to see if they did what he asked. He had a terrorist to catch.

32

KING LEFT THE DUCATI BEHIND AND GAVE CHASE AS HUSAAM Hammoud sprinted across the street. The sun was still unseasonably hot in the late afternoon, and since it was a Saturday, the streets were flooded with tourists meandering, making their way to and from the Acropolis. Just below the beautiful and timeless structures still standing high on the hill was the Plaka—several blocks of pedestrian-only streets full of gyro shops, jewelry stores, and trinket peddlers. And that's exactly where Husaam was headed. The crowd there was even more suffocating than the roads stuffed with cars.

Sweat poured off King as he ran into the Plaka. He threw his coat to the side and was still hot in just a T-shirt. He was doing his best not to run over anyone, but it was nearly impossible if he wanted to stay with Husaam. This guy was fast. It was also pointless to keep his gun in hand, because he would never take the chance of shooting around all these people.

King was having trouble keeping up with Husaam. And it was getting harder and harder to see him. The only reason King knew he was staying on the right track was because he could still hear pedestrians screaming at Husaam up ahead as he knocked them over. King had to jump one fallen lady entirely to keep from losing ground.

Then Husaam was gone. There was no more shouting from people up ahead, no more crowds parting in Husaam's wake. He had turned off, but the cross street went right and left. King slid to a stop, looking both ways.

Nothing.

He saw a man staring at him. The man was wearing an American flag T-shirt.

"CIA! Where'd he go?" King shouted.

The man opened his mouth, but he didn't have time to point before King felt something slam into him. Just like that, his feet were completely off the ground and flying above his head. Then his left elbow slammed into the stone-paved street below him, and he felt his shirt get ripped clean off. He could also feel his pistol become dislodged from the back of his belt line.

Then came the punches.

King reoriented himself, put both arms in front of his face in a defensive position, then waited for Husaam to make a mistake. The sixth or seventh punch was thrown with frustration, and that extra oomph behind it threw Husaam off balance. King took advantage. He slid his right arm between Husaam's legs and at the same time bucked his hips. This separation, and his arm placement, helped King escape from beneath Husaam as he threw him forward.

King jumped to his feet, and when he turned, he saw that Husaam had done the same. A crowd had gathered around the two of them now, forming a circle around the two men who were now squared off, ready to resume fighting. Husaam's physical appearance surprised King. He hadn't expected such a muscular man. His olive skin bulged with muscle from beneath the sleeves of his T-shirt. His black hair was pulled back into cornrows, a much more gangster look than King had imagined. But none of that mattered now. What was important was that he win this fight, and he needed to win it fast. There was no telling how many of Husaam's men would be coming at any moment. Much less the police.

King could feel the cameras from all the phones in the crowd—thirsting for that next great viral video of the bare-chested man who claimed CIA battling a full-blooded terrorist. King's days in the shadows were likely over. But there was nothing he could do about it now. He just had to make sure he had days left at all.

"Who are you?" Husaam shouted. "Tell me! Who are you?"

Husaam was spitting as he shouted. The mere sight of King was making him crazy. That's when the familiar slow-motion feeling King had always felt in high-adrenaline situations came back to him. He no longer could hear what Husaam was saying. The people who'd gathered around the two of them faded to black as King focused on Husaam's body. The body that finally began moving toward him.

King bent his knees, dug the ball of his left foot into the stone beneath him, and with his right leg, he push-kicked Husaam in the chest, changing Husaam's momentum—forcing him back. Then he waited for Husaam to come again, which he did immediately. He was being driven by rage, something King knew a lot about. Which meant he knew a lot about how to use that rage against him.

This time King let Husaam come all the way in. Husaam changed levels at the last second, ducking for a wrestling-style double-leg takedown. King countered it by catching

Husaam under his arms, kicking his legs back, and falling on top of him, pushing Husaam facedown onto the stone with his hips. Acting quickly, King spun on top of him like a turning bottle cap, lodged his legs down and around Husaam's hips while sliding his right arm under his chin.

Husaam countered back. He caught King's arm and turtled up; then he spun, turning into King so fast that King couldn't hold position on his back. But at least he was still on top of Husaam. King switched from full mount to half guard, intertwining his legs, which he had always preferred while training in top position. It was clear that Husaam had been versed in Brazilian Jiu Jitsu, so King didn't take any chances. As he pushed down with his hips, trying to lie as heavy on top of Husaam as he could, King forced his right forearm up under Husaam's chin, pushing with all that he had. Husaam had the wherewithal to push King's elbow across and trap his neck in a head-and-arm choke. King was surprised by the strength in Husaam's squeeze. It was clear they were fairly evenly matched on the ground, so King struggled out of the hold and popped up to his feet. From then on, this was going to be a fistfight.

Husaam shrimped back and hopped up to his feet as well. He wasn't tired. King could still see the bounce in his step. This wasn't going to be easy. And King felt it was time for a new approach.

King moved forward first this time, feigned like he was going to throw an overhand right, but instead he jabbed Husaam in the nose. Husaam stumbled back, then came forward, but was stopped by another jab, then another. Blood began to trickle from his nose. He wiped it with his forearm, stared at the blood for a moment, then stepped forward himself. When he swung a looping right hand, King weaved left and twisted his hips, whipping a hard left hook directly into Husaam's right kidney. Husaam grunted and dropped to his knees. King had hit the organ flush, which can bring more pain than almost any other blow.

While Husaam was on his knees, King didn't let up. He stepped forward with his left leg, then whipped his right leg toward Husaam's head. Husaam was able to block the Thai kick with two forearms, then back-rolled to give himself room to work. King tried to push forward and land a leg kick, but Husaam checked it by lifting his leg, and the shin-to-shin contact sent a shock rifling through King's entire lower half. Unspeakable pain.

Husaam knew how to fight a clean fight. So it was time to make this thing dirty.

King limped forward and faked another leg kick. Husaam reacted by lifting his leg to check the kick again, so King stepped in and locked his fingers together around the back of Husaam's neck in a Thai Plum clench. This was the third style of fighting King had attempted. If Husaam was also versed in Muay Thai, King would be shocked. King yanked down on Husaam's neck to test. It came down rather easily. For the first time in the fight, King had full control.

He wasn't going to let it go.

King pulled Husaam's head down again and drove his right knee upward. The impact popped Husaam's nose, and the crowd gasped as blood gushed from his nostrils. King didn't let go of the Plum. Instead, he pulled Husaam off balance by yanking his head left, then drove his knee right into Husaam's groin. There was no holding him up after that. Husaam grunted as his air left him; then he collapsed to his knees. As Husaam was writhing in pain, King stepped back, planted his left foot, and whipped his right leg around his body, blasting Husaam's forehead with the top of his foot.

The lights went out.

As King stood, chest heaving, over Husaam's unconscious body, his first thought was of Sam and whether she'd made it out of the hotel. The police still hadn't shown up at the Plaka. In King's mind, the fight had gone on forever. In reality, it was probably only a couple of minutes.

The crowd let out a roar of appreciation for the free show, and the flag-wearing man walked up and raised King's arm. King jerked his arm away and spoke to the crowd.

"There are more men like him coming with guns. Get out of here. Now!"

When the people scattered, King saw his Glock lying on the stone. When he went to pick it up, he was trying to decide what to do with Husaam. If he let the police have him, King couldn't help but think he'd be out in no time, with nothing gained by finding him. But he couldn't shoot him in front of everyone either. As he bent down to grab his gun, he saw flashing blue lights at the end of the pedestrian street. Two police officers were exiting the car. People huddled around them, pointing in King's direction to let them know where the trouble was taking place.

King tucked away his gun. Behind Husaam was a clothing store. He walked over, lifted Husaam from behind, and dragged him inside. The cool air felt good on King's back.

"Get out. Now!" he shouted at the woman behind the register. To her right was a dressing room. King figured this was as good a spot as any to force some answers out of him.

He dragged him inside and sat him on the bench, propping his back against the wall. Husaam finally started to come around, and his head bobbed upward, his blinking eyes finding the barrel of King's pistol.

"How did you know we were at the hotel?" King asked.

Husaam smiled. Blood leaked through his white teeth. King slapped the smile right off his face with the end of his gun.

King had to make this fast, so he changed his approach. "It was me who killed Andonios Maragos at his little lake house."

Husaam's demeanor changed instantly. His eyes widened, his shoulders perked, and the muscles in his arms tightened. There was no question now that he was involved with the Maragos family and their terrorist endeavors. The real question was, was he the only one?

"What's wrong? Don't feel like smiling anymore?" King taunted.

Husaam started to stand. King discouraged it with the tip of his pistol to Husaam's forehead. "I squeezed the life out of Andonios with my bare hands."

Husaam's jaw clenched.

"It was my team that killed his brother Gregor Maragos here in Athens. And yep, you're looking at the guy who stopped his sister, Anastasia Maragos, from killing the president of the United States. I watched her take her last breath too. Gotta say, pretty satisfying."

Husaam spit some blood on the floor. "If you kill me, you bastard, you'll never make it out of Athens alive. My bro—"

Bingo. Husaam stopped himself, but it was too late. Saajld—the "missing" brother wasn't really missing at all. He was hiding, pulling the strings, like every other cowardly terrorist cult leader before him. Husaam must have just been his whipping boy. And King had a hunch that Husaam never liked that hierarchy.

"It's okay," King said. "Go ahead, finish that sentence. I'll wait."

King could hear some commotion from the street outside the clothing shop. It was now or never. Husaam didn't finish, so King did for him. "Let me guess, Husaam Hammoud . . . You meant to say that your *brother* will make sure I don't make it out of Athens alive." King smiled. "I understand now. Because he's the one who's *really* in charge?"

"Fuck you!" Husaam rose up to challenge King.

King put a bullet in his forehead. The longstanding terrorist who'd murdered God only knew how many innocent people collapsed to the floor below.

"No," King said. "Fuck you."

33

A COUPLE OF HOURS AFTER THE SATISFACTION OF CHECKING another enemy off his list, King finally had the chance to sit down and catch his breath. After shooting Husaam dead, he'd grabbed a T-shirt and a hat from the clothing store and snuck out through the back entrance. During the time he'd spent running down and killing Husaam, Sam had tried to call a few times. She had taken out the two men in the lobby of the hotel, then another who was outside waiting for her. She had to hide around the corner for a while because the police were crawling all over the place.

After King told her he was okay, they both found separate transportation back out of the city to the airport. Using a different passport she happened to have on her, Sam reserved a room at the Sofitel Airport Hotel. They both took great pains to make sure they weren't followed—taking multiple cars on multiple routes. When they arrived, King told Sam to go ahead up to the room so she could shower in private, but the real reason he wanted her to go before him was because he noticed some bourbon on the top shelf at the hotel bar. He was happy to find their selection was impeccable.

King had taken a seat at the table in the corner of the one-king-bed hotel room—the only room they had available. He already had two glasses placed side by side, and with a slight smile he began to pour the Eagle Rare bourbon from the bottle he'd paid three hundred dollars cash for. He'd found the roll of money in his go bag, which Sam had managed to grab from the stairwell where he'd left it at the previous hotel before the shootout.

The scent of the bourbon as he poured was already helping him relax. As it always did. Eagle Rare was one of his favorites. The smell of vanilla, caramel, and oak reminded him of another time and place. One that didn't involve so much hate and violence. The bathroom door opened, and steam wafted out. Sam emerged in the white robe she'd exchanged for her clothes. Her long dark hair was wet down her back. She was beautiful in the dim yellow light of the bedside lamp.

"So, where are my clothes? And yours?"

King looked down at the robe he was wearing. Then back to Sam. "I had housekeeping come get them for a wash. Yours were starting to stink."

Sam tried to hide a smile.

"Was that a smile? The ice queen has a soul?"

"Been into that bottle already, have you?"

"No. I'm a gentleman. I waited for you."

For the first time in over a year, he got the classic Sam eye roll, and it couldn't have made him happier.

"Come here and have a drink with me, you old cow."

Sam walked over and took a seat on the edge of the bed. "You're no spring chicken. Thirty-one this year, right?"

"Still a decade younger than you." King held up his glass.

"Not quite. But close," Sam said, smiling. Then she picked up her glass.

"Cheers," King said. "To never growing up."

Sam clinked his glass with hers. "You've got that toast in the bag. Though I was beginning to have my doubts. You've been awfully dark at times this year."

King thought about it for a moment as he took his first sip. The familiar burn was a glorious indulgence. He supposed he *had* lost his boyish charm as of late. "Been a tough year."

"How's your arm?"

He'd suffered a road rash when Husaam slammed him to the ground.

"Nothing a little bourbon won't numb."

They were quiet for a moment as they sipped.

"It's good to see you, Sam. It's been way too long."

"I agree. I've actually missed you."

"Well . . . never thought I'd hear that. Cheers to Sam's mushy side." He flashed her a big smile as he took the bottle from the table and poured a little more.

"I guess I'd better fill you in on Bobby Gibbons."

King frowned. "Always right back to business. You almost set a record this time, though."

"Sorry to disappoint."

"I'll get you to relax one day."

Sam took the rest of her drink in one slug, then held out her glass for more. "If we were here selling insurance, I might be more apt to let my hair down. As it stands, someone is trying to rig your country's next presidential election."

"How the hell could you possibly know that?"

"I'm putting pieces together," Sam said. "Bobby Gibbons was the last person to meet with Mary Hartsfield at CIA headquarters before she was murdered."

"Why would he meet with her?" King was trying to make the connection. "And was it after hours?"

"It was. He called her worried about the car bombing in London."

"What?" King set down his glass.

"Have you ever heard of an ex-CIA agent named Doug Chapman?"

"Of course. Who hasn't? Guy's a legend. And an asshole."

"I'd use the term *infamous*, but yes, he has quite the history. Anyway, since the CIA ousted him a couple of years ago, he's become known in circles as a political 'fixer.'"

"Fixer?" King said. "You mean like Ray Donovan?"

"Don't know who that is," Sam said. King wasn't surprised. She never did anything but work, much less watch Showtime. "But Doug is a fixer in terms of when there is a problem in Washington that needs to be '*handled*,' apparently he's become the guy to call."

"Okay, what does that have to do with Bobby Gibbons and the car bomb I saved Bentley, or I guess Althea, from?"

"Bobby Gibbons hired Doug Chapman because Bobby had stock in Everworld Solutions."

King picked up his glass and took a drink. "Damn. I'm getting awfully tired of hearing that company's name."

"You and me both."

"I'm surprised. I didn't think Gibbons was like Senators McDonnell and Thomas. Always heard he was one of the good guys."

"I believe he is," Sam said. "I've talked with Mary in the past about him. She said he's a stand-up guy. When I talked to Bobby again after he and his wife left their house, he said McDonnell and Thomas just told him Everworld was a good investment. He said that was all he ever knew about it."

"But he knew how bad it looked to be seen as involved with a company that funded terrorists, so he wanted himself scrubbed from the records before the media found out about it."

It was starting to come together. Except the part about Bentley.

Sam continued. "Gibbons said Doug told him about the car bomb after it happened. Doug told him that Bentley, because of her presumed work on the numbers side of the Everworld business, was the only credible person left who could tie him back to the company."

"How did Gibbons react to hearing Doug would go to such lengths as to murder a seventeen year-old girl?"

"Not well. Apparently, that's when Doug put a gun to Bobby's head and told him to let him do what he was hired to do."

"Wow."

King let that sink in. All of it was a lot to process. He had to back up for clarification. "So what does all this have to do with rigging an election?"

Sam set down her empty glass. "I don't think Doug Chapman *only* works for Bobby Gibbons."

"Land the plane, Sam. You're making some huge leaps here."

"Mary and I had dinner and drinks last week before I left for Athens. She told me that President Williams was worried about the presidential candidate running against Bobby Gibbons."

"John Forester?" King said. "From the Forester family?

Why would Williams ever be worried about him? He's only the son of the most politically corrupt family this country has ever known."

"Right, your sarcasm is well placed," Sam said. "Well, Mary told me that President Williams was so convinced that Forester was trying to cheat that she actually put a top secret three-man task force together just to investigate him."

"Mary did that? Really? That's ballsy. She gets caught doing that, she's a goner. I can't believe she told you that."

"We've grown—had grown—close over the last year."

"I'm sorry, Sam."

"Anyway, I think that's why she was killed. She told me she wanted some advice when I got back from Athens, because she wanted me to look at some things they'd dug up on Forester. I never got a chance to see the file, but I'm guessing Doug Chapman found out what Mary was doing. I think he might be actually working for John Forester, and never was really working for Bobby Gibbons."

"You think Doug Chapman killed Mary? To keep info from coming out about John Forester? This is crazy."

King's head was spinning. He needed to break it down, one detail at a time. "Okay, so, speculation aside, you think Doug Chapman tried to have Bentley killed, and after I saved her, you think he continued to run her down all the way to the safe house in Belgium?"

"It certainly lines up," Sam said. "Doug is ex-CIA. Which means he's one of only a handful of people who could have known about that safe house."

That definitely rang a bell for King. He'd thought when it happened that it was probably an inside man.

Sam continued. "And my theory is that once Bentley was kidnapped from the safe house, Doug didn't have her killed because he was probably worried, since you'd saved her from the car bomb, that someone else was onto him. So now he's going to hold on to Bentley until he can make sure he isn't in danger of being outed."

"You think that's why the phone number was left on Agent Karn's shoe?"

"It's the only thing that makes sense to me. Like I said, if you called the number, he'd know he still has a mess to clean up. Now he thinks he's home free."

"I still don't get it," King said. "If Doug is not actually working for Bobby Gibbons, then why try to kill Bentley Martin? If he really thought it was her that knew Gibbons had money in Everworld, wouldn't he want her alive? If Doug is working for John Forester instead, and trying to sabotage Gibbons, Bentley would be one way to help him pin terrorist funding to Gibbons."

"You're right," Sam said. "We're definitely missing something."

"Unless Doug was never really trying to kill Bentley."

"I don't follow," Sam said. "You saved her from a car bomb meant for her. Paid for by an American."

"But actually I didn't. I saved Althea Salameh. Saajid's niece. Maybe Doug was working for Saajid and double-crossed him? There are holes everywhere, but maybe Doug's target was this woman posing as Bentley."

King poured them both another drink.

"Damn," Sam said.

"My head hurts." King held up his glass once more. "To tangled webs."

"To untangling them," she said as they clinked glasses.

Both sipped their bourbon. King was trying to pull at least one thing together for certain. "So how do you think this all ties back to Husaam and Saajid Hammoud? To Andonios Maragos and Althea Salameh?"

Sam shook her head. "Not sure, but they are clearly linked. This is why I said your election might be getting tampered with. I just spoke with intelligence before my shower, and they confirmed what you uncovered in the stairwell at the hotel, that Althea Salameh was Jamila Salameh's daughter. Saajid and Husaam Hammoud's niece."

"This is insane. But shows even more that the Maragoses and the Hammouds have definitely been working together for a long time."

Sam shook her head. "Something still seems to be missing. And I can't quite put my finger on it."

"A lot of things are missing. We've been doing a lot of reaching to make things fit. Bottom line is, we have to start pulling some things together. Where is Bobby Gibbons now? If Doug is crazy enough to do all the things we think he's done, why wouldn't he just kill Gibbons? Then it would be a free run to the White House for John Forester. If that is who Doug is really working for."

"I think in the beginning he thought it would be cleaner to have the media take Bobby down for all the scandals. Especially with being the last to see Mary Hartsfield alive. But now that Bobby has gone into hiding, and someone like you is out in his world mucking things up, he might find killing Bobby *is* the easiest option."

"Where has Bobby gone into hiding?" King said.

"Kentucky."

"You sent him to my house, didn't you?"

"And he should be there anytime now."

King looked down at the bourbon in his glass and gave it a swirl. He could feel the alcohol running through his veins now. Maybe that's why the thought of home brought so much emotion.

"Miss it, don't you?" Sam said.

"Like you wouldn't believe." He set down the glass without finishing the drink.

"Maybe if we clean all this up you can go back?"

"I don't think I can. I can't put my sister and my niece in danger like that again. I almost lost them both because of what I do. This was my choice, to fight, not my sister's. I have to live with the consequences. And if me staying away keeps them safe . . . then it's worth it."

"I understand."

There was a knock at the door.

"That's probably our clothes," King said, his head still swimming in his own sadness.

"Perfect timing," Sam said as she stood to get the door. "You up for a little field trip? For old times' sake?"

King looked up. He found an eager look on Sam's face.

"Come on, there are few things you love more than revenge."

That got his attention. "The traitor CIA agent who gave Husaam your location at the hotel?"

"You got it."

King couldn't help but think that was exactly what he needed to stop feeling sorry for himself. He stood up and walked over to his go bag sitting beside the television. He reached in, pulled out his Glock, and checked for the chambered round.

"Field trip it is."

34

RAFINA, GREECE

"I WANT BLOOD, Saajid! They've taken *everything* from us!"

Saajid had seen his sister Jamila upset plenty of times. It was her personality. But the fire in her eyes at the moment was something new. Of course he understood why, and he felt the same way. She'd just lost her daughter, and now they'd killed her brother. But Husaam getting himself killed was exactly what Saajid told him would happen if he didn't listen. Saajid had been explaining to him, to the point of exhaustion, that defeating the United States was something that didn't happen at the one-agent-at-a-time level. It happened as a result of a slow and perfect planning process. Like what he currently had in place with John Forester, erasing his political opponent, Bobby Gibbons, so that Saajid could control the highest office in the land.

"Are you listening to me?" Jamila continued. "Althea is dead! My own daughter! Husaam is dead! Our brothers and sister Maragos are all dead! Our *father* is dead! All by American operatives. And you just sit here. No retaliation at all!"

"Enough! You sound just like Husaam. And look what happened to him!" Saajid shouted as he stepped toward her. "Do you not remember what happened when I gave in to all of your shortsighted plans a year ago? I told you the nanotechnology Gregor produced would not work. Their defenses are too good! The only way to beat them is to *control* their defenses. We cannot fight fire with fire with the war machine!"

Jamila took two steps toward him, getting right in her older brother's face. "And you think your plan is going to work, Saajid? Are you kidding? You really think that once this presidential candidate that you will have helped reach the top of the American political food chain is actually going to listen to you once he becomes the most powerful man in the world? Wake up! He's using you. If what you say is true, and American forces are impenetrable, once this John Forester is president, he won't listen to *you*. He'll be untouchable. And he knows about you and our operation now, so he will just have you erased. Probably by the same man who killed your own brother today!"

Saajid held up his hand, ready to slap his sister across the face to shut her up. Instead, he turned away and paced the office. He refrained from lashing out mostly because what she was saying actually made sense. And he didn't like it.

"You know I'm right, Saajid." Jamila had softened her tone. "You are the smartest person I have ever known. But you are naive if you think some political chess piece in America is going to serve you once he has all the power in the world. You can threaten him, his family, whoever you want. It doesn't matter. He will make sure it's like you never existed."

All the work Saajid had done to get this plan in place began to feel like quicksand. Like each move he made had buried him and his family even further. Now he had lost so much. He still had his wife and his kids, but the cause was more important. Saajid's father had made sure he understood that before he died. But he didn't want to lose them. Not for nothing.

"Maybe," Saajid said, turning to face his sister, "maybe you are right. But you shouldn't have come here. You have put my family in danger by doing so. You are on every terrorist watch list that exists. You know they are watching you. How could you risk bringing attention to yourself here?"

"I'm sorry. You're right. I just didn't know what else to do. I lost Althea, Saajid. My baby girl. You have no idea what that feels like. She had such a bright future with us. She had so many skills. Do you want this to happen to your family? Do you want to feel the agony I feel right now?"

"Of course not," Saajid said.

"Then let's act now. That's why I have come. The American agents are still in Athens somewhere. We must find them. And kill them both. I know you have seen the videos, Saajid. The man who was standing next to Althea when she was shot is the same agent who was fighting with Husaam at the Plaka today."

"You may be right. They do look similar. But the man standing next to Althea in that video in London didn't kill her. She was killed by a sniper."

"Exactly," Jamila said. "This is exactly what I am talking about. Who did you hire to kidnap Andonios's other daughter, Bentley?"

"The same man who killed the director of the CIA."

"The same man who is helping you propel John Forester into the presidency?"

"Yes."

Jamila shrugged her shoulders. "You see, my brother, this Forester has already turned on you. Before he has even become president."

Jamila's words hit home. Was it possible that Doug Chapman had double-crossed him? Was he actually working for John Forester? Saajid's blood was boiling. He couldn't believe he had already paid Chapman. It had always been about the money for Doug, not getting Saajid power. He walked over to his desk, picked up his phone, and dialed Doug's number.

"Hello?" Doug answered.

"How did you know where to send your man to find Bentley Martin in Belgium?"

"I don't have time for this, Saajid. Why does it matter? We have her."

"Yes, but I don't have my niece. She's dead. You are the only person other than her father, Andonios, who knew her connection to me, and that she was posing as Bentley to confuse Bentley's involvement in Everworld."

"So what? Like I said before, you knew the risks of involving your niece. At least we saved Bentley, Andonios's other daughter, right?"

"But not my sister's daughter!" Saajid slammed his fist down on his desk. "Did you know that it would be Althea going for a run? Did you set that car bomb for her? Tell me, Doug, was she your target the entire time?"

The line went dead.

Saajid whipped his phone across the room, and it shattered when it slammed against the wall. His chest was heaving. He couldn't believe he had traveled so far down the road of his plan, only to see it come to a dead end. Only to have his sister be right. There was no taking control of the United States; he had been overly ambitious. And he had seen so much more loss because of it. He was tired of losing. He may not be able to control the US government, but that didn't mean he couldn't hurt it in ways no one had ever seen. Thankfully, his and his family's plan of attack was multifaceted. There were still plenty of things in place to make their mark.

"Green-light every faction we have in America. When they're in place, make sure they call me first, for the go-ahead. I want to time this a certain way." Saajid made sure his sister was looking at him. "No one moves without hearing from me first."

"Glad you're finally on board, Saajid. Let's show them what more than a decade of pragmatic planning can do, and use it all to strike at once!"

Saajid nodded. "Let's bring them to their knees."

35

LEXINGTON, KENTUCKY

THE GATES OPENED and Dbie Johnson pulled the car through. Bobby and Beth Gibbons had gotten to know her pretty well during the eight-hour drive they'd shared from Washington, DC, to Lexington, Kentucky. The grounds of Alexander King's home were spectacular. Just through the gate, the driveway stretched out straight ahead as far as the eye could see. On both sides of the road, massive trees arched and met overhead, forming a canopy for the long drive to the house. White wooden fencing ran along the property lines on both sides, just beyond the trees.

"Oh look," Beth said. "Is that a Thoroughbred pony and its mother running along the fence!"

Bobby watched the two black majestic-looking animals frolicking in the pasture. "I believe so. Gorgeous, aren't they?"

"Such beautiful animals," Beth said.

"Yeah," Dbie said from the front seat. "Even though Mr.

King is gone, Sam still makes sure the place runs the same as if he weren't. His sister and his niece visit pretty often."

Bobby didn't tell Dbie that he knew Alexander King was still alive. He kept that between himself and Sam. After a minute or so, a house appeared in front of them. Dbie followed the circular driveway that curved around in front of a neoclassical Southern mansion. It looked as if there was a main portion of the house, shaped like a box, with two shorter yet wider wings that stretched out on either side. The mansion was white with four gigantic white pillars that supported the entryway. Four white chimneys protruded from the gray pyramid-like roof. Both second-story sets of windows had balconies that extended outward from the front of the house, and there was an oversized gray front door with a large semicircular window above it.

"Why would a man who inherited all of this give it up to join the military?"

Dbie got out of the car. Bobby and Beth followed.

"If you would have asked him, he would have told you he never had a choice. After his parents were killed, all he ever wanted to do was make people pay for doing good people wrong."

"Who could blame him," Bobby said. They walked toward the front door. "The story you told us about the nanobots that you and King helped keep out of the White House was something else. You're a real hero too, you know."

Dbie shrugged it off and opened the door. Even if she hadn't told Bobby that she was a tech person, he would've guessed something like that from her appearance. She was a cute girl, but her overall look—short dark hair and dark glasses—had *I work with computers* written all over it.

"Well, like Alexander would tell you if he were here,"

Dbie said, "make yourself at home. I have work to do for Sam, but if you need anything, just call me. Sam is having someone cook dinner for you, but if you get hungry before then, just raid the fridge. Oh, and I'll see to it you have some clothes as well."

Bobby and Beth were still in their pajamas. He felt ridiculous being out during the day in them, but it was better than sitting in some interrogation room, explaining why he was in Mary's office so late and why he wasn't responsible for her ending up dead shortly thereafter.

"Thank you, Dbie," Bobby said. "You've been more than kind."

Dbie walked them inside. The interior of the home was as grand as the exterior, but Bobby didn't get the chance to take it all in before his phone began to ring. He didn't recognize the number, but he just knew it was Doug Chapman. He looked at his wife; she could tell Bobby didn't like who was calling.

"I have to answer it."

"Bobby, don't. If you think he killed Mary, all you will do is make things worse."

Beth was probably right, but he also didn't want Doug to come looking for him. "I have to." Then he asked Dbie, "Is there somewhere private I can take this call?"

"Alexander's office is right through there."

She pointed to the right, and he walked straight for the door, then shut it behind him.

"Hello?" Bobby tried to sound normal, but he felt like his voice came out in a squeak.

"What the hell's going on, Bobby?" Doug went right in on him. "You canceled your rally tonight in Virginia."

"Yeah, I don't feel well. Per the press release." Bobby had

rehearsed this conversation several times in his head. But when he rehearsed it, he wasn't short of breath and worried how it was coming out. "I lost a dear friend last night, Doug. Calling you was about the last thing on my mind."

"Yeah, I get it, but we have to stay in close contact. Where are you? We need to meet."

Bobby knew this would be one of the first questions Doug would ask.

"I'm in mourning, Doug. You said to let you do what I hired you to do. And that is what I am doing."

"Mourning? Bullshit, Bobby," Doug said. "Look, I need to know if you are the one who killed Mary Hartsfield. I can get out in front of this thing if—"

"If *I'm* the one who killed her? She was a friend, Doug! I would never—"

"Spare me," Doug interrupted. "I know you were the last one to see her. I've got eyes everywhere, Bobby. This is what I do. Been tracking down killers and liars for decades now. And I'm telling you, you are a marked man. I'm surprised the CIA or FBI hasn't already been beating down your door."

It was that sentence that let Bobby know everything he needed to know. Doug was talking out of both sides of his mouth. One second he has eyes everywhere, the next he doesn't know that Bobby isn't at home? That was the real bullshit. He believed with everything inside him that Doug killed Mary. Now, Bobby just had to make sure Doug didn't get to him and his wife before Bobby could expose him. He had to go back to thinking like a Marine.

"Doug, cut the shit. You keep acting like I'm some sort of lost puppy. I assure you, I'm not. You know good and well that I am not at my home. Whatever it is you're doing, it's not going to work. You aren't going to sabotage my run for presidency. I made a mistake the day that I got desperate and hired a wild card like you. Doug, you're fired."

"I agree, Bobby. It was a mistake to hire me. Probably the biggest you've ever made."

"Spare me, you scumbag." Bobby knew he should have ended the call, but he just couldn't hold his tongue.

"Now you're just a loose end. People in my line of work don't like loose ends."

"Is that a threat, Doug? You think I'm afraid of you?"

Doug answered by ending the call. Bobby couldn't have been happier that he was nowhere near Washington just then. The separation from an apparent lunatic helped him feel safe. But he'd be lying if he said he wasn't worried. He'd heard the stories of the kind of ruthless agent Doug was before he left the agency. Men and women like him, when their skills were pointed in the wrong direction, were all kinds of dangerous.

Bobby peeked out the office door. No one was around. On the desk across from him he noticed an unmistakable trophy. The Kentucky Derby gold cup. But what was just beyond the trophy really caught his attention. He walked over to the gun case with a silent prayer that it would be open and supplied. His prayer was answered, as he was faced with a Glock 19 alongside a full magazine. He picked up the gun, locked in the magazine, and tucked it down his pajama pants.

Bobby wasn't about to underestimate Doug anymore He said himself that he had eyes everywhere. If that were true, Doug may already know where Bobby and his wife had gone. He didn't think that was the case, but Bobby wasn't going to take any chances. Not anymore, anyway.

With that mentality, he picked up his phone again and dialed the last lifeline he had. A woman he'd never met. He knew Sam Harrison had connections to a *dead man* who Bobby hoped could turn out to be his secret weapon.

36

King didn't like being back in the Athens city center so soon after all the madness of the afternoon. Normally after something so public, especially when such a high-value target like Husaam Hammoud was taken out, an agent, or team, would leave the area immediately. And stay away. But King and Sam both knew that there would absolutely be retaliation for Husaam's death. Even if Sam was right that Saajid's preposterous yet ultimate goal was to rig the presidency, he was still a terrorist, and terrorists can't help but react. At least that had always been King's experience in the decade or more he'd been fighting them.

The cab pulled up to the back side of an apartment complex in a neighborhood called Gazi. They'd driven around the neighborhood four times, checking for anything suspicious or anyone who might be keeping an eye on the place. They both thought it looked clean enough to go on in, though they knew it wasn't a thorough search.

"I thought you said it was busy down here," King asked as he looked at the fairly empty street.

"It's only ten p.m. Another hour and this entire area will be crawling with barflies."

"Then let's get after it."

King and Sam exited the vehicle. The street behind the apartments was dark, but the neon glow of bar signs was blaring just on the other side. The cab pulled away and left them with the few pedestrians who were making their way to the popular side of the street.

"After you," King said, extending his arm in the direction of the apartments.

Sam moved ahead. "His name is Fred Johnson. He's been here for two years."

"Long enough to get bought by the bad guys?"

"I hope not," Sam said as she headed up the stairs. "But I don't know how else anyone could have known about me being here."

The stairwell was pretty well lit. Fred was staying on the fourth floor. King's biggest concern about the visit to the agent's place wasn't that he might be waiting with a gun, it was that if he had been turned by Hammoud, Hammoud's people would most likely be watching. Sam had tried several times to contact Fred so they could meet at a different location, but in the end both Sam and King knew it wouldn't have mattered. If they were watching Fred, they would have just followed him. At least here, in a private location, fewer people could get caught in the cross fire.

Sam walked away from the stairs and straight over to Fred's door. The play was to act like she didn't suspect anything, and hopefully extract at least some little helpful nugget of information from him. After Sam's third attempt at knocking on the door, King had lost all hope that this would happen.

"Kick it in," Sam said, motioning toward the door.

"It's 2020, Sam. You kick it in," King said with a wink.

As usual, she didn't find him funny. But she did kick in the door. King moved right around her, his gun drawn. The room was pitch black, but he didn't need the gift of sight to know what they had walked in to. The stench told both of them all they needed to know.

Fred was dead.

"Ugh." King covered his nose and mouth with his T-shirt. "When was the last time you met with him? 'Cause it smells like he's been dead a while."

King felt along the wall for a light switch.

"Impossible. I just met with him yesterday."

"Well, something is sure as hell dead in here—"

King's hand found the light switch, and the source of the smell was sitting in a chair just a few feet from them. There was blood everywhere.

"That Fred?" King said.

Sam moved around him, checked the room behind the chair, then inspected the dead man with her shirt over her mouth as well. King took in the room around them. It was in total disarray. It looked like someone had ransacked it without actually taking anything.

"Not sure. His head has a couple of holes in it," she said. Then she reached for Fred's pant pocket. He was turned a little to his side, giving her access to his back pocket. Fortunately for her, it was about the only part on him that wasn't covered in blood.

While she checked for identification, King walked back out into the outside hallway. He walked all the way to both sides of the building, making sure no one was coming. It looked clear.

"X," Sam called.

As he headed back toward the front door, the smell was making its way outside now.

"I don't believe it," Sam said. "The ID says Gerald Parsons."

"So?"

"That was the cover Fred Johnson was using here in Athens."

"But you said you met with him yesterday," King said. "Bodies don't start smelling like this for something like a week."

"I met with someone claiming to be Fred Johnson. But I'd never seen him before."

King took a few steps closer. His eyes were watering from the smell, but like all intense smells, it had begun to fade the longer he was in the room.

"You're telling me that whoever killed Fred here had all the check-in codes and all of that? Enough to pass protocol when you reached out to meet?"

"What do you want me to say, X? You know I always follow protocol. The man I met with passed every single one of them. Whoever did this must have tortured him for that information." Sam pointed to several blood stains and puddles in the small living room. "Hence all the bloody mess here. We have to go. Now."

Sam began walking toward him. King held up his hand. "Not until we search the place."

"For what? If he had any information that would be of any use to us, they would have taken it with them."

"Maybe, if it was out in the open. But we're agents. We

think like him. We know the places to hide things that a bunch of terrorist thugs may not think of."

"You know they're watching this apartment."

"You knew they were when we pulled up. What's the difference, Sam? They aren't here now, and I don't want to leave here without gaining *something*."

"We have gained *something*," Sam said. "We know our agent wasn't turned after all."

"No, he was tortured and killed. Way worse." King moved to his right into the kitchen. "Just watch the door. I'll only be a minute. I have to look."

Sam didn't answer, she just walked out of the apartment to look out for any trouble.

King immediately pulled the refrigerator out of its nook between the cabinets. He found nothing but a lifetime of dirt and grime. Next he moved into the bedroom—the only bedroom in the apartment. He flipped on the light and walked into the bathroom, lifted the lid on the back of the toilet, but there was nothing.

"Any luck, Sherlock?" Sam shouted.

The quip only added to King's growing frustration. He *needed* to find something. If Fred was indeed a good agent, and hadn't flipped, then he had two years of research on the terrorist game in Athens stowed somewhere. This was their only chance to uncover any clue as to Saajid's whereabouts. There was no way King and Sam could find out in a day what Fred had been hunting down for two years. And twenty-four hours is all King felt like they had before the retaliation came for Husaam's death.

King exited the bathroom and gave the bedroom a once-over. It was ransacked just like the living room. The television was on the floor, paintings ripped off the walls, and the bed tossed upside down. He went back out into the living room. There was a large painting facedown on the floor at the foot of the mantle. The only reason it caught his eye enough for a second look was because the light was hitting the bottom corner of the painting in such a way that he swore he saw it shimmer. When he moved to his left, it disappeared.

"X, we have got to go." Sam ducked her head back inside the room. "Right now. You know they're coming."

"One more second."

King moved around the couch and crouched down by the painting.

"What is it?" Sam said.

"Not sure, but it looked like . . ." King picked up the painting, and sure enough, he had seen a slight shimmer. "Tape." King lifted the tape on the brown paper backing of the painting.

"Seriously?" Sam said, with a look of bemusement.

King lifted the paper and found a thin four-by-six-inch notebook tucked underneath. He pulled it out and lifted it up. "Bingo."

"All right, now let's go. We can look through it once we get the hell out of here."

King briefly flipped through it and noticed that all but the last few pages were covered in notes. Sam was right. They couldn't take the time to scour the thirty-plus pages of scribbles. King tucked it in his pocket and headed for the door.

"All right," Sam said, moving for the stairs, "if we don't encounter anyone, let's just walk up the street and pop into a bar. We can spot anyone coming in after us that way."

King agreed. "We can buy some time inside to skim the notebook."

"Put your arm around me. Let's at least look the part of a date night out."

"You'll use any excuse to get close to me, won't you?" King was feeling good after finding the notebook. And he was happy to be doing it with Sam. A little of his old personality was coming out. It was a breath of fresh air to feel some normalcy finally. But he knew what was at stake, and his focus was 100 percent.

Just before they stepped out of the light, he got the classic eye roll. But it also came with a hug around the waist. "Good to have you back, mate."

King felt good to be getting back to who he really was. He also knew how lucky they were to find a lead in that apartment.

They would need a lot more luck if they hoped to stop the magnitude of what they knew must be coming.

37

KING OPENED THE DOOR FOR SAM. THE OBNOXIOUS MUSIC poured out of the bar.

"Couldn't have picked a place with better music?" King shouted as he followed behind her.

It was evident he hadn't been in a hot spot like B327 in a while. Not too long ago, he and Kyle would have reveled in the loud music, dark vibe, overpriced drinks, and under-dressed women. Now, every aspect of it offended his senses. The dark part, however, would work in their favor.

There had already been a lot more walking traffic on the streets since they'd entered Fred's apartment, so the bar was crowded. Sam and King weaved through people holding cocktails and conversations. The DJ in the back was playing hip hop music, which had lost its luster for King in the last couple of years. Either he was getting old or the music just wasn't as good as it used to be.

The two of them walked around the bar so they could grab the only two seats facing the front door. King could tell by the look on Sam's face that she didn't much care for the *vibe* of the place either. She'd never liked these sorts of places, at least as long as he'd known her, but he once met a friend of hers who revealed that Sam had been quite a handful in the clubs back in the day. King had tried desperately to get some juicy stories on his favorite girl, but the friend closed up like a vault when Sam gave her that "don't you dare" stare.

A cute bartender finished pouring a beer from the tap and bopped over to the two of them. She tossed a couple of cocktail napkins down. "What can I get for you?" she shouted over the thump of the bass.

Sam held up her hand to say nothing for her. The bartender looked at King.

"She's driving," he said with a wink. The wink fell flat. She just stared at him waiting to take his order. He had never felt older. So he ordered like the old man he must have seemed to her. "Old-fashioned. No water. Top shelf."

The bartender moved to her station and began working on it.

"For a former spy, you sure don't know how to blend in," King said to Sam.

She kept her eyes glued on her phone. King glanced up at the door. No one had come in behind them yet.

King fished the notebook from his pocket. "Now's a good time to see if anything's in here." He tapped Sam on the arm, but her gaze didn't falter. "Sam!"

Sam held her phone just inches from his face. It was an update sent from the deputy director of the CIA. A lump formed in King's throat as he began to read. It was a note letting all available agents know about an all-hands-on-deck situation: a commercial airliner had just crashed into the Miami Marlins baseball stadium, right in the middle of an exhibition game.

King looked away, anger pulsing through his body. Sam

brought his attention back to her phone. She pointed a little farther down in the note. King couldn't believe what he read. A Twitter account created in the last twenty-four hours had two tweets, both with the hashtag #MiamiMarlins. The first went out an hour ago. It read, "It's a great day for a game." The second Tweet went out just minutes after the plane crash. "That was for father."

King was sick. He knew there would be retaliation for Husaam's death. He had no idea it would come in such a massive way. The reported number of the deceased in Miami was already well into the hundreds. The bartender sat King's drink in front of him, and he took it down in one gulp. It lay sour on his stomach.

"It's him," Sam shouted over the music. "It's Saajid. If he's ticking off attacks for the people he's lost, there's at least a couple more coming for his sister's daughter and for his brother."

King's jaw was clenched. He hadn't realized he was still holding his glass; it shattered in his hand from his squeeze. Luckily, it only nicked him. He wiped the blood on the cocktail napkin.

"Go find something in that notebook," he told Sam. "If he's close, we have to find him. Tonight."

Sam left her seat for a better-lit area of the bar. King was stewing as he stared at the door, praying one of Hammoud's men would come looking for them. Finally, a man walked in who fit the bill. King rose from his seat. The man was scouring the bar with his hands in his pockets. King rounded the end of the bar, his hand on the grip of his pistol at the small of his back. The man was about halfway to King when they locked eyes. King began to pull his pistol as the man was removing his hands from his pockets.

Suddenly a woman jumped in front of King and threw

her arms around the man. King stopped dead, tucked the pistol back in his jeans, and took a deep breath. He needed to get a grip. The last thing he needed was to let his anger about what was happening in Miami force a bad decision.

The door to the bar opened again. This time two men walked in, and they were in a rush. King slid over to his left and tucked himself in between two people standing at the bar waiting to be served. He pulled his phone from his pocket and pretended to be typing intensely. He glanced around the head of the woman in front of him, and the men were walking his way, their heads swiveling. These were Hammoud's men. With a cooler head, King could feel it.

This time, however, he would be patient.

38

THE DJ PLAYED THE SONG "*GOOD FEELING*" BY THE RAPPER Flo Rida. The beat thudded in King's chest. Immediately the people all around him began to dance. It was perfect timing—he had a *good feeling* he could take these guys out. The dancers gave him cover as the men walked right by where he stood at the bar. As soon as they passed, he put away his phone, grabbed his knife while his hand was in his pocket, and followed right behind them.

It was too dark to see any bulge from a concealed weapon, so he had to wait patiently while they made their way to the back of the bar. When they didn't find what they were looking for, they exited the main room to the hallway outside the bathrooms. King had watched Sam go this way to read the notebook, so if they checked the bathrooms, King needed to be right on their heels. Fortunately, they had yet to look back. But he was ready if they did.

Moving into the hallway to the restrooms was a bigger problem than King expected. Mirrors starting waist high stretched all the way up to the ceiling. There was no hiding. King glanced back over his shoulder. A couple more men dressed in black walked through the bar entrance. Hammoud had sent an entire team.

King moved fully into the mirrored hallway. His instincts told him to go ahead and kill the two men. But after almost pulling a gun on a civilian just a minute ago, he had to wait until he had absolute proof that these men were there to do harm.

He didn't have to wait long.

The man in front noticed King following close behind them in the mirror he was walking toward. Before turning, he tried to reach subtly for his weapon, but King's focus was sharp; any movement of the sort was going to get the man killed.

King jabbed the blade of his knife directly into the jugular vein of the man directly in front of him. As he pulled the knife out, he front-kicked the same man in the back, sending him crashing into the man reaching for his gun. The force of the bleeding man knocked the other over, giving King the chance to advance. He kicked the gun from the hand of the man on the bottom, stepped on his arm, then jabbed the blade twice into the man's neck.

There was no need for King to wait around, as he knew these men were dead. The ladies room was on his right, so he pushed inside. Sam was reading the notebook as she leaned against the wash counter. When she looked up and saw blood running from King's blade, she didn't even flinch.

"I'm assuming you found Hammoud's men then?"

"Two more coming from the entrance. Probably more waiting outside the back of the bar."

Sam tucked the notebook in the back pocket of her black jeans, pulled her Glock 17, and chambered a round. "We should probably wait here for them."

King nodded. "Anything good in the notebook."

"Plenty, but we can chat about it later."

The muffled beat from the music made it impossible to hear much out in the hallway, but the scream from a woman who'd apparently found the bleeding men on the floor rose above the noise. Then more screams followed. King knew the bar was about to empty out. This would be their best chance to escape—moving with the sea of people rushing the exit. He exchanged his knife for his gun and leaned his shoulder against the door.

"We need to go now," Sam said, confirming his thought.

"Stay with me," King said as he pushed open the bathroom door.

He held his gun at eye level as he entered the hallway. He knew that anyone swimming upstream toward him would be the two men in black who had entered the bar, because everyone else would be running away from the bathrooms. That's why the instant he saw a black-haired man walk around the corner, only a few feet from him, he was able to hit him twice in the head. The gunshots were deafening in the enclosed space. And the blasts took the crowd from scared to panicked as they raced for the exit doors. The music continued to play as more screams of panic erupted. When King squeezed the trigger, he stopped in his tracks, expecting the other man he'd seen earlier to follow close behind. Out of the corner of his right eye, in the mirror, he saw the reflection of that man just outside the doorway, turning to run.

King understood the *flight* mentality the second of Hammoud's men had after seeing someone get shot, but he also knew it was a mistake. There was no way the man was going to get through the crowd to the door in time to escape King. Though his odds were terrible either way, they would have been better if he'd held his ground and fired back.

These are the calculations that untrained terrorists never learn, and it's the reason they aren't a lot more dangerous than they are. It's also the reason they bomb people in secret, because they could never fight an actual war.

King gave chase, sprinting through the bar. The man had already run into a sea of people crowding the exit. He would turn to shoot in desperation at any moment, putting a lot of innocent people in danger. King surged forward, and just as the man turned, King greeted his forehead with the butt of his Glock. The man dropped hard onto the floor. King looked back, and just as he knew she would be, Sam was watching the back exit.

Most of the people in the bar were quickly clearing out. Their window to escape amongst the crowd was closing. King rushed over to Sam.

"Does the notebook give us Saajid's location?" he shouted over the music.

In the dim light Sam smiled and nodded.

A shot of adrenaline coursed through King's veins.

"Then let's get out of here!"

King turned for the front door. There were about twenty people still shoving to get out. The panic had died down a bit, which wasn't good. The man King had taken out in the crowd, who was still unconscious on the ground as he stalked by, changed all of that. As the people noticed him and went into hysteria once more, King made a hole through the middle, and Sam followed. A few seconds later they were running outside in the middle of a crowd. The street was packed with the usual morons who just *had* to see what was going on, even though there were gunshots coming from the bar. It didn't bother King. It merely further complicated the situation for anyone who might be looking for him and Sam.

King tagged along behind a couple holding hands as they raced to get away from the scene. The man held a set of keys in his left hand, and it seemed the most promising way out, so King stuck close behind. Sam had her hand on King's back to let him know she was with him so he wouldn't have to keep checking on her. One of the thousand little things a professional like her did to keep things moving optimally. Only things you could learn with years of experience.

Every detail mattered.

They crossed the street with this couple, and in front of them the lights on a four-door sedan blinked twice. The couple took their places in the front seats, and King slid in the back before the man could lock the doors. The woman screamed when Sam shut the door behind her. King brandished his Glock the moment the man was behind the wheel.

"We're the good guys," King said. "Just drive us out of here and we'll leave you alone."

The man's face softened under the yellow light of the interior. He said something in Greek to his girl, then started the car. Maybe the fact that King was an American put him at ease; King could tell they didn't speak English. Whatever it was that helped them trust him, it didn't matter, because the car was moving away from the chaos, and that was what was important.

As they drove away from the bar, toward the unknown, the only thing playing in King's mind was that airplane crashing into the crowded baseball stadium in Miami. And he couldn't help but worry what they might hear next.

39

RAFINA, GREECE

"WHAT DO you mean they got away?" Saajid was furious at Rayan, his head of security.

"We had them pinned down in the bar. I sent four men in after them. When the shooting started, it was chaos. They escaped with the crowd."

Saajid paced the produce area located above his operations bunker. He had a strict curfew in the isolated village he'd created, so other than his sister who was coordinating the attacks in the US, he was the only one around. He needed the fresh air after being below ground the entire day.

"I'm sorry, Saajid," Rayan said. "I failed you."

Saajid began processing.

Fred Johnson had been getting way too close to discovering that Saajid was the head of the organization in Athens and even where his compound was located in Rafina. When

Saajid had him killed a week ago, he knew torturing him for information would pay off. The man had sung like a bird, handing over call signs and passwords in order to save his life. It had worked to intercept the meeting with the female agent who was staying at the hotel. Sending someone who looked like Fred Johnson to meet her was brilliant, and making her think Fred, though he'd been there two years, had found nothing on the "terrorists" in the region was the icing on the cake. It had effectively thrown her off the scent. But Husaam had stirred the hornet's nest by attacking her despite Saajid telling him not to. So Saajid knew the female agent would seek out Fred Johnson to see why he had flipped on her.

Rayan should have taken her out at Fred's apartment. But she had help with her. Honestly, that was the thing that was bothering Saajid more than anything. Who was assisting her? He was already past Rayan's failure. He couldn't think backward. He was focused only on what to do next. His people in New York City were almost in place. That was what was important. But he also needed to find out the identity of the man with the female agent who was after him in Athens. Saajid was 99 percent sure who the man was; he just needed a final confirmation.

"Did you see his face?" Saajid said. "Is it him?"

In his office Saajid had been focused on determining whether the man in the London video was the same man in the videos that were now viral on YouTube showing Husaam's fight in the Plaka. Once he was able to determine they were the same person, he could take it a step further and compare a still photo from one of the videos to a picture he'd kept for the past year of the news coverage in Washington DC. The story was about the man from

Kentucky who died the same day Saajid and the Maragoses attempted to assassinate the president of the United States.

Alexander King.

The man who stopped Saajid's plot to kill the president had also killed Saajid's childhood friends, Anastasia and Gregor Maragos, that week, and he was lauded by the United States with a funeral ceremony fit for a hero.

Now, that same dead man who killed Saajid's friends looked *exactly* like the man in the video who had just murdered his brother. And he had to know for sure.

"Well?" Saajid said, raising his voice. "Is it the same man who murdered Husaam?"

"It is," Rayan said with confidence. "And now he's disappeared."

Saajid slammed the phone on the ground, then stomped on it for good measure. Jamila came up from the underground facility.

"What is it? What's happened?"

"It's him." Saajid paced the floor. The wood beneath his stomping feet rattled and shook the covered produce from their baskets.

"Him who? What are you talking about? It's getting late. You'll wake the entire village."

Saajid turned toward his sister so fast he nearly fell over. Her face was aglow in the light of the moon, and he could tell by her frightened look that his eyes must have been on fire.

"I don't give a damn if I wake up all of Greece! The same man that killed Anastasia and Gregor killed our brother today! And he was standing beside Althea when she was murdered as well! Your own daughter!"

The color drained from Jamila's face.

Saajid continued his rant. "This is such an American thing to do. Fake the death of an agent, only to send him in the shadows to steal what's left of our family!"

Jamila wiped the tears from her face, took a deep breath, and tried to think forward. "Where is he now?"

"Rayan had him and lost him. This man is like a cockroach. But I'll burn the entire city down if I have to."

"At least we're safe here. No more harm can come to our families."

"Right, because other than us, they're all dead!" Saajid was seething. "Now it's our turn to hit back again. Even harder. I want every American to fear for their lives the way our families have feared for theirs for decades now."

Jamila cleared the emotion from her throat. "That's what I came up here to tell you. New York City is ready."

"All six of them? And they know their sacrifice?"

"All six, and they all are happy to die for what is right."

Saajid knew that while the plane that had crashed into the baseball stadium in Miami would frighten Americans from flying, what was coming next would scare them from moving from their homes at all. His people in New York City had been scouting the subway systems for months. Now, six of them were headed there with backpacks full of explosives, and every five minutes, for a half an hour, they would detonate them as the trains came into the stations. It would be the most terrifying thirty minutes in America's history. The way social media worked today, by the time the third blast went off, all of New York, and the world, would be watching while the next three blew up in their faces.

Saajid turned to the sky and looked up at the moon. The same moon that would be passing over a broken New York City in a matter of hours. He remembered a question his brother had asked him the day they executed their first attack well over a decade ago. Husaam had said, "Do you think taking other people's lives is the right way to go about spreading the word of our god?" This question had always stuck out to Saajid because he had asked his father the same question, the morning of the day the Americans killed his father in cold blood.

His father's answer was the same one Saajid had given Husaam. He told him that killing isn't the evil that society makes it out to be. It is a cleansing. Islam is the only religion that should be recognized, and all who denounce it, especially Western Christian societies that claim to be so righteous, need to be cleansed from the earth, to make way for the *true* people of God. Saajid told Husaam that day what he still thought about the men who were willfully dying today in these cleanses in the US, that they will be rewarded for showing the world that things, and beliefs, *must* change. And in order for there to be change, there must be a cleansing.

The New York City subway stations at Eighty-First Street/Museum of Natural History–Manhattan, World Trade Center, E–Manhattan, Forest Hills–Queens, Lorimer Street–Brooklyn, 161st Street/Yankee Stadium–Bronx, and Times Square Forty-Second Street, would all be cleansed in the next half an hour. And because of social media, Saajid would be able to tell the world why it happened, without fear of consequence.

The only thing Saajid was worried about at the moment was the ghost haunting him thirty kilometers away in Athens. However, he felt good about the fact that at least this agent who was able to stop their plan last time was nowhere near the United States to help them now. This was Husaam's gift to his people, and to his god. He gave his life to show Saajid this agent was here. He gave his life to set these cleanses in motion. And even if it was the last thing Saajid did, he would initiate these cleanses, one by one, all around the *so-called great* nation of the United States.

His brother would not die in vain.

40

A HALF AN HOUR AFTER THE COUPLE HAD DRIVEN THEM OUT of danger, King and Sam had boosted a nearby four-wheel drive and were driving in the dark, looking for their turnoff for the road, EO83. Rafina was just a few miles ahead, a coastal town that neither of them had ever heard of. However, the notebook that King had extracted from the painting in Fred Johnson's apartment explained that the compound, or village, that Saajid Hammoud had built was somewhere near the foot of the Penteli Mountains.

"There was a notation at the top of the page that the informant was a bartender," Sam explained. "Looks like Fred had received word from another informant that this bartender was a cousin of the Hammouds, but like a black sheep. He was trying to work his way back into the fold, and his duties were to work in Athens and be a scout for trouble, and recruit for future business."

"Let me guess," King said from the driver's seat. "The Hammouds treated him like shit so he squealed."

"In a way, I guess. They got his girlfriend killed and he wanted revenge. Fred even put a star in the notes with the words *lucky break* written beside it." Sam pointed at the sign that glowed in the headlights. "Turn off here, then take a left."

As King exited the highway and turned left, other than some lights spotting the darkness around them, there wasn't much to see.

"Loyalty might be the only redeeming quality of a terrorist. After all, they're willing to kill and die out of loyalty to their faith."

"Yes," Sam said. "But you also have to realize that because they're so extreme, men like Saajid are so disconnected from basic morality, they're also willing to lose people close to them for the same reason."

"I suppose people quit trying to figure out these wackos a long time ago. That's why we just started blowing them up, right?"

Sam didn't answer. King glanced over at her, and in the light of the dash, he could see that something was bothering her. Over the years, King had gotten to know all of her faces, and what each of them meant.

"What is it?"

"It's nothing."

One of the reasons it took King so long to get to know Sam, to *really* get to know her, was because she was always so closed off. Time had lessened this trait but hadn't stolen it completely.

"Come on, Sam. We've got nothing else to talk about for a bit."

"I can't believe I let that man fool me."

King was lost. "Fool you? What man?"

"The man who met with me, posing as Fred Johnson. If I'd sniffed that out, I might have kept us out of danger this afternoon."

"Yeah, and I might not have had the chance to take out a wanted terrorist."

"Still . . ." Sam trailed off.

"You really don't like getting something wrong, Sam. Believe me, I understand. I'm the same way. But you didn't know Fred, and the man you met with had all his check downs because they tortured it out of Fred. Nothing you could do."

King looked over again and could see her clenching her fist. "You want to find that guy when this is all over, don't you?"

Sam whipped her head in his direction, and her face held a scowl. "I do."

Her expression was priceless, and her determination was inspiring. And knowing just how much she meant it, how much she was stewing over this, made it funny to him. Especially considering how much more serious the drama that lay just ahead of them was.

"I just hate open endings," she said.

"I know," he said and gave her a pat on the shoulder. "Don't worry, we'll close it."

King's phone rang. It was Agent Roberts. He put it on speaker so Sam could hear. "Talk to me," King answered.

"Bentley Martin left the country."

King and Sam exchanged a glance.

"What do you mean?"

"I mean, surveillance identified her at the airport earlier today," Roberts said.

"Alone? Where'd she go?" King said.

"As far as we can tell, she went alone. And . . . we're not sure where she went."

"What?" both Sam and King said at the same time.

"Well, run her name then, Roberts. She had to have ID to get on the plane," King said.

"I'm not a rookie," Roberts said. "I ran her name. Nothing came up. But I'm on it. We're all over this."

King searched his mind for answers. For something that made sense. Then he remembered the conversation he had when he first snuck up on the car with the woman watching him walk down the street. When pushed, Bentley had admitted that Karen—now known as Althea—and her were like twins, and that she was letting her go for the run while Bentley put the tracking device in Althea's hat. Therefore, Althea was posing as Bentley. What if now . . .

"Run the name Althea Salameh with the airlines," King said abruptly.

"What? But she's dead."

"Just do it. And call me back as soon as you know something."

"Okay—"

King ended the call.

"What are you thinking?" Sam said.

"I'm not sure. Just that if Bentley is unaccompanied at the airport after being *kidnapped*, yet there is no record of her getting on a plane . . . since they've posed as each other before, if Bentley is up to something we don't know about, maybe she figured she could use her dead look-alike's passport to try to get away unnoticed."

"Not sure what else it could be. Good thought. And good timing too," Sam said as she pointed to a barn just off the side of the road. "There's our marker."

King slowed and pulled off the road. The rocky surface gave way to dirt. He pulled around the right side of the barn. "We just going to walk in from here?"

"Notes end right here." Sam was reading in the dash

lights. "Last thing it says is that the commune is at least a mile toward the mountain. And apparently that's where Saajid operates underground."

King couldn't dwell on not having more information. These notes put him and Sam in the game. Without them, they'd be stuck in Athens while these maniacs continued with their cowardly revenge. He could wish all he wanted that the instructions were more detailed from there, but wishing wouldn't make it so. All they knew was that any car that made it beyond that barn was going to get scrutinized by the security measures Saajid had set up to keep out trespassers. At least that's what the notebook said.

King watched as Sam took pictures of the notes with her phone. "I'm sending these to Deputy Director Rodgers so he knows where we are. He's telling us to wait. He said he is putting together a team in Athens to help us out here."

"You told him there was no time to wait, right?"

"Of course. He said to use my good judgment."

"He must not know you very well," King said. "Good judgment doesn't really come into play when we get together."

"Good thing he doesn't know about you then, right?" Sam said, closing the notebook.

King watched as she sent the photos to the man filling in for Mary Hartsfield. He heard something ding on her phone, but she was already halfway out of the vehicle. King got out and shut his door. Before King made it to Sam's side, he heard her gasp.

"Oh my God, X."

King rounded the back of the vehicle, and Sam was staring at her phone.

"Don't scare me like that, Sam. I thought someone had a gun on you or something."

When she looked up at him from her phone, he knew whatever it was she was reading was worse.

"Three suicide bombers have already blown up three trains in New York City."

"What?" King's stomach dropped.

"Each of them five minutes apart. Deputy Director Rodgers thinks there will be three more."

"What? How could he know that?"

"The Tweet," Sam said, then showed him a screenshot on her phone.

King recognized the name and profile photo of the Tweet immediately. It was the account that had claimed the plane crash into Miami Marlins stadium. It was Saajid. The Tweet said, "*For my brother. Enjoy the next thirty minutes.*"

King hung his head. This one had some extra sting to it. Though he would never change killing Husaam Hammoud —it was the only thing he could've done in that situation— all of the lives lost in New York would never have happened if he'd just let him go.

"It's not your fault, Alexander." Sam read his mind. "That is what Saajid wants you to think. You think that, he wins."

"He already won. His message is being spread like wildfire."

Sam looked over her shoulder into the darkness. "Not for long."

King followed her gaze. The black night in front of him matched what moved over his heart when he saw that Tweet. All he wanted to do was get his hands on Saajid. To stop the killing.

King snapped out of it and cleared his mind. "Why haven't they shut down the Twitter account yet?"

"They did. This one was made as a new account with

one letter different. We can't keep him from telling the world he's a monster. But we can keep him from being one. At least in this lifetime."

"Then let's go shove a bullet up his ass," King said.

"You lead the way."

41

"WHAT IS THAT NOISE?" SAAJID ASKED HIS SISTER.

Saajid, Jamila, and three of his top lieutenants were watching the coverage of the bombings in New York City on the news. In between silent moments created by the commentator as the footage rolled, Saajid swore he could hear something going on above them.

"I don't hear anything. Maybe you are a little paranoid? Let's just enjoy the show our brothers are putting on for the world."

Saajid listened to Jamila and turned his attention back to the television. There was sheer chaos erupting in New York. All the intricate planning and money that Anastasia and Gregor had put into building the nanotechnology a year ago had been a waste. Losing their lives was a waste. These subway bombings and the crashed plane into the stadium proved to Saajid that good old-fashioned planning and patience *were* more important than technology and over the top plans. The men who had sacrificed for Saajid today, and for Allah, they had done far more for the cause than everything Anastasia and Gregor, and Andonios's money, had ever accomplished. He was feeling better about his brother's death as well. Already his death had proven to be worthwhile. Without it, none of these cleanses would have happened. Instead, they would be waiting months for the presidential election to see if the work paid off. This was much more gratifying.

"Wait," Jamila said. "Turn that down. I think I do hear noises above us."

Saajid muted the television, and the five of them all heard *something* coming from the street above them.

"What the hell is that?" Saajid said, jumping up from his chair and rushing out of his office. He walked over to the steps that led to the door in the floor of the market, and tuned in. "Is that . . . is that singing?"

Saajid rushed up the stairs and threw open the door. As he climbed out, the singing became louder. Everyone followed behind him, and when he rounded the tables, he saw fire.

"A fire?" Jamila said, gasping.

Saajid's blood boiled. In the middle of the street, there was a gathering of people, all standing around a bonfire. He couldn't believe his eyes.

"Stop!" he shouted. "Stop singing!" He turned to his men. "Get something to put out the fire. Now!"

The three of them ran off to find something to extinguish it.

"I said, stop singing!" Saajid jogged over to the people. They were singing a death hymn, and all around the fire were pictures of Husaam. They were holding a vigil. A wave of sadness rolled over him as the fact that he would never see his brother again crashed through him like a tidal wave. But he pushed the feeling aside and refocused on the people's blatant disregard for one of the most important rules Saajid had made when he started this village: no lights and no fires!

"Stop singing! Who made this fire? Who did this? This will get us all killed!"

He felt Jamila grab his arm, but he ripped it away. In the kind of darkness that surrounded the compound, a fire could be seen for miles. Even a small one. His men ran up and began pouring bags of sand over the fire to put it out. Another man attempted to tame it using a large blanket. The sobs of those gathered grew louder with Saajid's interruption. And then he noticed his wife and his children across the blaze. He nearly lost it entirely.

"What are you doing? You know the rules! Get back to the house. Now!" He closed the distance between him and his wife. "Did you do this?" He got right in her face. "Did you?" His children were looking on in fear, at their own father as if they didn't recognize him.

His wife put a defensive arm in front of her face. "The children wanted to remember him, Saajid."

Saajid punched her in the mouth. His wife dropped to the ground. Jamila tried once again to stop him, but he shoved her away.

"You know better than this! Get up!" Saajid shouted as he kicked her in the backside. "Get up and get the children inside. I'll deal with you later!"

Jamila finally pulled him away. The fire was still going, and in the commotion, pictures of his brother were pushed into it. Saajid was heaving with madness as he watched his brother's face turn to ashes in the flames.

"Get this put out! And everyone get inside!"

He moved back over to his wife and picked her up off the ground. Her lip was bleeding and she was shaking. His children were crying, holding onto their mother's leg. "Do you not understand? If someone sees the light from this fire, they won't just kill me, they'll kill us all! You know what the Americans have done to my family. They will line up everyone in this village and shoot us dead. Get to the bunker, now! Take the children to the back room. Go!"

The fire was on its last legs.

"All of you," Saajid said to his men and Jamila, "get back in the bunker. Let's go!"

He pushed them all in front of him down the dirt road. He was a ball of emotions. Anger, sadness, fear, they were all swirling in him, making him crazy. He couldn't believe his wife would put everything in jeopardy after all the work and sacrifices he'd made. Saajid continued to usher his family and his men down into the bunker. He moved down the stairs, pulled the door closed overhead, and prayed to the god he was so valiantly serving, hoping that if anyone was looking for them, no one saw the fire. His village deserved that much, at least, for all that he had done for the cause in just the past twenty-four hours.

Saajid turned away from the stairs after climbing down and stalked down the hallway. Jamila grabbed for his arm as he stormed past the office, but he ripped away from her. When he entered the back room of the bunker, his children were sitting on the beds against the far wall.

"It's okay," his wife said to the children. "Just lie down and sleep. Everything is okay."

She barely got the last word out before he choked off her words by grabbing her by the throat. If they were lucky enough to have the fire not be seen, he needed to teach her a lesson and ensure that this would never happen again. He felt like squeezing until she passed out. But he loved her. And aside from this one incident, she had been a good servant. But just like Husaam, all servants must also have their day. Maybe this was hers. He would let Allah decide and allow him to work through his body whether she lived or died. He was okay with either outcome.

"Stop it, Father! You're hurting her!" Saajid's son shouted.

Saajid ignored him, and continued to squeeze. Jamila rushed into the room and pulled at his shoulders.

"Leave us! This doesn't concern you!"

Jamila backed away. Saajid continued to squeeze. He could feel his wife's grip loosen around his wrists. He knew she was close, but he hadn't heard from his god to stop.

"Father, please!" his daughter shouted this time.

He didn't stop.

"Father!"

He felt his daughter's and then his son's hands pulling on him. His wife's eyes rolled back in her head. Maybe his god was telling him to stop by having his two children be brave enough to challenge him.

Saajid let go of his wife's neck. She sucked in air so hard that it choked her, but she was going to be fine. His children sobbed as they hugged their mother. Saajid stood and looked down at them.

"This could all have been avoided if you'd just followed the rules." He backed away toward the doorway behind him. He took a few breaths to steady his rage. The adrenaline running through him was causing his hands to shake. "Not one sound from this room. Not one."

He shut the door and went back to the office.

"The other bombings have been successful," Jamila said.

Saajid gave her a nod, then looked at his men. "All of you, perimeter check, right now. Make it thorough. Take your weapons."

They nodded and left the bunker.

"Do you think anyone saw the fire? You think all the brush and trees did their job?" Jamila said.

Jamila was talking about the natural wall they'd planted a decade ago to form a barrier. At the time, it wasn't meant to hide light, but he supposed it had grown up enough around them that maybe it had.

"I-I don't know. It's late, maybe that will help."

"We should be fine," Jamila said, hoping to reassure him.

"It's fine. Let's worry about things we can control now," Saajid said, pointing at the television footage of smoke rising from one of the bombed subway stations. "Are they ready in Los Angeles? Let's not let up now."

"Ten minutes."

42

"I'm telling you, I saw a light," Sam whispered to King.

They had been jogging blindly for more than ten minutes, at least a mile and a half. It was pitch black around them. The clouds had moved in overhead, so even the moon couldn't help them. The terrain was rough, causing both of them to stumble on a few occasions.

"I didn't see it. Surely they wouldn't be dumb enough to use electricity or fire after the sun went down."

"It was there, and when we moved to our right, it was gone. But I'm angling toward it now, and it wasn't far."

The two of them jogged forward. King believed Sam; he just didn't understand how he'd missed it. Regardless, he soon knew exactly what the source of the light was.

"You smell that?" he said.

"Smoke," Sam confirmed.

It smelled like burning wood. It reminded him of another lifetime when his high school would put on a bonfire for the homecoming football game. And judging by how the smell was becoming stronger, they absolutely were close. King put his hand on Sam's shoulder in front of him to slow her down and make sure they stayed together. It was that dark. He took the bottom of her T-shirt in his hand to keep tethered. He held his Glock in his other hand. He could feel the questions creeping up in his mind. Was this really Saajid's village? If so, what was the security? And if they could get past security, where was Saajid and this underground facility?

The brush had become thicker at their knees. So much so that Sam had slowed to a walk. Every noise they made was loud. Visibility was about ten feet, and King couldn't tell if his mind was playing tricks on him or not, but he swore he heard a breeze rustling some trees. Sam slowed to a stop. She had heard it too.

She pulled him close and whispered, "Trees in front of us. The smell is stronger. We're here."

King pulled her down to a knee. He heard something over her shoulder on his left. If this were his little village in the middle of nowhere, and he didn't want it to be found, he would keep it dark like this too. And he would also have armed guards patrolling the perimeter. Always.

King tucked his gun at the small of his back. He reached in his pocket and pulled his knife.

"I'm going to try to keep this quiet. Just watch my back," he whispered.

Then he felt Sam move around behind him. The clouds cleared a bit, and some yellow moonlight showed them the line of trees. It was terrible timing. King would have preferred no light at all. All the same, he moved forward, and he immediately heard a rock kicked just at the tree line ahead.

He kept his breathing even by slowly pulling in air through his nose and releasing it out his mouth. The breeze sent a cool chill down the bit of sweat he'd built on the jog there. He tuned his ears forward. His eyes searched the trees for any shadow passing in the moonlight. He was putting one foot in front of the other in what felt like slow motion.

He heard four quick footsteps off to his left, but before he could turn, he felt the burn in his shoulder at the same time he heard the rapid *pop-pop, pop-pop-pop* from the suppressed gunshots. He and Sam both dropped to the ground. As soon as their bodies met the dirt, Sam was firing behind her. Her gunshots sounded like mini bombs exploding in that quiet night. They didn't have access to suppressors in Athens, and Sam's gunfire may as well have been an air-raid siren. All King could see when he looked in the direction of the sounds were small sparks of light from the end of the shooter's gun. He tucked his knife back in his pocket and pulled his Glock.

King managed to get his free hand around Sam's arm, and he dragged her behind the brush in front of him. The claps of the suppressor stopped. He felt the blood from the wound in his shoulder running down the outside of his left arm. The adrenaline helped him to ignore the pain. King scooted to a knee, raised his head just above the bush, and his gun hand followed immediately when he saw a shadow moving toward them.

He pointed, fired three times, but the shadow had moved to the right.

"You hit the shooter?" he whispered to Sam.

"I think so."

The suppressed shots hadn't returned after he was shot, so he had to assume that she had hit the gunman a moment ago.

"I missed," he said. "And they went right. Let's go left."

. . .

KING STAYED LOW, moving around the brush and into the trees. The light in the sky was just bright enough now that he could see the man who had shot him lying on the ground about ten feet away. Sam had hit him. King thought for a moment about picking up the man's suppressed weapon, but at that point, the cat was already out of the bag. And if his magazine ended up being empty, it would have been a wasted trip. They didn't have time for that. A wave of gunmen could be on their way to him and Sam. They needed to stay the course.

King moved quickly toward the pine trees ahead. He heard what he thought was a man's voice, but it was faint and far away. They moved around some branches, just a few feet, enough for Sam to detect a flame flickering beyond the tree line. King, too, could see embers still smoldering in the pile now, right in the middle of a dirt road, which was flanked by several small adobe-style houses on both sides.

But he didn't see any security.

He figured that however many guards there were, they must be in the trees nearby.

As he stared ahead at the secret village, it seemed crazy to him that people had volunteered to live out here with such a madman. Of course, they probably thought he was a prophet or savior of some kind. King recognized that the longer it took him and Sam to find Saajid, the more of these blind followers would end up dead. Normally, he would wait for security to come to him, but there was no time for that. They had to keep pushing forward. No element of surprise this time.

He looked to his left and noticed the first building in the row of structures. He tapped on Sam's arm to let her know he was moving in that direction. The snapping branches beneath his feet sounded like mousetraps going off. He picked up his pace. He rounded the adobe wall of the small structure. If there was anyone inside, they were likely awake. After the gunshots they'd heard, the entire village would be. He assumed they were trained to stay inside, to stay quiet, if anything like this ever happened. But he also assumed they would have known not to light a fire.

That gave King an idea.

He took the handle of the door, turned it, and pushed his way in. The end of his gun found a shadow inside. He came a hair away from pulling the trigger. Thank God he didn't. What little moonlight he'd let in showed a woman covering her baby's mouth, trying desperately to keep the child from making a sound. King could see the whites of her eyes were wide, but he could also see that her free hand was moving.

King dove forward onto the woman. Turns out, he'd kept her from raising cast-iron pan she had under a blanket instead of a gun he'd worried it might be. He put his knee on her arm and covered her mouth with his left hand. This gave him hope that maybe no one else living in the surrounding houses were armed either. Sam had swooped in behind him and took the child in her arms. She was doing her best to coach it into not crying. So far it was working. When the woman saw her baby in the arms of an intruder, she struggled against King with the strength of a man. But King was able to hold her down, and he was able to muffle her cries. He didn't want to hurt her, but he might have to knock her out to keep her from getting herself killed.

King pulled the woman over to the wall. There was a towel lying on a small table. He set the pan down, grabbed the towel, and tied it in her mouth around the back of her head to stop her from screaming. But she was still making noise, and it didn't take much out there to be heard. He had no choice: even though it was the last thing he wanted to do, he put his gun to her head.

"I'm not going to hurt you," he whispered. "I just want Saajid. Tell me where he is, and we'll be gone in minutes and your baby will be fine."

The woman continued to breathe heavily, struggling against him. Tears ran down her cheeks. He knew she wouldn't give away Saajid's location, but he had to ask. She didn't, so he was forced to move on to the plan B that he'd thought of on his way toward the village.

"Find some matches," he whispered to Sam.

Sam was bouncing the small child as she walked over to the table where a few pots and pans were stacked. No lights were turned on, but their eyes had adjusted enough to see big objects. Finding something like matches would prove impossible.

When a shadow passed in front of the only window facing the dirt road, he knew it didn't matter. This was happening without a plan. When King stood, he noticed Sam was already setting the baby down. She had seen it too. They were about to go to war.

Sam looked at him and nodded.

There was no one in the world he'd rather have by his side.

43

SAM SLID OVER AND CROUCHED AT THE BACK WALL DIRECTLY IN front of the back door. King moved to the wall right beside the front door. He'd taken the knife from his pocket and thumbed open the blade. King and Sam spoke without words. He knew he was to take the kill. Sam would only fire as a last resort. Though their presence was likely already known, there was no need to make any unnecessary noise, making a nearly impossible situation harder than it already was.

The woman was squealing in the corner. The baby was beginning to whimper from hearing the mother in distress. The door opened inward, and just as soon as it was wide enough, King saw the tip of the gun and kicked it to the right. He followed that with a blind stab that landed in the man's shoulder. The man dropped his gun, but King couldn't get to his throat before he screamed. When King stabbed the man's larynx, his shout went hoarse. King dragged him inside, Sam shut the door, and King made sure the man would never make any sound again.

The woman squirmed away, trying to push herself up

the wall. Her muffled attempts to scream were too loud. Just as he was pondering that they were going to have to shut her up,

Sam rushed over and knocked the woman unconscious with the butt of her gun. But now the baby was really starting to wind up. They had no choice but to move.

"We have to find the underground bunker," King whispered.

Sam stood. "We don't have time to go door to door here."

King crouched and searched the man's pockets. He found a Zippo lighter, and plan B came back to the forefront.

"Can you cover me?" he said to Sam.

"Against what?" she whispered. "We have no idea how many people with guns live in this little messed-up place."

She had a point, but it didn't matter. He was going to have to take risks if they wanted to stop Saajid. Sam checked her phone. When she looked back up at King, he could tell it was more bad news.

"Three more bombs in New York."

King was sick. He was right here, right next to the man who was killing King's people on their own soil. It didn't really matter what he had to do, he had to stop it.

"I'm gonna light this fire," he said as he stood. "Cover me as best you can."

"You can't just run out there, X. I can't—"

He was out the door before she could finish. He couldn't debate with her any longer. If it cost him his life, so be it; this is what he signed up for. What he couldn't take was hearing about more innocent Americans dying while he played hide-and-seek with a sick freak.

The wind blew through his hair as he streaked across

the dirt road. As if nothing else existed, he focused on the pile of wood in front of him. He sprinted toward it with all he had, the lighter in one hand, his gun in the other. As he approached the pile, he could make out someone on the other side of it running toward him, about fifty yards away. King ran up behind the wood and crouched. He flicked the flint wheel, igniting the flame. After tossing the lighter into the embers near the middle of the pile, he took his gun in both hands. He stood, edged his way around the pile until he could see the person running for him. A spray of bullets forced him back behind the pile.

Behind him came bullets as well. He whipped his head around and found it was Sam who was firing. The flame was just beginning to catch. Not fast enough. He laid down on his stomach and gently blew some air toward the flame. Sam continued to fire behind him. He heard a second set of gunshots coming from beyond the pile. He had to get this flame going. If they could see their targets, he and Sam were far superior shots. He gave it another blow, and the orange magnified at the bottom of the wood.

He popped to his knees and fired a few defensive shots in the direction of the shooters. Then he dropped back down and fanned the flame with more breaths. King wanted the shooters to have to decide which was more important: keeping the flame down or attacking their intruders. Either way it helped his cause. At the very least, the villagers would be distracted.

"We've got you surrounded!" a man's voice, thick with a Middle Eastern accent, interrupted the gunfire. "It's no use!"

Surely that couldn't be Saajid. In no scenario did King ever think the coward, accustomed to killing people from afar, would ever crawl out of his hole and join the danger. There was just no way.

"It's me you want," the voice said. "Come out now and I won't kill your entire family."

Rage pumped through King's system. He should have kept his mouth shut, but he fell for the terrorist's bait.

"You already tried that last year," King said. He blew on the flame again. Just like the fire that lit inside him when he heard the terrorist mention his family, the fire began to light in front of him. The wood was going to catch. Saajid was going to have to make a decision. "But I did kill every person you sent, you coward. You think I'm afraid of you?"

The fire was really starting to burn now. So much so that King could focus on the one thing he came for.

"So it is you," Saajid shouted. "Very clever, convincing the world you don't exist. Don't worry, it doesn't matter if you are alive or not. It hasn't stopped a single one of my plans. In fact, you're the reason for all of them today."

King tightened his grip around his pistol. The fire was really going now. King had to take a few steps back. Out of the corner of his eye, he noticed Sam moving quickly from house to house, coming closer to his position.

"Why don't you ask your brother if it matters if I exist?" King paused for effect. "Oh . . . right. You can't. Just know, he begged for his life before I blew his brains all over the wall."

Gunfire erupted from the other side. King dropped to his stomach. It felt good to be able to push Saajid's buttons. If King could avoid being hit, this was the best-case scenario. It would cover Sam's movement and pull all of their focus toward him.

If he could keep this up, Sam might have the chance to end this right here, right now.

44

THE FIRE IN FRONT OF KING WAS RAGING. IT LIT UP THE entire village that Saajid had built in his effort to disappear from society. King himself was completely exposed out in the open. He searched the night behind him for any sign of movement; he found none. Sam was in position now. He couldn't see her, so he would have to react to her gunshot. It would be easy to tell hers from all the others. Sam's gun was the only one that wasn't a rifle.

King shuffled over to the side of the fire opposite from where he assumed Sam was taking position. As soon as she began to fire, he would help close the men in. He took a quick glance down the road and saw only three men. Though the fire was really going, he still couldn't see well enough to know which was Saajid. As soon as they saw King stretching for a look, they began shooting. He pulled himself back behind the fire as bullets penetrated the wood just in front of him.

King closed his eyes and let his mind go quiet. The wood was crackling. The heat was beginning to make him sweat. For some reason Bentley came to mind. Had she escaped her kidnapper and made a run for it? Did she use Althea's passport to do so? It seemed unlikely that Bentley would have had another woman's passport, but he'd seen crazier things. Maybe she had been planning to use Althea's identity the entire time.

He pushed those thoughts aside and focused on the gun resting in his hand. On getting ready to shoot.

Three gunshots from a pistol finally broke the silence. King spun to his right around the fire and shot three times at the first man he saw. The gunfire from the terrorists came heavy. None of it was aimed at him, so he had to make Sam's distraction count. He fired twice more at the man down the road, who finally dropped. He moved his weapon to the next man who was turning his automatic rifle in King's direction. King squeezed the trigger three more times, hitting the man somewhere in the chest. Then he saw two men running in Sam's direction.

He heard her fire a few more times, but the men kept running. King shot twice more at them, but before he could hit either of them, the slide locked back on his Glock. His magazine was empty. He jammed the gun down in his pocket and ran around the fire in Sam's direction. If he ran at the right angle, he might be able to catch up to the shooters in between houses. Sam flashed by in the gap between walls; she was firing behind her as she ran. King hit a sprint in two steps. As he entered between the two houses, a man came running right in front of him. King dove and missed the first man, but managed to get his right arm hooked around the man's waist who was running behind the first, taking him down to the ground.

The man rolled over and popped up to his feet. Thanks to the light of the fire from behind him, King could see the man point his gun at him. King rolled and kicked the inside of the man's left thigh, knocking him off balance. The man's shots went wide, thumping into the ground right beside King. The gun was so close that King's ears were ringing from the blasts. He popped up to his feet and managed to get his hands around the barrel.

Pop-pop, pop-pop-pop!

He heard shots off to his right and behind him. His hearing was still off, but it sounded like a pistol. King pushed the man's gun away from him as he kicked down on his kneecap. The man buckled and King was able to rip the weapon away from him, smash his nose with the butt of the AK-47, then turn it around in his hands and hold down the trigger until the man clutching his knee fell over dead.

The AK clicked and the magazine was empty. Other than the crackling of the wood in the fire, there wasn't another sound for miles. Then he heard a man groaning out in front of him on the other side of the house, somewhere out in the dirt road.

King began walking in that direction. He dropped the AK, took his Glock out of his left pocket and his only spare mag out of his right. He slid it in place and racked the slide.

"Sam!" his shout was loud in the silent village. "Sam!"

"I'm okay." Her voice was several yards behind him.

He was relieved to hear her. It had been her pistol that had made the other gunshots a moment ago. He walked around the last house and into the open road. In front of him, on his right, was what looked like a small outdoor market. The dirt road turned into wood planking beneath some tables and a tent. Through the legs on one of the tables, he saw a man disappear into the floor, pulling a door shut over his head.

Saajid wasn't dead.

King scanned the perimeter. He didn't see any other

movement. There were a few figures standing in the door-ways of the houses now. King imagined if this monster had a family, they were probably watching. He kept his gun at the ready. Sam had caught up to him and walked along with him on his right.

"I think it's him," Sam whispered. "I thought I hit him in the head. Must have been a little low."

They both walked around the tables set up on the wood-planked floor, over to the door on the floor, beside some baskets used to hold fruit. As King kneeled down, they saw blood on the wood beside the door. Sam was right, she had hit him. But now he couldn't help but feel as though they were getting ready to step down into a hornet's nest.

King felt Sam's hand on his arm. When he looked up at her, she was looking off into the distance. She pointed to her ear, then back behind them. King tuned in, and he could hear what she was talking about. There was a faint sound of a vehicle kicking up dust. Someone was coming.

Saajid had called for backup.

It was time to end this before Saajid could wriggle his way out of it. Hundreds if not thousands of lives depended on it. King took the handle of the half-hidden door in his hands. He could hear what now sounded like a large truck rolling closer and closer. He pulled open the door and pitch black stared back at him.

Pure evil awaited them below. Facing it was the only way to keep it from spreading up above. King looked back up at Sam, and she gave him a nod.

They were ready.

45

KING LOOKED BACK AND WATCHED SAM LOWER THE DOOR behind her. There was still an orange glow from the fire visible through the cracks behind her. She walked down the steps and sidled up to him. He then turned back to the darkness. There was no more crackle from the fire to be heard, no wind blowing through the trees, just the sound of King's own heartbeat thrumming in his ears.

The hallway they were walking through was only about six feet wide. The smell was wet dirt, and the temperature was a few degrees cooler than outside. King was hoping his eyes would adjust, but no matter how long he was down there, he wouldn't be able to see in such darkness. He stepped forward slowly. One foot in front of the other. His gun held firmly out in front of him—finger on the trigger. He was staying low, as if that would somehow protect him if bullets began to fly.

King put his left hand out and felt for the wall. He dragged his fingers along until the wall disappeared. He moved to his left into the void and began to feel around. His hand came across something wooden. It felt like a dresser, maybe a desk. He ran his hand along the top of it. It was smooth, and it was strange to feel something so modern down in what seemed like a dug-out cave. His fingers ran over a book; he could feel the hardback cover give way to pages. He continued on until he felt something metal. It felt like the base of a lamp. He followed the metal upward until his hand hit a chain. He pulled it, the light came on, and to his surprise, his eyes found a fully functioning office. Even more surprising was that he was alone in the room.

Sam hadn't followed him in.

Panic moved through him. He was standing in an office that reminded him of his father's office from the early '90s. Cherrywood furniture everywhere. It was like he had walked down into a cave and gone back in time. It disoriented him for a moment as he tried to process what he'd found.

He heard a door slam and a woman scream. It wasn't Sam, but that didn't make it any less harrowing. King moved back out into the hallway where he could finally see. Ahead there were two more doors and also an intersection with another hallway.

"Put it down or I'll shoot."

He heard Sam's voice, but it was muffled. She must have made it inside one of the doors. King knew she had to have heard something she thought was dire, otherwise she would never have moved in without him. King rushed forward and pushed open the first door past the intersecting hallway. It was a bathroom, and it was empty. He ran forward to the only other visible door and pushed it in. When he entered the room, he saw one of the most terrifying scenes he'd ever witnessed. The room was cast in the yellow light of a small candle. Immediately on his right was

Sam. She was holding her gun out in front of her, ready to fire. It was what she was aiming at that took his breath.

Saajid Hammoud was standing against the back wall, holding a large knife to the throat of a young boy. Saajid was wearing a white traditional thobe, a black turban on his head, and his white beard glowed against his dark tan skin. His eyes were wide—mad with rage. Blood covered his white garment, probably from Sam's bullet on the street. King and Sam were staring at a man who had lost his mind. On the floor, at his feet, was a woman lying on the ground, blood running from her throat. In the corner a young girl was in a fetal position, whimpering softly.

"I said put it down, or I will shoot you," Sam said again.

King tucked his gun at the small of his back. "Do what she said, Saajid."

Saajid moved his wild eyes from Sam to King. "It's you, isn't it? You killed my brother. You had Anastasia, Gregor, and Andonios killed, didn't you?"

"Put down the knife."

"I won't let you kill any more of my family. I'll take them with me to the next life myself."

"Saajid, put it down," King said. "Your family doesn't have to die for your bad decisions. They can still live a happy life."

"Where? In America?!" He spit on the ground. "I'll never let you corrupt my family! At least in death they will remain pure!"

King's approach wasn't working. If there ever had been any humanity inside this man, it was gone now. King would have just shot him, but the way Saajid was holding his own son—holding him up by the back of his shirt with the knife under his chin—King was afraid that when Saajid dropped dead, the knife might kill the boy anyway.

"Just put the knife down, Saajid!" Sam shouted.

King could hear the truck now right above them. Perhaps it was Saajid's strategy to hold out until his backup arrived. If it was Saajid's men, King and Sam were dead. What he couldn't do was let Saajid kill these children. The look on the horrified boy's face was enough to take years off a man's life.

King took a step forward. He was hoping that being unarmed would give Saajid the notion that he had a chance at killing King.

In his periphery King heard a crash. He jerked his head around and watched Sam fall face-first onto the floor, a vase clattering down around her. He turned and punched the woman running at him in the forehead so hard he thought he broke her neck. She dropped as fast as Sam had. Both were unconscious.

King spun back toward Saajid just in time to get a forearm up to stop the knife from sliding into his neck. He saw the boy jump over Sam and dive into his sister's arms. Both of them were safe. Now he could focus on Saajid.

Saajid was a small man—tall but wiry. The complete opposite build as his brother. And unlike Husaam, Saajid would not be able to put up much of a fight.

King grabbed Saajid's knife hand by the wrist. He bent it in such a way that it cracked in half. Saajid screamed in pain, and the knife dropped to the floor. The right hook King landed to Saajid's jaw knocked several teeth out of his mouth as the impact pushed him back against the wall. The kids in the room screamed. They had no idea that their father was a maniac. A man who'd already killed hundreds, if not thousands, in the name of extremism. They only saw their father getting destroyed. And when King realized they had probably just watched their mother get killed right in front of them, he paused before he made his next move.

King knew exactly what those children were thinking. He had been in their shoes, over fifteen years ago. And though he didn't know it at the time, his father was a maniac as well. King had never recovered from watching his mother die. It was the very reason he was standing in the middle of a foreign country, putting his life on the line, so that his fellow Americans wouldn't ever have to experiences situations exactly like this. Though it had brought King years of endless pain and suffering, the tragedy he witnessed on his own front lawn was the reason he could keep more bad things from happening to innocent people. And it was probably the only way these children wouldn't grow up to be like their father. So he knew that for them there was still hope. But he couldn't make it worse. They didn't need to see what he was about to do. Because it was going to be worse than any nightmare they would ever have otherwise.

Sitting in the corner opposite his children, Saajid was trying to stop the blood that was running from his mouth.

Meanwhile, Sam was coming to.

"Are you okay, Sam?"

She rose to her knees, looked slowly around the room, and nodded.

"Can you get them out of here?" King said, gesturing to the children.

Sam stood and gathered them in front of her. They didn't fight her. They didn't want to see what was about to happen. The woman King had knocked out rolled over on the floor. She was still disoriented.

"That's Jamila Salameh, Saajid's sister," Sam said, shuffling the kids out into the hallway.

King picked up Jamila under her arms and placed her on the floor by the wall next to her brother. Though he didn't want to do it, he was going to have to say things to them that he would never do, trying his best to convince them that he would.

King just hoped it was enough to make both Saajid and Jamila stop whatever destruction they had planned next.

46

King moved over to the bed and took the blanket that was lying on top of it. He walked over and covered the dead woman on the floor.

"Who is this?" King said as he pointed to the woman.

Saajid and Jamila both stared back at him.

"You had so much to say out by the fire, Saajid, what happened?"

Saajid spit more blood on the floor.

Jamila decided to be his mouthpiece. "What you have done here, there is no reason for you to feel proud of yourself. It means nothing."

King walked over and stood in front of them. "I'm fully aware that *you* mean nothing. It's your brainwashed followers that concern me now. Tell me what else you have planned."

Jamila laughed at him. King recognized that he had something in common with these terrible human beings. It seemed that like him, they weren't afraid to die. He assumed that because they had caused so much death, they were desensitized to it all. The way they interpreted their holy book, they likely believed they would be rewarded for all of their "*work*."

"Never," Jamila said.

King looked at Saajid. His black eyes were focused on King's, as if trying to will him to fall over dead. "If you don't tell me what the next plan is, I'll kill both of your children, right in front of you." The words tasted sour as they exited King's mouth.

"If you knew anything about me," Saajid said, his words coming out stilted, probably from a broken jaw, "and if you knew anything about my faith, you would know that threatening me with my children would make no difference. We willingly sacrifice for our god. You wouldn't know anything about this."

"You're right," King nodded. "I wouldn't. My God would never ask me to make that sacrifice."

This was the first time he saw a reaction. There was a look in Saajid's eye that suggested he wouldn't tolerate King questioning his faith. It was his button.

King began to push. "Furthermore, my God wouldn't ask me to live in solitude while I did it. If what you believe is so righteous, why do you have to hide from the world?"

King realized once again that he had more in common with this terrorist than he thought. He too had been living in solitude for the past year; he too had been hiding from the world.

Saajid sat up. "Because the world doesn't understand. Most of my own people don't understand. They take the word of God and twist it to whatever fits what feels good to them. And Allah's word says that this type of behavior must be punished!"

"And you think murdering people is the way to do that?" King said. "Have you ever thought that maybe it is you who is twisting the words of your god to fit what you want? To feel powerful? To impose your beliefs on others as if you are God yourself?"

Saajid rose to his feet.

King pulled the gun from the small of his back. "Tell me what you have planned, or I'll kill your sister right now."

Saajid's daughter came running back into the room. "Our people won't do anything in America without him telling them to!"

"Aaleyah!" Saajid shouted. He lunged forward, but King stepped in front of him and threw his shoulder into Saajid's chest. Saajid whipped backward and crashed to the floor.

"I heard him say it earlier, before he hit my mother," Aaleyah continued.

"Aaleyah, stop!" Jamila shouted.

King looked back at the girl. There was resoluteness in her eyes. She'd seen her father do enough; King could tell she was ready to end this too. King had no choice but to believe her. And it didn't matter if he didn't, because Saajid wasn't going to reveal his plans regardless. King just had to trust those plans would all fall apart without their leader.

Sam pulled the girl back out into the hall while King pulled Saajid up to a sitting position, pressing his gun to his head.

Saajid looked into King's eyes. "Now who is playing God?"

Sam came back into the room. "I hear people above us. We have to go!"

As the words left her mouth, a pop and a hissing sound rang out in the hallway behind them, followed by the children's screams.

Tear gas. King knew it immediately. What also calculated instantly was that it wasn't Saajid's men. It had to be the crew that Deputy Director Rodgers had sent from Athens. They knew Sam was here, so he didn't think they would just come in shooting, but he couldn't take that chance. He sprinted past Sam and the kids in the hallway. He closed his eyes and dragged his hands along both sides of the wall to guide him.

"Americans!" King shouted. "We're Americans!"

The tear gas was getting thick, and when he shouted, he took some in. His throat and eyes began to burn, and he was coughing as he tripped over the first step. He heard the door open above him. "Sam Harrison is down here!" He coughed again as he held up his arms. "I have Saajid, don't shoot!"

Through watery eyes he saw the four men lower their guns.

"Get Sam and the children out. I'll get Saajid!" King said in between coughs.

King turned back into the gas. When the hidden door opened, it had created a sucking effect, and the gas was coming right up the stairs around him. He almost just waited at the stairs until the gas dissipated. Sam surely heard him tell the men they were down there, so he knew she would be following soon, but he also remembered the fork in the underground hallway, and he had no idea where the other hallway went, maybe to another exit.

King took a step back, got a large breath of fresh air, then went back down. He ran into Sam on his way through, but he ran right past her. When he got to the back bedroom, sure enough, through the blur of his watery eyes, he could see that Jamila and Saajid were gone. Once King left the bedroom and turned left down the second hallway, the tear gas was all but gone. But so was the light. He didn't have time to worry about what he would run into. As he sprinted down the hallway, extending his hands to the walls again, his breathing not quite as bad as before. What *was* bad was smashing into a wall in front of him. The hallway turned left, but he didn't know it until the dirt in front of him knocked him on his ass.

King picked himself up and hurried left. His eyes and lungs were burning, but he could see a faint light up ahead. He pushed forward and ran for it. He rubbed the last of the water from his eyes, and the coughing had finally subsided. He could see that the light was the same orange glow from the fire in the street near the first door where they had entered the underground bunker. Finally able to see better, he spotted a ladder and then the lower half of a leg moving up the rungs. He surged forward and was able to grab the ankle. When he yanked down, Jamila squealed and fell downward. He half caught her and half threw her down to the ground.

With little regard for her, King shot up the stairs, and when he saw the direction Saajid was going to try to make a run for it, he knew he had him. He pulled the ladder up behind him to make sure Jamila was trapped in the tunnel for the men to capture her, and then he turned to run.

His back was to the fire, a fair distance behind him now. The fire had reached its limit for offering visibility, and once King dashed into the trees, he was plunged back in darkness. The light from the moon was still as it was before, enough for King, once he was beyond the wall of trees, to see Saajid running for the base of the mountain. He knew he was going to kill him as soon as he got his hands on him. There would be no bureaucracy. Not with this kind of evil. King was going to give him the chance to face the god Saajid had killed so many for.

Catching up to Saajid took only seconds. The man was frail, and King was in top shape. He grabbed Saajid by the back collar of his thobe and yanked him down to the ground. He grunted in pain after being laid out on his back. He tried to get up, but King put the bottom of his sneaker on Saajid's chest and pushed him back down. King was done talking.

Saajid was not.

"I know you think you've won, King. But we will never stop fighting for what is right."

King looked back toward the village. No one was coming yet, so he had a minute. He wanted some answers.

"Who shot your niece, Althea, in London? And who kidnapped Bentley Martin?"

The terrorist under King's foot actually smiled. "This is what I mean, Mr. King. You think you have all the answers, but killing me is not the end. It will just make you feel like you've accomplished something when in fact you've actually stopped nothing. Not in the long term."

King had no desire to debate. He learned a long time ago that you can't reason with crazy. So he simply repeated what he hoped Saajid would shed some light on before he died. "Who shot your niece in London? Who kidnapped Bentley Martin?"

This time, Saajid laughed. "Althea gave her life much the same way my brother did. Sacrificing so that we may continue the fight to show the world the true meaning of God. And God has many tests for his people. Unfortunately for Althea, she did not pass. But at least she died trying, and with honor."

Telling King how he'd put his own family in harm's way seemed to be a source of pride for Saajid.

"What is that supposed to mean?" King said.

"Bentley and Althea have been competing for a long time. Ever since they were both here in Greece, and even more when Bentley moved to London. They both wanted to take the next step in being a soldier for their god, but their rivalry was making them sloppy."

Listening to this poor excuse for a human slur out this ridiculous story was hard to do. But curiosity kept King from putting Saajid's tirade to a halt.

Saajid went on. "I told Althea and her half sister, Bentley, that yesterday was the final test. That whoever survived would be the one to fight alongside me. It didn't surprise me that it was Bentley. Althea was smart, but Bentley . . . she is special."

King couldn't believe his ears. He'd heard of things like gang initiations requiring taking someone's life, but to play this sort of game with your family was sick—yet also par for the course when it came to an extremist like Saajid.

"But Bentley didn't survive," King said. "You had Althea killed for her."

"I couldn't let Althea be taken by the police," Saajid reasoned. "Or worse, British intelligence. She knew far too much about everything. My hope was that Bentley would be able to kill you, too, when you least expected it."

King's mind was reeling. He couldn't believe that he had fallen for Bentley's act. She had been beyond convincing.

Saajid continued with a smirk, "Instead, seems as though she killed your man."

King pictured Agent Karn dead on the couch, lying in his own blood He knew right then the doors he'd found busted in at the cottage was just part of Bentley covering her tracks. Making it look as though someone had been there to kidnap her. But Bentley had killed Agent Karn from the inside. It was also the reason Karn's car was gone: Bentley must have driven away in it. He then pictured Bentley sneaking up on Karn and sliding the knife in his throat.

And King had brought Karn there to protect her, only for her to end up killing him. It should have been King who was dead. King took his gun out and held it down by his side. He stepped forward and kicked Saajid in his crooked mouth.

Saajid might not have been much of a man, but he was resilient. He spit out more blood and rolled back over. "Bentley was always a lot more like me than her father. She was taught by the best. You will never find her now. But one day, she'll find you. After all, you did murder her father."

The terrorist, who was about to discover what truly awaited him in the afterlife, was wearing a proud smile.

King flashed back to when he first noticed Bentley in the car. The reason she hadn't pulled away when she noticed King was because she wanted him to kill Althea for her. That was why she'd stuck around when King left her to go back to his flat. She wanted to make sure Althea was gone.

"You'd already be dead if she'd known it was you who killed Andonios," Saajid said. "She's that good."

"She did know," King said. "I just left too soon for her to try."

"The holy book is a powerful thing, really," Saajid continued to rant, something King noticed people often did when they knew they were about to say their final words. "It's inspiring how someone as smart as Bentley, someone so good with numbers, wanted to follow in *my* footsteps. Wanted to follow the work of God."

"What's really amazing is that you don't know when to quit running your mouth." King stepped forward, raised his gun, and aimed at Saajid's head. He'd heard all he needed to hear.

Saajid stared down the barrel. "Just tell me this one last

thing. If you shoot me, what makes you different than me? You say I'm playing God when I kill. What is it that you are doing when you do the same?"

It was a question King had asked himself at least a thousand times, and one to which he never had an answer, because maybe there was no difference at all. But he knew one thing for sure: in the end, he and Saajid Hammoud were nowhere near the same person.

"Maybe me killing you is playing God, Saajid, and maybe it's not. But make no mistake, *we* are not the same."

King could see that Saajid was about to interject, but he was tired of listening. He squeezed the trigger once, and once was all it took.

The Hammoud reign of terror was over.

47

Lexington, Kentucky

BOBBY GIBBONS POURED a cup of coffee from the carafe on the kitchen countertop. The sun was shining through the window above the sink. He and his wife had had a wonderful meal last night. Being in Alexander King's home had begun to feel like a vacation, which he and his wife hadn't had in a long time. She was still fast asleep upstairs, so Bobby took his coffee outside to the oversized patio. He said good morning to the guard at the back door whom Sam had put in place for him. There was a guard outside the front door as well. He walked over to the stone rail of the raised patio. On both ends of the patio were stairs that wound down to the pool below. He paused for a moment to take it all in.

It had been unseasonably warm all week in the northeast. The weather this morning was beautiful, but the view was even more stunning. The rolling hills laid out in front of him were expansive. There was a horse stable a few hundred feet away off to his right. Down in the paddock to the left of the stable, a few Thoroughbred horses grazed on the shimmering bluegrass. It struck him once again, how could a man ever leave all of *this* for a life of fighting the most horrible people in the world? He knew firsthand that motivation was a funny thing. No matter what you have, or where you come from, one thing can happen to you, changing your life forever. It was the same for Bobby when he joined the Marines. He could have stepped right in after high school and taken over the family business, but when his friend was killed overseas, he was compelled to go and try to do something about it.

Bobby sipped his coffee and took in a long breath. While the past day here in Kentucky had been nice, he couldn't help but feel dragged back into worrying about Doug Chapman. His worry wasn't about whether or not he could still become the president of the United States in a few months; it was more about whether he and his wife could simply survive the next few months at all. He'd made a lot of mistakes over his lifetime, but he feared none had been bigger, more dangerous, than getting involved with Doug. Then again, when he really thought about it, he may have never had a choice.

The sequence of events that led him to hiring Doug suddenly seemed like they had been planned, or arranged, by someone else. And while he ultimately made the call to hire him, in hindsight he felt manipulated, and for that he was very disappointed in himself. Especially that he'd dragged Beth into it along with him. She'd always stuck by his side no matter what, and this is how he repaid her: by putting her on the run from a crazy man trained to kill.

Suddenly, the coffee that had tasted so good a moment ago was beginning to upset his stomach. He pulled out his phone and called Sam Harrison again. Once again, she didn't answer. This wasn't a surprise; he'd spoken to her as she and King were boarding a plane from Greece over twelve hours ago. They should be close to landing, but clearly they hadn't yet. He put his phone away and walked down the patio stairs. Any time things became scrambled in his mind, a long walk always helped. So that's what he decided to do.

A half hour later, Bobby was walking back toward the house. The walk had been spectacular both for what he saw and how it cleared his mind. He decided he wasn't going to run from this thing. If he was going to be the leader of the free world, which was where he felt he deserved to be, he would want people to look back on this and see that he stood up to people who were trying to run over him.

To see that he was a fighter.

His pace back to the house was determined. Sam's ability to help Bobby and his wife escape, keeping them from being brought in by either the CIA or Doug Chapman, had made an impact in his mind. Getting away from the campaign trail for a day, leaving Washington, had given him a chance to gain perspective that he wouldn't have been able to have while he was stuck in the throes of it all. His passion for going after the highest office in the land and having a positive impact on the country he loved had been renewed. He would run from this trouble no longer. He was going to face the situation, and Doug Chapman, head-on. Just like he would want a president to do if he were looking on as a citizen and contemplating a vote.

Bobby walked past the pool and jogged up the stairs. He was excited to tell his wife about the walk and the clarity it had brought him. However, when he saw the man who'd been guarding the back door lying on his back in a pool of blood, his first thought was to hope his wife would be alive at all.

He ran over to the body, only to see that the gun was missing from his shoulder holster. He blasted through the double doors and into the kitchen. The gun he took from the box in King's office yesterday was up in the bedroom, so he ran to the counter and grabbed the largest knife in the block. On his way to the stairs he glanced out the front door, stepping outside briefly. The guard out front was in a similar position as the man at the back. He had been no help in protecting Beth.

The phone began to ring in his pocket, but there was no time to answer it.

Multiple gunshots rang out from upstairs. Bobby's heart leapt into his throat.

"Beth!"

He hadn't meant to scream as he turned to run; it was just a reflex. He ran back inside, made sure no one was on the bottom floor of the house, then sprinted up the stairs. He turned left, and ran down the long hallway toward the door where he and his wife slept. There were drops of blood on the carpet leading to the door. He'd never been more afraid to open a door in his life. When he pushed it open, a gunshot blasted in the room. He heard a bullet hit the wall beside him as dove onto the floor.

"Bobby!"

He sprang back up to his feet when he heard his wife call his name. He saw her cowering in the corner, still holding the gun in her hands.

"I almost shot you!"

He rushed over to her and took the gun from her hands, then took her in his arms. "You're okay!"

She pushed him away and pointed toward the door. She was shaking, and by the look on her face he could still see that she was terrified.

"Where is he?" Bobby said. "Are you okay?"

"I shot him. I was coming out of the room to go downstairs to find you. When I opened the door, he was walking right toward me. I remembered you setting the gun on the nightstand, so I ran right there and turned just in time to shoot him."

"Beth, where is he?"

She hadn't said that it was Doug, but Bobby knew it. He had no idea how Doug found them, but he wasn't surprised —the man used to be a secret agent.

"I don't know. I shot a couple of times, he grunted, then ran out of the room."

"Did he have a gun?"

"Yes. He was holding it when I turned around."

Bobby walked over in front of the door. "Was he standing here?"

"Yes, then he turned and ran when I kept firing."

Bobby slowly dropped to his knees. He could've sworn he saw something under the bed when he'd dived to the floor a minute ago. He crawled forward, ducked down, then reached under and picked up the gun. This didn't mean that Doug was unarmed—Bobby remembered the guards' weapons were missing—but it meant at least both he and his wife had a gun. And while that didn't equalize things— Doug was much more skilled— it would make a difference. He had kept his own skills sharp since leaving the marines, and knowing his wife was also armed gave him confidence as well.

Bobby also knew that while they were far outmatched tactically, now was the time to move, as Doug was likely tending to his injury. Giving him time, a chance to stop the bleeding and regroup, would be the worst thing they could do.

"Let's go, Beth. We can't wait here."

As Beth walked over behind him, his next worry was for Dbie. He didn't know exactly where in the mansion she was staying, but he sure as hell hoped she was okay.

Bobby poked his head out the bedroom door. For the moment, the hallway was clear. If the gunshot wound Doug suffered was bad enough, it would take some time to stop the bleeding. It was go time.

He reached back and took Beth's hand, pulled her along into the hallway, and speed-walked with his gun held out in front of him as he made his way to the stairs. Bobby noticed that the drops, and in some places puddles, of blood continued past the stairs to where Dbie had said was the master bedroom. Regardless, Bobby was halfway down the stairs in the next heartbeat, breaking for the front door.

Beth was clutching at his hand as she tried to keep up. He made it to the door, swung it open, and ran for the circular driveway in front of them. Before they reached the blacktop, a black Cadillac Escalade, coming straight for them, slammed on its brakes and screeched to a halt where the driveway and the front lawn met.

The windows were all blacked out, so Bobby didn't know if he and his wife were about to die or if their lives had just been saved.

48

KING SLAMMED ON THE BRAKES AND THE ESCALADE SLID TO A stop. His emotions were all over the place, but it was clear that he needed to get his shit together, and he needed to do it fast. This was the first time he'd been back to his home in over a year, and seeing it made him realize how much of a void he felt from not being there for so long. But he sobered up immediately when he saw presidential hopeful Bobby Gibbons and his wife running toward them in their pajamas, both of them carrying guns.

King had known from Dbie's phone call to Sam a few moments ago that something was terribly wrong, but seeing this sight upon arrival jolted him, and readied his system for a fight. It had been a busy few minutes since they landed at Lexington's Blue Grass Airport. Agent Roberts had called right after Dbie, with an update on Bentley Martin. Or a lack thereof. He'd had Heathrow Airport in London run the name Althea Salameh like King had asked. There was no one under that name flying on any airline. By the time they were able to match up Bentley with the fake passport she'd used to book the flight, she had already exited her plane in Germany. And if Saajid had been even remotely honest about Bentley and her training, he knew they weren't going to see her use that same identity again. She was off to the shadows. Maybe one day they would meet again.

"Keep them safe, and get them the hell out of here," King said to Sam in the passenger seat. "I'm going in to get Dbie."

"Xander." Sam grabbed his arm before he could jump out of the SUV. "If this *is* Doug, this isn't like going after Saajid. Or even dealing with Saajid's men. He's been trained as you have, and he's good."

"He'd better be."

King opened the door and stepped out into the sunshine. His shoulder was still aching from the mini surgery Sam had performed on the plane ride back to Kentucky. She'd pulled the bullet out herself and stitched him up. Patching it up had hurt worse than the gunshot wound itself. He took a quick look around at his property. The familiar smells of home on his Thoroughbred horse farm engulfed him, and once again he swallowed his rising emotions. He rounded the SUV to find two guns pointed directly at him.

"Sam is in the car, Mr. Gibbons. Are you all right?"

"We're fine," Bobby said. He lowered his gun with a sigh of relief. "But I don't know where Dbie is."

"What do I need to know?" King said.

"Doug Chapman took out the guards at the front and back. My wife shot him upstairs, but not sure how bad he's hurt. We didn't see him again, but the blood from the wound trailed off to the right of the stairs on the second floor."

King's bedroom.

His adrenaline spiked, because that's where Dbie said she was when she called. Dbie was only involved with King and Sam because of her tech skills. She was not trained in weapons or tactics. If Doug was in there with her, she was in trouble. King and Doug had crossed paths a couple of years back when King was doing vigilante work. One of King's targets was also a target of the CIA. King had gotten there first, and the entire reason the CIA caught wind of King and his underground missions was because Doug ratted him out. The next time, and the last time, King saw him, it took three men to separate them. This time there was no one around to step in, and King hoped he could have another shot at him while Dbie moved to safety.

"Get in the car," King told them. "You're safe with Sam."

King moved toward the front door, his Glock and a full magazine in his hand. He walked over to the fallen guard, but he didn't have to investigate to see that Bobby was right about him. The pool of blood told the story. He listened at the door for any sound, but as expected, he heard nothing. Then a memory came to him. A couple of years ago he was asleep in the master—where Doug and Dbie supposedly were right now—when he was attacked by a mercenary group that had come to kill him. They nearly killed both him and Natalie, the woman he was seeing at the time, that night.

One of the ways they got to him and Natalie was by entering through the windows upstairs.

If Doug was in King's bedroom, he would be focused on the bedroom door. While King didn't have a helicopter to swing through the window from like the men who attacked him that crazy night had, he did have a ladder. It wasn't a fancy *James Bond* way of getting to the bad guy, but it was a

Kentucky boy way of doing it, and as long as he made it to Doug, that was good enough for King. Sometimes knowing your surroundings was as helpful to winning a battle as anything else. And there was no place he knew better than his own home.

King sprinted for the garage. The side door was open, and inside he found the twelve-foot ladder where he'd always kept it. He rushed over and picked it up, walked it out the door and around to the back of the house. He walked up his back patio, staying as close to the house as possible in case Doug might glance out the window. He stepped over the other dead guard, and a few feet later he was situated under his bedroom. Directly under the bathroom window. He was hoping this would allow him to have look inside without being noticed.

As quietly as he could, he opened the ladder and locked the spreaders in place. The patio was raised close to eight feet, so the twelve-foot ladder would easily reach. He took out his Glock and climbed until his head was just below the window. Inch by inch, he raised his head even higher. The angle at which he was looking enabled him to see through the bathroom door into the bedroom. But just by a sliver. And he saw nothing in that sliver. He knew the window wouldn't be unlocked, but he tested it anyway to be sure. No such luck.

King ducked back down and took out his phone to call Sam.

"What do you need?" Sam answered.

"Have you left yet?"

"We're not quite beyond the driveway. What do you need?"

"A distraction. And make it a loud one."

"Count to thirty. I can give you five seconds."

King put the phone back in his pocket, took the barrel of his pistol in his hand, and counted. Twenty-seven seconds later, he made himself ready.

Three.

Two.

One.

Gunshots rang out from inside the house, and they didn't quit. Sam must have borrowed the two guns Bobby had as well, because it was a chorus of gunfire. King struck the window in front of him with the butt of his gun, once at the top and once at the bottom. The middle of the window hollowed out, and just as the last of his five-second cover blasted through the house, he pulled himself inside the bathroom, immediately raising his pistol in front of him. He was ready in case Doug had heard the shattering glass.

The silence after the fact was as loud as the gunshots beforehand. The crunch of glass underfoot as King moved forward was impossible to avoid. It was most certainly the reason Doug had been ready to fire as soon as King peeked his head out of the bathroom door. King jerked back inside the bathroom. The bullets crashed through the first window in the bedroom as Doug fired from inside the bedroom back toward the bathroom doorway. Doug was at the bedroom door along the same wall as the bathroom door, only a wardrobe cabinet and fifteen feet separated them. King hadn't seen any sign of Dbie, but he'd only had a brief glance.

"Let the girl go. Let's keep this between you and me, Chapman."

"I expected someone to be guarding Bobby, but I didn't expect it would be a ghost. Though the man in the video in Athens looked awfully familiar."

King kept the conversation focused on the moment at

hand. "You've already lost Bobby Gibbons. And now that you've come here to kill him, it won't be hard to prove you also killed Mary Hartsfield."

"You think so?" Doug said. "But if I kill you, then go and get Bobby, there's nothing linking me to any of it."

"Sam's already called it in, Chapman. There's no way out of this. Save yourself an extra life sentence and surrender now."

Doug laughed. "Is that what you'd do in my situation, King? Surrender?"

"I'd never be in your situation. I have this little thing called loyalty."

For the first time, he heard Dbie squeal. It sounded muffled, like something was over her mouth.

"You're still young, King. Give it a few years. The CIA will screw you over too. You're nothing but a pawn to them."

King answered by firing around the door a couple of times, trying to catch Doug off guard. He immediately jumped out the door and behind the wardrobe cabinet. Doug returned fire, and King gave the wardrobe cabinet a push with all the strength he had. It immediately began to topple over, and Doug had no choice but to move outside the bedroom to avoid King's follow-up gunfire. The bullets splintered the door just beside Doug as he jumped into the hallway.

"Get back here!" Doug shouted.

Dbie had squirmed free. King knew Doug wouldn't hesitate to shoot her. King hopped up on the side of the fallen cabinet, sprang forward off of it, and as soon as his shoes hit the carpet, he dove diagonally out the door, plowing into Doug's legs. Doug's gun went off, but as King was beginning to climb on Doug's back, he saw Dbie run around the corner and down the stairs.

She was safe. But the impact jarred King's gun free, and now he had to deal with Doug. Already that was proving to be anything but easy. On his way down to the ground, Doug managed to turn toward King,

and he brought his gun around with him.

49

As Doug's gun was swinging around toward King, King managed to get his right forearm up and knocked the gun's aim toward the ceiling. Doug was on his back, so King pressed forward and put both hands on the arm holding the gun. He was able to pin Doug's arm down on the floor, but it threw his weight off on top of him, and Doug was able to shrimp out from beneath him, causing King to lose his dominant position. King would have to worry about that next, because all that mattered in that instant was working the gun free. Which he was finally able to do, but not until after the final round was fired and the slide locked back.

The second Doug dropped the gun, he rolled over on top of King. King's Jiu Jitsu instincts kicked in, and he immediately repositioned to get his legs free, wrapping them around Doug's waist in a closed guard. This kept Doug from advancing, so when King wrapped his arms around Doug's shoulder and neck, Doug was prevented from raising up on top of King and raining down punches. King could feel wet against him, most likely blood from where Bobby's wife had shot Doug somewhere in the torso.

It must not have been too bad, because it wasn't slowing him down.

"I can hold you here all day, Chapman. The police will be here any minute."

Saying nothing, Doug struggled against King's arms to free himself. But King was too strong.

"Ain't gonna happen," King said.

Doug switched gears and kicked his leg over to get into a side mount. But his transition was too loose, and as soon as King felt Doug's weight shift in the same direction, he pushed off with his arms, and shrimped his butt and legs back away from Doug. Once he was free, King popped up to his feet. As soon as King was gone from beneath him, Doug did the smart thing and stood up himself.

Seeing Doug's face made King even more enraged. The man who had killed his friend, Mary Hartsfield, was standing right in front of him. And he couldn't wait to get his hands on him.

"Did you really think Saajid Hammoud could fix a presidential election?" King said through labored breath.

"Fuck Saajid Hammoud. I only wanted his money. I'll be as good as president myself when John Forester gets elected."

Sam's theory had been right. Doug was really working for Forester, Bobby Gibbons's only real competition.

"You tipped Saajid off about our agent in place in Athens, didn't you?"

Doug smiled. "I had to give Saajid something. Otherwise, he wouldn't trust me enough to give me the last of my money."

King stepped forward and took a couple of swings at Doug, but Doug was quick to move, and he pushed King away with both arms. But he didn't advance further.

"You were the one who interfered in London with Bentley Martin, weren't you?"

"It wasn't Bentley," King said. "But why would you want her dead anyway? She could have only helped you bury Bobby Gibbons by tying him to Everworld's terrorism funding."

"As I'm sure you've found out by now, Bentley Martin isn't who any of us thought she was. She was closer to Saajid than anyone. They talked almost every night. That's why I had to lie to him when she was missing from the safe house in Bruges. If I hadn't said I got her back, he wouldn't have wired the money. Crazy thing, huh? My guy that went to get her back said the scene he found was nasty. He said what that little teenager did to your agent friend was brutal." Doug laughed. "Bet he never saw that coming."

King stepped in again and tried to wipe the smile off the smug bastard's face. When Doug shifted again, King merely hit him in the shoulder. Doug countered with a right hook to King's stomach. It was a good shot but didn't deter King too much.

"You weren't the one who sent him into that lioness's den, were you?" Doug mocked King as he stepped back toward the stairs. "Wait, you were, weren't you?"

King stood and stared a hole through Doug.

Doug continued goading him. "That was *you* on the phone when I shot that bitch in her office, wasn't it?"

The rage inside King grew.

Before he had a chance to react, they both detected sirens in the distance. Sam had called the police after all. Doug's smug grin dropped as he turned to run. King glanced behind him to locate his gun, but in the shuffle it must have been kicked back into the bedroom. He didn't have time to search for it. King knew the surrounding landscape well. There were plenty of places to hide. If Doug ran out of his sight, he might get lucky and manage to get away.

King couldn't let that happen.

He bolted for the stairs and watched Doug rounding the bottom, heading toward the back door. The sirens were close now. King raced down the stairs and headed for the back patio. Doug was already outside, moving toward the patio stairs. King put his head down and sprinted after him. He crossed the patio, turned, and jumped down the stairs, keeping his stride as he passed the pool. Doug veered right and took to the pavement that led to the stables. Beyond that, there was nothing but pasture, thousands of acres worth, stretching out in all directions.

Doug had missed his opportunity to go where there were places to hide, to the right away from the patio. Now there was no way he could escape. Even if Doug was in his own top shape, there were few people alive who went harder at staying fit than King. Over the last year, working out and taking out targets had been the only things for him to do with his time. And King wasn't one to half-ass anything.

Doug ran past the stables. King was catching up to him with every stride. After another hundred yards or so and a third glance over his shoulder, Doug realized he wasn't going to get away. And rather than exhaust himself before the fight of his life, he made the decision to stop and wait for King to catch up.

Tactically, it was a smart move.

Realistically, King still had the upper hand, and he couldn't wait to tear him apart.

50

When Doug turned around to face him, King slowed his run to a fast walk.

Doug moved into a fighting stance. "I figure it will be easier to get away after I keep you from being able to chase me."

King didn't stop walking. "Then stop running your mouth and get to it."

Doug began walking too, and King lowered his head and rushed right in to tackle him. Doug sprawled, dropping his hips on top of King and pushed himself off. King kept coming at him. Doug threw a left jab. King parried right while twisting his hips right, then uncorked a right hook to Doug's ribs. King followed it with a left uppercut that not only shut Doug's mouth but also broke a couple of teeth when it connected with his chin.

King could still hear the gunshots from the phone call he had been on with Mary. The picture played in his head of this man shooting his unarmed friend. Doug had staggered back after the uppercut, and King landed an overhand right to his forehead that hit so hard, he heard bones in his own hand break.

Doug fell to the ground, badly injured but not unconscious. King flexed his hand open and closed. It was definitely broken, and it hurt, but it wasn't bad enough to stop him. His adrenaline was so high that the real pain wouldn't come to him until the fight was over. King walked over to where Doug was struggling back to his feet. He was on all fours. When King reached down and grabbed his collar, he felt something sharp slide into his left thigh. Doug had pulled a knife. For a moment King had been too overconfident, and it cost him.

Doug pulled the knife out and took another swing, but King was able to jump back, the knife just missing him this time. King stepped forward before Doug could get to his feet and soccer-kicked him right in the nose, making a loud *pop* sound. Doug collapsed face-first onto the ground.

King looked back over his shoulder. He could see three people running down the stairs of his patio. While he couldn't make them out individually, it was clear they were all dressed the same. He knew it was the police. A couple of things computed at once.

One: he couldn't let the police see him. He was supposed to be dead. And though his blood was on the knife that Doug had stabbed him with, and probably on Doug himself, King knew Sam could keep all of that under wraps. Perks of being CIA. But what he wouldn't be able to overcome would be the police that would have to arrest him. And he obviously couldn't be brought in. This wasn't *Men in Black*. There were no magic wands that could erase people's memories, and there would be far too many people who would see him to keep the truth from getting out. A viral video of a man, who looked like King, fighting a terrorist in Athens was one thing. Fingerprints and probably some people at the precinct who knew him would be another story—impossible to cover up.

Two: he wanted to end Doug's life himself. Saajid Hammoud could call it the same as playing God, like Saajid killing for his religion, but King knew better. His moral compass might not be that of the most upright, God-fearing civilian, but it read pretty damn true. He knew the difference between right and wrong, and giving this scum the chance to escape his confines was something King just couldn't leave up to chance.

The three police officers disappeared behind the stables as they ran toward him. King pulled out a knife of his own. He walked around behind Doug Chapman and straddled his back. This monster wasn't going to come back and haunt King. There were enough ghosts from his past to worry about in the world as it was. He grabbed the hair on top of Doug's head and pulled it back toward him. He flipped the blade open on his knife, then sliced in such a way that no one would ever be able to stop the bleeding.

As he stood, King grabbed Doug's knife , then turned to his left and began to run. He heard "Freeze!" shouted from a distance, but he did not comply. It was an odd feeling being the good guy who'd just killed the bad guy, but running away from the scene. It was even crazier that he was doing so on his own property. It was a cruel twist to this story that was his life as a person trying to get revenge. A man only trying to do good. Running away couldn't have felt more wrong. But he knew it was the only thing he could do.

As he jogged through the tall green grass and the adrenaline began to subside, his hand began to ache. The wound in his leg was stinging, but it would heal. Then he thought of all that had happened over the past week. He'd taken out some of the most horrible criminals on the planet and probably saved a lot of lives in the process. But as he had come to know over the years, the harsh reality for a man like him was that he only remembered the ones he couldn't save. The friends who weren't as lucky as he was to make it out alive. The innocent victims caught in the cross fire at the hands of a deranged enemy. All a man could do when he faced the worst humans alive and lived to tell about it was continue to fight through the sadness. Somebody had to do it, and he felt fortunate that he was one of the few who could make a difference. No matter how small, or large, that difference seemed.

He pulled out his phone and dialed Sam as he jogged. Pain shot through his broken hand as he held the phone to his ear. The police behind him were a distant memory. They would never catch him before he met up with Sam. He knew this backcountry far too well.

"Took you long enough," Sam answered. She always played the tough woman when she was worried about him. He'd grown to find comfort in it.

"Yeah, there were some complications. Thanks for the diversion. Dbie and the Gibbonses okay?"

"All good."

"Pick me up on Williams Lane at Big Sink Road in half an hour. We'll need a cleaner for Chapman's body. He's got my DNA all over him."

"I'll take care of it. See you in half an hour."

King looked down at his leg again. His pants were fairly bloody from the knife wound, but no arteries or anything serious had been hit. He would be fine. But with today's injuries, he was sure as hell going to be sore tomorrow.

But at least he had a tomorrow.

As he continued his jog toward the pickup point, he was aware of the surrounding beauty juxtaposed against the darker side of his life. The deep blue sky, the horses playing near a massive oak tree, the vast green pasture—all of it couldn't have been more different than the dark alleys and disgusting people that comprised the rest of his life. It didn't seem fair. But he knew that even though he hadn't chosen the life he currently led, he would choose to keep living it that way. And the beauty of where he came from only gave him more reason to fight—to preserve it and protect the people who peacefully enjoyed it.

He knew not every American appreciated what he and his fellow servicemen and women did, but the ones who did care were the only ones who mattered. And though he'd lost another friend, he knew that in the grand scheme of things, Mary was willing to sacrifice her life if it meant justice would prevail in the end.

It was funny . . . one of the things King had always hated most in life were secrets. Especially the types of secrets that allowed someone like his father to betray one's entire family. And secrets like Saajid Hammoud was able to keep long enough to kill so many innocent people. But now that King's entire life was a secret, it gave him pause. He couldn't hate all secrets if his secret gave him the ability to protect people.

King turned and ran backward for a moment. He could no longer see the spot where Doug lay dead. It was too far away now. But he certainly felt good about the fact that that man's secret life of wreaking havoc was over. And when he turned back around, with only open pasture in front of him, he realized he was happy about one other thing.

Now that he understood that some secrets were bad and

some were actually good, as he looked down at his hands covered yet again in someone's blood not his own, a final truth came to mind about his undercover lifestyle.

Some secrets are deadlier than others.

And because of that truth, he could fight on.

EPILOGUE

JANUARY 21, TEN MONTHS LATER

Eastern Market, Washington, DC

THE WIND WAS HOWLING on a cold night in Washington, DC, and a snowstorm was threatening to pummel the surrounding area. Alexander King walked into the Acqua Al 2 restaurant as he had been instructed to do. There was no one inside, which wasn't a surprise seeing as how it was three in the morning. He unwrapped his scarf and unbuttoned his overcoat. He hated the cold, so being called back to the northeastern United States in the middle of winter wasn't exactly something he was happy about. But it was Sam who told him he needed to be there, so he did as she asked. It was her secrecy in all of it that he didn't understand.

He moved past the dining room and found the long empty hall that Sam told him to look for. He walked up the stairs, then down another corridor overlooking a different restaurant. He knew that was where he was supposed to be, but no one was there to meet him. The hallway had come to a dead end and he was staring at a wall.

When something moved on that wall, he instinctively reached for his concealed weapon. A portion of the wall began sliding to the right, and he prepared himself for the worst. Could this be a trap? Instead, he saw Sam walk through the opening, grinning from ear to ear, and he relaxed.

"It's good to see you, Sam, but what's with all the theatrics?"

She gave him a long hug. It had been a couple of months since he'd seen his friend, his *"handler", as was her CIA term.* It had been a long end to the year after everything that happened with Saajid Hammoud and Doug Chapman back in March. He took a month to recover from his wounds while everything was sorted out at the CIA. Once everything shook out, the president and the Senate ended up bypassing the deputy director and made Robert Lucas the new agency head. It was a controversial choice because he'd been involved in a lot of questionable situations during his time as an agent. He was known for his no-nonsense approach. It was a good thing for King, though, because Sam had actually known Robert for a while. She was able to discuss everything that had happened regarding the Phoenix program, and how Mary was the only one who knew Alexander King was still alive. Robert, a man not one to avoid blurring the lines, actually enjoyed the idea of having a "secret weapon" that no one else knew about. Which is why King didn't understand the need for this face-to-face meeting with some unknown person about whom Sam refused to give him any information.

"You'll see why the theatrics in a moment," Sam said. "Are you certain you weren't followed?"

"Sam." King shook his head, giving her his "come on" look. He didn't understand why this was such a big deal.

"All right, but we can't be too careful."

She nodded her head in the direction of the room behind the wall. When they walked through, he could see a dimly lit bar; the rest of the small restaurant was dark. Sam had called him to a speakeasy. Normally this was something he'd be keen to check out, but his personal love of a good drink wasn't at the top of his priorities at the moment. The shadowy figure sitting at the far end of the bar was more his concern.

As Sam walked him around the bar, the man stood, and Sam was right: King now understood the theatrics.

"Mr. President," King said as he held out his hand. "Certainly wasn't expecting to see you here."

The fit, silver-haired man reached out and gave King's hand a firm shake. "Call me Bobby."

King had watched Bobby Gibbons be sworn in as the new president of the United States just yesterday afternoon.

"Okay, Bobby," King said. The president motioned toward an empty seat at the bar, and both of them sat down. "Well, this is your first full day in office, and you called for me. This can't be good."

"That's an understatement," Bobby said. "And yeah, they didn't even give me a warm-up day. They came right at me with some terrifying news."

Sam took the seat behind King. He knew she had already heard all about this *problem*.

"Would you like a drink?" Bobby asked.

There was a bottle of Blanton's bourbon sitting on the bar beside two glasses.

"Always," King said.

Bobby poured. "I'm normally a scotch guy myself, but I knew better than to offer a Kentucky boy such an inferior dram." Bobby gave him a wink.

The two of them clinked glasses and gave cheers. King couldn't help but think he was getting buttered up for something horrible.

"Why meet in person and go through all this trouble?" King said.

They both sipped.

"Right to it then. Well, first I wanted to thank you for saving my wife and me from Doug Chapman. We'd both be dead, and I wouldn't have fulfilled my lifelong dream of becoming president if you hadn't made it there and did what you did. I felt I couldn't thank you properly without shaking your hand."

"Just doing my job. But you're welcome. Now give me the bad news."

Sam laughed behind him. That confirmed his fear. Whatever the president wanted next was going to hurt.

"Well, Alexander, I need your help."

"Ah," King said, nodding, "the start of all painful conversations. Whatever you need, Mr. President. Just don't beat around the bush."

"I need you in Alaska."

And there it was. The big ask. It was also the reason Sam had laughed: she knew how much King *hated* the cold.

"I couldn't be more excited," King said.

Bobby picked up on his sarcasm and hung his head. "I know. Sam told me you're allergic to cold."

That was actually a good way to put it. It felt like an allergic reaction when temperatures dropped below forty-five degrees.

"What's in Alaska that would need my attention?" King said. "Or should I say, *who* is in Alaska?"

"It's both really. Let me start from the beginning. It was just brought to my attention this morning so it's still fresh. You obviously remember the panic over the coronavirus this past year."

"Of course," King said, then took another drink.

"Well, some of the seedier types in the world took notice of not only the panic the virus created but how quickly such a virus can spread."

"You think someone is going to weaponize a virus?"

"I don't think so, son." Bobby's tone hardened. "It's happening. We just need to get to the root of it."

"And you think that's Alaska?"

"I do, but this is where it gets tricky. Did you hear about the small town on the northern coast of Alaska this past week?"

Things began coming together for King. "Almost an entire town of two hundred people died in like a couple of days, right?"

"Yes."

"You think it was biowarfare?"

"We think it was a test."

King let that sink in. He remembered seeing that one person had become sick, then the entire town died off in a matter of days. But the reports on TV were that it was a tragic accident that had to do with something contaminating their drinking water. It didn't surprise King that the news didn't have it right.

"Okay, that's the what. Now where's the *who*?"

"Dmitry Kuznetsov, a world renowned biochemist and virologist, flew into Seattle from Moscow several months ago for a world health conference . . . and he never left."

"Bridge the gap for me here, sir," King said.

"I'll get you the full briefing, but long story short, we think Dmitry might be in Barrow, Alaska. And we have reason to believe he is concocting a virus for the Russians that will cripple America and either make us vulnerable for a traditional attack, or the virus itself will *be* the attack."

"Shit. That's an awful big leap. I'm assuming there is some smoke for all that fire."

"There is," Bobby said.

King finished the last of his bourbon. "Where do I fit in?"

Bobby looked at King like he was about to tell him King's dog just died. King braced himself.

"Senator Fraley from Alaska knows a man who helps staff companies in Barrow. Not far from the town that was infected. You'll be starting as a security guard in three days."

King picked up the bottle of bourbon and poured another drink. As he put the glass to his lips, he turned to Sam. "You're loving this, aren't you?"

Sam gave a look as if she'd just tasted the most delectable dessert. "Oh, you have no idea."

"Nice," he said as he nodded and turned back to the president. He pointed with his thumb back over his shoulder. "She's supposed to be my friend. Who needs enemies, right?"

"My sister treats me the same way," Bobby said with a laugh. Then the smile disappeared. "Look, I owe *you*, not the other way around. So if this isn't something you want to do, you can say no. I just need the very best on this, because I think this might be one of the most important things we stop in our lifetime."

"Why not just send in a team and smash the thing up?"

Sam hopped off her bar stool and walked around King.

"Because we need to know who is behind this as much as we need to stop it. If it really is the Russian government that has implemented this, we need to know—"

"Because that would warrant a catastrophic retaliation," Bobby interjected. "And we *have* to be sure."

King took the entire drink down in one slug. "I'll do it." He stood and shook the president's hand. "But my next assignment better be in paradise."

"You bring this thing down and I'll meet you on the beach myself."

"I'll give it all I've got."

"That's all I'll ever ask." The president stood. "Thank you, Alexander."

"Don't thank him yet," Sam said. "One cute bartender and the entire country could suffer."

"I'll take my chances," Bobby said.

"At least someone has some faith," King said with a smile.

"Good luck, soldier."

King gave the president a nod and followed Sam toward the exit. She walked him all the way to the entrance of the restaurant. Outside the glass door he could see that it had already begun to snow. The large flakes floated down out of the dark sky and under the lights standing tall above the street.

Sam leaned in and gave King a hug. "Whatever you need, whenever you need it."

She handed him a new phone. He gave her the one he'd been using. "I'll be waiting for the brief and whatever else I'll be needing." Then he removed his scarf and his overcoat. He only had a thin button-down shirt on underneath.

"What are you doing?" Sam said. "You'll freeze."

King opened the door and walked out, turned back

toward Sam, and held his arms out from his sides. "I'm gonna have to get used to freezing, it seems." He looked up at the snow falling all around him. "No time like the present."

COLD WAR - Alexander King book two
AVAILABLE NOW

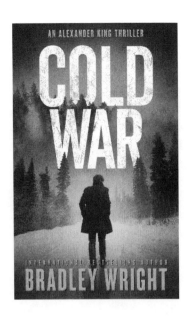

COLD WAR
by
Bradley Wright

Book Two in the Alexander King series.

ACKNOWLEDGMENTS

First and foremost, I want to thank you, the reader. I love what I do, and no matter how many people help me along the way, none of it would be possible if you weren't turning the pages.

To my family and friends. Thank you for always being there with mountains of support. You all make it easy to dream, and those dreams are what make it into these books. Without you, no fun would be had, much less novels be written.

To my editor, Deb Hall. Thank you for continuing to turn my poorly constructed sentences into a readable story. You are great at what you do, and my work is better for it.

To my advanced reader team. You continue to help make everything I do better. You all have become friends, and I thank you for catching those last few sneaky typos, and always letting me know when something isn't good enough. Alexander appreciates you, and so do I.

And finally, to the man or woman who first placed that corn whiskey in a barrel and aged it long enough to be called a bourbon. I speak for all of us who imbibe, I love you. Cheers to you, you beautiful soul.

About the Author

Bradley Wright is the international bestselling author of action-thrillers. The Secret Weapon is his tenth novel. Bradley lives with his family in Lexington, Kentucky. He has always been a fan of great stories, whether it be a song, a movie, a novel, or a binge-worthy television series. Bradley loves interacting with readers on Facebook, Twitter, and via email.

Join the online family:
www.bradleywrightauthor.com
info@bradleywrightauthor.com